RYLEY'S REVENGE

A GLOVES OFF NOVEL

NEW YORK TIMES & USA TODAY BESTSELLING AUTHOR

L.P. DOVER

Cover design by Regina Wamba of Mae I Design
Editing by Victoria Rae Schmitz, Crimson Tide Editorial
Formatting by JT Formatting

Printed in the United States of America
First Edition: December 2014
Library of Congress Cataloging-in-Publication Data
Dover, L.P.
Ryley's Revenge (A Gloves Off Novel) – 1st ed
ISBN - 13: 978-0-09903964-6-8
ISBN - 10: 0990396460

1. Ryley's Revenge—Fiction 2. Fiction—Romance
3. Fiction—Contemporary Romance

http://**authorlpdoverbooks.com**

Ashleigh

"ARE YOU IN love with him?" Colin asks.

We'd just walked through the door of my apartment, only long enough for me to sit my bags down and grab a bottle of water from the refrigerator. We were in Vegas because Colin and Bradley had a baseball tournament. Well, that, and to be with my best friend, Gabriella. That's what I told myself anyway. Deep down, it was because I knew Ryley was going to be there too, fighting. Seeing him again had only awakened what I kept buried inside of me.

I didn't know what to tell Colin as he stood there looking at me with those bright green eyes of his. The eyes which belonged to a man who was everything I could ever want—smart, loving, caring, and sexy as hell. Not to mention he had a body to die for. Colin was our school's star pitcher, and on his way to bigger and better things in the MLB.

I still haven't answered him yet, but if I let the truth come out of my mouth, I won't be able to take it back. Not even a day ago, I was afraid I was pregnant with Ryley's child. It was the scariest moment in my life, but what frightened me more was the look in Ryley's eyes when he thought he was going to be a father. He wasn't ready . . . hell, I wasn't ready.

The only problem was, right after I left him for Colin, he went straight back to his old ways with his identical twin. It's like I was erased from his mind, no longer the girl he fell in love with.

I have too much pride to go back to him, knowing he'll be whoring around with other women. Colin's a good guy and he deserves more than a woman whose heart's divided. I love him a lot, but I'm *in* love with someone else.

"Ashleigh, please," he murmurs, taking my hands. "You've avoided me all day. Did something happen while we were in Vegas?"

I was never good at lying, and Colin's always the first person to know when something's wrong. Sitting down on the couch, I take a deep breath and close my eyes. My stomach is in knots because I know I'm about to break another guy's heart. Colin's my safe place, my guarantee at a normal, functional relationship. I just know that if I stay, I'll never be fully happy. He doesn't own my heart, but he shares a part of my soul.

I have to make a choice. Opening my eyes, the warm tears fall down my cheeks. Colin doesn't speak because in my actions he already has his answer. He lowers his head and slowly lets go of my hands, running them through his hair.

"I don't think I can let you go, Ashleigh. At least, not without a fight."

Sighing, I wait for him to lift his head, and when he does I lean in to give him one last kiss. "I'm sorry, Colin, but you don't have a choice."

1

Ashleigh

Present Time (One Month Later)

"SO WHEN ARE you coming back to California?" Gabriella asked.

When I get the balls to face Ryley again.

But in all honesty, I didn't know. For the past month, I'd been in Aspen with my family, trying to get away from anything and everything that reminded me of Ryley and Colin. Working in my family's hotel helped. I loved talking to the tourists and getting them all settled in. It was a good distraction.

I'd been afraid Gabriella would've told Ryley by now about my breakup with Colin. So far, she'd kept my secret. Colin, however, refused to give up on me and made sure to keep in touch by calling almost every single day. He'd even visited Aspen twice already. He was my friend before we became lovers, but once you cross that line, it's almost impossible to go back.

"I don't know yet," I admitted. "I'm tempted to stay here for a little while longer. I miss being with my family." It wasn't exactly a lie, but it wasn't the full truth either.

There was something I hadn't told her, or anyone for that matter. I thought maybe running away to Aspen would make my problems disappear, but I was starting to think it was just going to make them worse. For the past hour, I'd done nothing but trace and stare at the phone number on the paper in front of me. I was just too afraid to call it.

Gabriella's laugh echoed in the phone, catching my attention. "Well, all I can say is, you won't believe the shit that's happened here the past couple of days, especially when I was in Vegas for the fights."

Perking up, I held the phone closer to my ear. There weren't any people in the lobby so I had a few minutes to spare. "Oh yeah, like what?"

Anything with Ryley?

Gabriella sighed. "Well, Tyler's super serious over a girl now. And, get this . . . It turns out, she's Kyle Andrews' sister. Who would've thought that, right?"

I gasped. Everyone hated Kyle Andrews. "Oh my God, that's insane. Have you met her? Are you okay with that?"

She snorted. "Yes, I'm okay with it. It is for the best. I miss talking to him though. Anyway, I met Kacey the other day. She's actually really nice—although, a little quieter than me."

"Everyone is quieter than you, Gabriella," I laughed.

"Oh, whatever. Well, now that Tyler won the title,

and Kyle's paralyzed in the hospital, all is right in the world."

"I'd say so," I agreed. Nothing like that ever happened at the hotel; it was quiet and drama free. Only in Gabriella's life was it interesting. "It sounds like you had a lot going on. How are you and Bradley doing? Still just friends?"

"For the time being, we're more like friends with benefits. We've been spending a lot of time together. Colin asks about you all the time though. I actually feel bad for the guy. We did come to the conclusion that something's wrong with you. He's noticed a difference and so have I. I think it's time you tell me what's wrong. And I don't want to hear anymore bullshit excuses. I know how to kick your ass, so don't make me come all the way to Aspen to force it out of you."

Sighing, I held up the post-it note and closed my eyes. If I didn't tell her something, I could definitely see her flying out here to live up to her promise. "I'll tell you as soon as I find out, Gabby. I promise."

"Are you okay?"

"I don't know, but when I do, you'll be the first to know. Needless to say, it might take a couple of days."

"Just as long as you get it figured out. I want my best friend back. It's not the same here without you."

I smiled, but the ache in my chest made the burn behind my eyes build. "I miss you too," I whispered, trying not to choke on my tears.

"Make sure to call if you need me . . . or if you just want to talk. I'm about to head out to the gym and get some training in, but after that, you know I'm free."

I nodded like an idiot, knowing very well she couldn't

see me. "I will. Have fun with your training. I'll talk to you soon."

We said our goodbyes and I hung up the phone. Once I verified no one was in the lobby, I took a deep breath and picked the phone back up. I'd tried calling the number sitting in front of me numerous times, but always hung up after the first ring.

"Good afternoon, Dr. McCord's office, this is Lisa, how may I direct your call?"

"Um . . . hi, Lisa. I'm a patient there . . . or at least, I used to be before I moved to California. I'd like to make an appointment. My name is Ashleigh Warren."

"Of course, dear, just give me a second." She typed away on the keyboard and then came back on the line. "Date of birth, please."

I told her my birth date, which happened to be just a couple of weeks ago. Even though I was only twenty-three, it felt like I had aged beyond my years over the past month. Things that used to be important, just *weren't* anymore—not when I had responsibilities looming over my head.

More clacking on the computer keys. "Okay, is this for a yearly check-up?"

Hands shaking, I closed my eyes and cleared my throat. "Not exactly."

"And why do you need to be seen? Is this an emergency?"

Halfheartedly, I chuckled and lowered my head to the desk, my laugh turning to tears. "In my life, Lisa, yes I'd say it's an emergency." I took a deep breath and blew it out slowly. "I think I'm pregnant."

CHAPTER 2

Ryley

NEVER IN MY twenty-four years of existence had I been knocked down and fucked in the dry tailpipe like I'd been three days ago. Everything I once believed in was a goddamned lie. What made it worse was finding out the truth from Tyler, and not Gabriella. For a whole month I was led to believe Ashleigh was with her pansy-ass fluffer of a boyfriend, only to find out she dumped him when they got home from Vegas.

It was during that particular trip when I had her in my arms again, thinking she was pregnant with my child. A sick, twisted part of me had hoped to God she was pregnant so that I could have a fighting chance with her. Now, with her running away to Aspen, I didn't know what to think.

The second Tyler told me what was going on I pretended it wasn't that big of a deal, even though deep down I wanted to hit something so fucking hard it'd make my knuckles bleed. For two days, I trained nonstop with my coach and Camden, ignoring every single phone call and text; especially, the ones from Gabby. My mind was a jumbled mess of shit. Ashleigh Warren had head fucked me into falling for her and then she left. I was a fool to fall, but dammit to hell, I wanted her back.

I was Ryley 'The Rampage' Jameson. I had women falling all over themselves just to suck my dick and do whatever I wanted them to. I loved it . . . or at least I pretended I did. It didn't help that I envisioned Ashleigh every time.

Sweat poured down the sides of my face, arms, and back as I pounded the punching bag, over and over again. My teeth were clenched so tight I could feel the pulse in my temple beating out of control. I was confused, angry, and most of all, I wanted answers. Tyler was right, I needed to find out what was going on.

"Ryley."

I heard my name, but didn't want to stop. Hitting and fighting was what I was good at, it kept my mind occupied from the tension pulling at my chest. Just a little bit more and the pain would be in my arms and the muscles in my back, not in—

A hand came down hard on my shoulder, drawing me back. "Ryley, stop!" my coach barked. "You're overdoing it, son. You need a break."

"Just a little bit more."

"*Now.*" The warning in his tone made me stop. Grabbing my wrists, he lifted my hands, snarling at my busted knuckles.

Danny Echols was my dad's best friend and the only father figure I'd had for the past couple of years. His silver hair was damp with sweat, and over his shoulder I could see my brother in the ring, taking off his gloves and looking on in confusion. Camden had no clue what was going on with me.

Breathing hard, I stepped away and looked down at my hands. They were bloody and split wide open.

"Look, I don't know what's going on, but you better figure it out soon. Surely, it's not because of the title fight is it? I know you and your brother will be battling it out soon, but that's no reason to let it fuck with your mind."

Bursting out in laughter, I shook my head, fisting my hands by my side. My knuckles split open even more and I welcomed the pain. The fight with my brother was the last thing on my mind. "Trust me, Danny. I'm not worried about the fucking fight. I have other things on my mind right now."

"Oh, don't worry about him, coach," Camden called. "He just needs a good lay or two." He winked at me and smiled, thankfully drawing the attention of our coach.

Danny sighed and waved me off. "All right, I'll back off. But I want you to soak those hands and get them healed. I don't want to see you around here tomorrow. You got that?"

Turning on my heel, I grumbled, "Yes, coach," before waltzing off toward the locker rooms. He knew I wasn't going to stay away.

Luckily, no one was in the showers. The only people who ever used the locker rooms were the fighters who trained in the gym, which happened to only be a handful of us. After turning on the shower, I stripped out of my blue and white fighting shorts and tossed them on the bench. A little blood smeared on the white cloth, but I didn't care.

Once the room was filled with steam, I stepped into the near scalding water and hissed as it hit my open wounds. Hanging my head, I placed my sore hands against the wall and let the water run down my body, washing away the sweat and tension. It wasn't long before my muscles began to relax. However, they tightened back up when a set of soft, feminine arms wrapped around my waist from behind. Her hands slid down, one cupping my balls while the other wrapped around my cock, massaging me.

"Don't tell me you forgot me already?" she whined in my ear.

Her touch did nothing but piss me off. Pulling her arms away from my body, I turned off the water and stalked past her to my locker. She was naked, her body glistening as the shower head dropped its last few drops on her skin. I wished I wanted her, but I didn't. For the past couple of weeks she'd been mine . . . but not anymore. The only reason I kept her around was because she looked like Ashleigh, with her dark hair and wide-set green eyes. But no matter how I diced it, she just wasn't the same.

"I'm not in the mood today, Natalie." Grabbing a towel, I ran it over my body quickly and reached into my locker for a clean T-shirt and jeans.

"Not in the mood? Since when are you not ready for me? We've been doing this for how long now?"

Almost every day for the past couple of weeks.

Arms crossed over her chest, she glared at me with anger radiating from those emerald green eyes of hers.

"It doesn't matter," I replied, "I'm done."

"You're done?" she scoffed. "Just like that?"

Zipping up my jeans, I nodded my head and started for the door. "Yep, just like that."

I'd been told by many women I was an ass. It didn't bother me. Not even when Natalie called me every single name in the book as I walked away from her, screaming as loud as she could. Today was shaping up to be one spectacularly shitty day.

My prediction was confirmed when I walked out of the locker room and locked eyes with the one person I'd been avoiding. Dressed in her tiny black shorts and red sports bra, Gabriella was ready to train. It was amazing how fast her body had transformed from slim to outright muscle. But from the looks of her, she didn't know I knew about Ashleigh.

She was up in the ring talking animatedly to Camden and my coach. When she spotted me, I didn't smile back at her. She said her goodbyes to my brother and hesitantly walked down to me, stopping a couple of feet away.

"Why haven't you answered my calls?" she asked.

About that time, Natalie stormed out of the locker room, her hair dripping water all over her tight, white tank top. "Get used to it, honey. I wouldn't waste your time on this dickwad."

Biting her lip to keep from smiling, Gabby watched Natalie walk away before turning back to me. "Um . . . o-kay. It looks like you're not having a good day." She set her gym bag down and stretched her arms over her head.

"More like the past few days," I snapped, crossing my arms over my chest. "Is there something you need to tell me? Or maybe something you *forgot* to tell me?"

Nervously, she laughed. "Not that I know of. Can you

give me a hint?"

"Vegas."

Sighing, she closed her eyes and hung her head, her midnight hair covering her face. "Tyler told you?" When she looked up, I nodded once. "Goddammit," she hissed, grabbing my arms. "She made me promise, Ryley. What was I supposed to do? She's my best friend."

"Well, so am I."

"I know you are, but it's not the same. Tell me what I can do to make it better."

"You can start off by telling me what the fuck's going on."

Letting my arms go, Gabriella flung hers in the air. "I wish I could, but she keeps brushing me off. I've been trying to get her to talk, but she won't confide in me."

Taking her elbow, I pulled her along beside me and out the front door. "Well, right now she's not going to have an option."

"What do you mean? Ryley, where are you dragging me to?"

I opened the passenger door to my black Mercedes G-class and ushered her inside. "*We* are taking a day trip to Aspen. You're going to take me to her."

Ashleigh

"HONEY, ARE YOU okay?" my mother asked.

I had taken the day off. My nerves were shot to hell because of the doctor appointment, and to top it off, my parents didn't know of my situation. I thought it best to keep them in the dark as long as possible.

Hands shaking and drenched in sweat, I put on a fake smile and nodded my head. "Of course, I'm fine. I just wanted to get some sun and relax today." It was a beautiful day in Aspen and the view of the mountains from my family's cabin had always been breathtaking. I could spend hours out on the back deck and lose all sense of time.

It was a shame it wasn't raining. The last time it rained, I let the cold droplets pour down on me, remembering the way it felt when Ryley made love to me at his cabin, under the open sky. I wanted those memories back, so I could make them real again.

Setting down a cup of tea, my mother kneeled down beside my chair and sighed. We looked almost alike with the same chocolate brown hair and green eyes. Her hair, however, was cut short in a pixie style while mine was long. I was also a head taller than her.

"You miss California, don't you?" she asked softly.

There were so many things I missed, I didn't know where to start. "I do. All of my friends are there."

Taking my hand, she squeezed it gently, her gaze warm. "Then why don't you go back? It's obvious you're not happy here. I know you want to be with me and your father, but we understand you have a whole other life. What about your degree? Don't you want to find a job doing what you love?"

Just a couple of weeks ago, I graduated with a degree in Marine Biology. I wanted to pursue a career in it, but right now wasn't the right time. "It's complicated, Momma. As far as California, I'm scared of what I'll find when I go back. So many things have changed."

She patted my cheek and slowly got to her feet. "We all change, Ashleigh. But that's when you grow closer with the ones you love. I don't know who or what you ran from, but I do know you won't be content again until you face it head on. I didn't raise you to be a quitter."

My throat tightened, but I held back my tears. "I don't want to disappoint you or daddy. It's been nice being back home. I'm gonna miss you all, especially Mimi." She was going to hate me leaving again.

"She's going to miss you too. And just so you know,

you could never disappoint us. We love you and will always be here for you. Don't be afraid to follow your heart."

Follow my heart. My heart was in California. All this time I knew what I needed to do, I was just too scared to do it. "You're right. I'm going to go back."

She smiled and nodded. "Just make sure you come visit soon."

"I will."

Rushing off to my room, I packed my bags, and booked the first available flight to California—which happened to leave in just a few short hours. With only two hours to spare before takeoff, I got my parents to drop me off at the airport and said my goodbyes. Security had always been a pain in the ass, but once I was through it all and checked in, I pulled out my phone and made a call.

"Good afternoon, this is Lisa at Dr. McCord's office. How may I direct your call?"

It was the same woman I had talked with to set up my appointment. "Hi Lisa, this is Ashleigh Warren. I called yesterday to make an appointment."

"Yes, Ashleigh, how may I help you?"

Biting my lip, I took a deep breath and hung my head. I was running away from one problem, only to run head first into another. "I need to cancel it. I'm sorry for it being last minute, but I have to go out of town."

The keyboard clacked through the phone as she typed. "No worries, Miss Warren. I understand things come up. Would you like to reschedule?"

"Actually, no. I don't know how long I'll be gone. I'll call as soon as I figure everything out." I said goodbye and hung up quickly.

Maybe it was just stress that caused my period to be late. There was one time I was three weeks late when I was in high school. It just so happened I was a virgin then, so I knew pregnancy wasn't an issue . . . but still, I was late. I was pretty sure it could happen again. If I didn't start in another week, I'd get a test and just get it over with. People always said ignorance was bliss. It wasn't bliss for me though, it was outright terrifying.

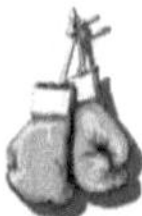

When the plane landed, I called and texted Gabriella but she never answered. Even by the time I got my luggage, she still hadn't responded. I needed someone to come pick me up and the only other person I knew to call was Colin. I didn't really want to call him, but I also didn't want to take a cab. The phone rang only once when he picked up.

"Now what do I owe the pleasure of this call?" he answered, voice deep and smooth as silk.

Lightly, I chuckled. "Hey, Colin. Actually, I'm in town. Is there any way you can come pick me up at the airport?"

"Really? So you're back for good this time?"

"I think so," I replied nervously. *At least I hope.*

I heard him fumble with his keys and then the sound of his truck roar to life. "I'll be there in ten minutes. I can't wait to see you."

The hope in his voice made my heart ache, but I

didn't have the energy to tell him that I wasn't back for him. I knew at that point, I shouldn't have called him. Hurting him was one of the hardest things I ever had to do, but being without Ryley pained me even more.

"I'll see you soon," was all I could say before hanging up. My stomach was in knots and I was scared to death. There was a ninety-nine percent chance Ryley would slam the door in my face, but I had to try to get him back. *He needs to know I love him.*

After twenty minutes of playing games on my phone, I almost dropped it when a set of arms wrapped around my waist and lifted me in the air. "Oh my God," I shrieked, laughing as Colin twirled me around. "You're gonna make me sick."

Setting me down, Colin chuckled and held my face in his hands. He had his green baseball cap covering his whitish-blond hair and he stared down at me with his bright emerald eyes. "It's so good to see you again. I'm glad you called." He pulled me to him and held me in his arms.

I breathed him in and held him tight, instantly relaxing against him. After everything I put him through, he still cared about me—which was a miracle. Sometimes I wished he would just hate me; it would make things so much easier.

"It's good to see you too," I murmured softly. "Do you mind taking me home? I'm exhausted." I was more than exhausted, I was comatose and nauseated as hell. My body felt like it was going to crash any minute.

Putting his arm around my shoulders, he kissed the top of my head and grabbed my suitcase. "Let's get you home then."

Tomorrow was a new beginning.

Ryley

WHAT THE FUCK . . .

I couldn't believe my goddamn eyes. We were walking into the airport and there, a hundred feet dead ahead, was Ashleigh . . . in the arms of the man who was supposed to be her ex. I sat there in total disbelief as I watched her leave, snug against his body, cradled protectively under one of his arms.

"Ryley, what's wrong?" Gabriella snapped her fingers in my face.

Shaking my head, I squeezed the handle of my bag and glared down at her. "I'm done. This will *not* happen again." Starting toward the door, Gabriella raced along beside me.

"What the hell are you talking about? Where are you

going? Stop." She tried to pull on my arm, but I ignored her and continued on my path. "Ryley, stop! Our flight leaves in an hour."

"We're not going anywhere," I growled. "I just saw Ashleigh and her fucking boy toy leave together."

"Who . . . Colin? They aren't even together anymore, Ryley."

By the time we got to my car, I threw my bag in the back and tossed Gabby's in there as well. "Yeah, well, the happy couple didn't look to be having any issues with their arms all over each other. Get in, I'm taking you back to your car."

We'd left her car at the gym, which was perfect because I needed to hit something—hard. Since it was late, my coach would be gone and I didn't have to worry about him bitching at me. Although, I honestly didn't care if he did because I sure as hell wasn't going to listen. Gripping the steering wheel with all my strength, I could feel the sores on my knuckles begin to split open again.

Gabriella angled her body toward me and huffed, crossing her arms over her chest. "Ryley, you have to trust me. They are not together, it's just not like that between them. You're acting like an idiot."

I sped down the highway. "It's kind of hard to trust you when you didn't even tell me about them in the first place. If there's nothing going on, why didn't she call you to tell you she was coming back?"

"Are we really going to argue about this? I already told you why I didn't originally tell you, jackass. And as far as her not calling me . . ." she snapped, pulling out her phone, "it's probably because my freaking phone is dead. I haven't had a chance to charge it up since I was kidnapped by you. And for your information, other than me and Colin, she doesn't have anyone else to call."

Pulling into the parking lot of the gym, I stormed out of my car with Gabriella close on my heels. "Look, it doesn't matter. Going to Aspen was a mistake anyway."

"You're wrong," she growled, slamming her hand on the gym door to block my path. "It was the first intelligent decision you've made since the break-up. Whether you want to admit it or not, you're in love with her and I *know* she's in love with you. So, stop being so stupid."

Turning my head, I glanced through the glass door to the people inside. "You want to know what I'm in love with, Gabby? Take a look in there," I said, gesturing to a blonde chick with huge tits. I managed to score a blow job from her the other day and I knew she'd let me fuck her whenever I wanted. "*That* is what I'm in love with. Girls like that, who don't want anything more from me than a good time. I don't have the patience for anything else. You need to stop pushing your ideals on me. I don't want fucking June Cleaver," I spat, turning to point violently at the blonde, "I want Baywatch Big Titties."

Snarling in disgust, Gabby turned on her heel and marched to her car. "Whatever you say, Ryley. You and I both know that's not what you want. But if you want to fuck Tits McGee in there, I'm sure as hell not going to stop you. Apparently, it's going to take a miracle to get your ginormous head out of your tight ass."

Once Gabriella left, I stormed inside and ignored everyone as I made my way to the one thing I wanted, to the one thing that could take my mind off of everything. Ripping off my shirt, I threw it on the floor, my heart pumping wildly in my chest. "It's just you and me tonight. It's time to bring on the pain."

I swung hard, landing a hard right hook. Blood smeared on the leather punching bag, but I kept on going until all I could see was red.

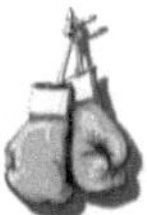

By the time I made it home, it was one o'clock in the morning and my hands burned like fire. They looked like raw meat and it felt fucking amazing.

"You are one sadistic son of a bitch," my brother pointed out, looking at my wide smile and then down at my hands. He was seated on the couch, head cocked to the side so he could see me.

When I turned the corner into the living room, I didn't expect to see a woman on her knees, slobbing his knob. She was naked and rubbing her clit as she sucked him off.

"Don't you have a bedroom for that shit?" I grumbled, throwing my bag down. Turning away from them, I marched into the kitchen and poured a tumbler of whiskey.

"Yes," Camden called, "but I have two other guests in there getting warmed up for me. Why don't you go say hello? I'm sure they'd love to . . . ease your tension."

Walking past him toward the stairs, I didn't even give him a second look. "I'm not exactly in the mood for that shit, bro."

"What's gotten up your ass lately?" he hollered.

"I'll give you one guess. And you of all people should

understand how this one can get up your ass."

Everything grew quiet and if my brother figured it out, he sure didn't say anything about it. I shouldn't have made that quip, but I was pissed and I wanted him and everyone else to leave me alone. I still vividly remembered the night when Ashleigh called and told me to drive to Malibu to get my brother; that she had tied him up to the bed and left him. He had been a complete dick to her and she paid him back by making him come all over himself by fingering his ass and jacking him off. Camden deserved it.

My brother and I used to pass women to each other left and right. It was a game I'd rather enjoyed playing, until Ashleigh came along. Even after she left, I still couldn't play the game. But, I'd gotten pretty good at giving the illusion I was back to my old tricks. I couldn't let Ashleigh know how bad she fucked my shit up.

Ashleigh

AFTER GETTING HOME from the airport, I fell asleep on the couch the second I sat down. I'd heard voices, but they'd muted to nothing before I was picked up and taken down the hall to my room. Once I was tucked in bed, underneath my sheets, I felt at home—and it was wonderful.

"Are you going to sleep all day?" A finger poked me in the shoulder. "Hey, I'm talking to you, lazy ass. It's ten o'clock in the morning."

The sound of Gabriella's voice brought a smile to my face. "It's good to see you too," I chuckled. "I see you finally made it home."

Opening up my eyes, I had to blink them a few times to see Gabriella's face clearly. She was dressed in a black sports bra and black shorts with her hair pulled high in a ponytail, sitting on the edge of my bed. It must be training time.

"Yes, I made it home and if you weren't passed out, I was going to jack your ass up. However, since Colin told me you weren't feeling so hot, I left you alone. He headed out shortly after you fell asleep." Jaw firm, her serious green gaze bore into mine; something was wrong.

Sitting up, I rubbed my eyes and looked on cautiously. "Why are you staring at me like that?"

"Oh, I don't know. Maybe it's the fact that you and Ryley are going to be the death of me. I swear I don't know what the hell to do with you two."

"What are you talking about?"

She held up her hands, halting me. "Hold on a sec. I'll admit, part of this whole thing is my fault since I didn't get your text message. If I did, then I'm sure you wouldn't have called Colin to pick you up."

"Trust me, I didn't want to call him." Throwing off my covers, I slid off the bed and took off my T-shirt and shorts so I could get ready for a shower. I felt disgusting. "I didn't know who else to call, Gabby. What's so bad about him bringing me home? We're friends." Grabbing a towel, I headed into my bathroom and turned on the shower.

Gabriella joined me in the bathroom, crossing her arms over her chest. "I know that, but Ryley sure as hell doesn't. He was under the impression you and Colin called it quits."

Eyes wide, I shut the shower door and turned to her. "How did he find out? Did you tell him?"

Sighing, she shook her head. "No, I didn't, but Tyler did, and what's worse is that Ryley saw you at the airport with him."

You have got to be fucking kidding me. "What were you two doing at the airport?"

"Oh, you're going to love this. We were going to Aspen."

The moment Aspen fell out of her mouth, my heart stopped in my chest and I felt sick. He was coming for me.

"Yeah," she continued, "and I guess, you and Colin happened to look like more than just friends. Or as Ryley put it 'arms draped all over each other' or some shit."

"Oh my God. *No*," I shrieked, holding my stomach. "It wasn't like that. I came home for Ryley. I want to get him back!"

Gabriella pursed her lips, her countenance weary. "I know you want him back, but things have changed, Ash. He was livid when we left the airport. After seeing you and Colin together, I think it knocked him over the edge—he was seeing red. It's the second time he feels like he got slapped in the face."

Eyes burning, I threw my towel on the floor and rushed to my closet. "I have to see him, Gabby. Do you know where he is?" I grabbed one of my pink tank tops and a pair of jeans out of my closet, sliding them on as fast as I could. I didn't care if I needed a shower. I couldn't let another minute go by without talking to him.

"He's probably at home," she confided. "Judging by how hard he's worked the past few weeks, I'd say he needs a day off."

Slamming my closet door, I ran back to my bathroom, washed my face and brushed my teeth. My skin wasn't as tanned as it used to be since I'd been working indoors at the hotel. Now, with the shock of finding out what happened yesterday, I looked downright pale. Not to mention, my cheeks had sunken a bit from being sick. I looked as weak as I felt, but I was determined to find Ryley. I'd spent a month away from him and I was tired of torturing myself. Even if he didn't want me back, he was going to let me explain.

"I'm going over there," I announced, marching out of my room. "Nothing happened between me and Colin last night. He has to know the reason why I came back."

Gabriella followed me to the door and grabbed the keys to my car off the counter, handing them to me. "Whatever happens, don't give up on him. He's angry at you, but if you keep trying I know he'll come around. You can do this."

Holding my keys in hand, I took a deep breath and nodded. "You're right, I can. I won't give up."

Once out of the apartment, I rushed down the steps to my car and was on my way to Ryley's house. The fight to win him back wasn't going to be easy. But I had a lot to make up for.

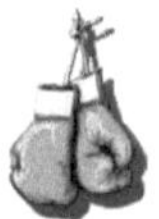

When I pulled into his driveway, I looked up at the balcony to his room. It was the same balcony where I ended our relationship just one short month ago. Taking a deep breath, I got out of my car and slowly walked up the stone walkway. Before I could back out, I rang the bell and took one step away from the door. All I could hear was the heartbeat pounding in my ears as I waited for someone to answer. Through the glass door, a silhouette appeared and the door opened. I was hoping it would be Ryley, but it was Camden, with a sneer on his face.

"Well, well, well . . . look who it is. I didn't think you'd ever show your face around here again," he chided. His hair was the same golden blond Ryley's used to be before he dyed it brown.

"I need to see Ryley. Is he here?"

Camden chuckled and opened the door wider so I could see his full body. He was shirtless and showing off his many tattoos, wearing only a pair of black boxer briefs that displayed how well-endowed he was. Even though he had the same body as Ryley, his did nothing to affect me.

"Oh, he's here, sweetheart. I'd say he's about ten inches deep in the hot blonde I sent his way last night."

By the mischievous look in his eyes I knew he was lying . . . or at least I hoped he was. "Fine, I'll just wait for him to get done."

His eyes widened then grew hard; I'd caught him off guard. "Fuck no. You're not welcome here. Not after you left me tied to a fucking bed and then dumped my brother."

"You deserved what I did to you," I hissed.

"And did my brother deserve what you did to him?" he countered.

I stiffened and looked away. No, he didn't deserve it and I regret what I did, every second of every day.

"Yeah, I didn't think so. The only way you're getting inside of this house is if you beg for my forgiveness. I can think of plenty of ways for you to use that lovely mouth of yours."

Disgusted, I scoffed and backed away, glaring at him. "Fine, you win for right now, but I'm not giving up."

"Even when he's in his room right now fucking a woman who just left my bed? You would still want him after that? I bet you don't even know how many people he's been with since you left."

The thought made me sick, but there was nothing I could do about it. I left him and the consequences of my actions were going to haunt me for the rest of my life. "Fuck you, Camden," I growled. "This isn't over."

"Actually, sweetheart . . . it is." He slammed the door and that was the end of round one. I lost, but it was only one of three. *Ding, ding, ding.* Round two.

6

Ryley

THE SOUND OF a door slamming woke me up and all I could feel was how bad my body ached. My hands didn't hurt as bad as I thought they would, but my muscles were on fire. Groaning, I slowly slipped out of bed only to be stopped by a voice behind me. "Good morning, sexy. I can work those kinks out for you."

Turning around, a tall, naked female with long blonde hair prowled closer. "What the fuck are you doing in here?" I snapped.

She pouted her lips, and then licked them as her hungry eyes raked up and down my body. "Your brother sent me. I had to promise I could make you come."

My brother was a fucking idiot. "Okay, fine, consider your job complete. Now get the hell out of here."

Her eyes went wide. "But . . ."

"*Out!*" I shouted, pointing to the door. "Damn woman, are you deaf? Or are you just too stupid to do what you're told?"

Huffing, she stomped to the door and slammed it open, only to be met by my brother.

"Well, someone must've woken up on the wrong side of the bed this morning," he teased, looking over at me. He stepped out of the way and didn't even acknowledge the woman as she sidled past.

"Who was at the door?" I asked, reaching into my drawer for a pair of shorts.

"Oh, just someone trying to sell me their bullshit. Don't worry, I got rid of them. What are the plans for your day off?"

After sliding on a pair of black workout shorts, I searched through my closet for a shirt. Settling on a black and green MMA Pride T-shirt, I slid it on and turned back to my brother. "I'm not taking the day off," I grumbled, reaching for my gym bag. "I have a fight against Nate Anderson in four days and I want to make sure I'm ready."

"You're going to kick his ass, Ry. The real question is . . . are you going to be ready for the title fight against me?" he asked slyly. "You know I'm not going to go easy on you."

"Yeah, I'm real worried about it, asshole. You might want to get rid of your playthings and get to the gym yourself." Camden was a good fighter though, and I had no doubt our fight would be the hardest I'd ever had to face. Grabbing my bag, I stalked past him and out into the hall.

"I'll be there soon," he called after me. "There's something I need to do first."

I grunted something unintelligible and continued on my way. It was too nice outside to take my car, so I opened up the garage and slid my helmet on before wheeling my sport bike out into the driveway. I loved speed and there was nothing like cruising down the highway with everything flying past you. It was one of my escapes, and I needed one desperately.

Ashleigh

FUMING, I MARCHED up the steps to my apartment and slammed the door shut. Why was Camden such an asshole? Gabriella had already left, so I pulled out my phone and dialed her number. There was no way I could tell her everything in a text.

When she picked up, she sounded out of breath. “So what happened?”

“Camden wouldn’t let me in,” I grumbled. “He’s such a dick. Are you already at the gym?”

“Yeah, I’m running on the treadmill. Matt’s giving me the evil eye. Have you tried calling him?”

“No, not yet, but I will. If he shows up at the gym will you call me? I have to see him.”

“Of course. But I have to go before my brother makes

me run another five miles."

We hung up the phone and I immediately dialed Ryley's number. Each time it rang, my heart beat louder and louder. When his voicemail came on, it was the first time I'd heard his voice in a long time; I missed it. As soon as his phone beeped, I cleared my throat and left a message. "Ryley, it's Ashleigh. I really need to talk to you. Please call me back and I'll explain everything."

That was a lie. I couldn't explain everything because I didn't know everything. And even if I did know, I couldn't tell him yet. Telling him now would be a disaster. The last thing I wanted was for him to give everything up because of his obligation to the baby. It would only foster resentment toward me.

When my phone beeped with an incoming text, I thought it was going to be Gabriella telling me Ryley showed up. However, it was Ryley himself. I knew he was pissed at me, but I didn't realize to what extent until I read what he wrote.

Ryley: Do me a favor and stay the fuck away from me. Don't come to my house, don't come to the gym. I don't want to see or talk to you. It's over.

Ryley: Leave. Me. Alone.

Closing my eyes, I could feel the burn behind my lids and the rejection in my heart. I knew it wouldn't be easy to get through to him, but he *did* try to go to Aspen to get me. That was my last thread of hope. Before I could reply, Gabriella called.

"Hey," I choked.

"Hey girl, I just watched him pull up on his bike. If

you want to see him, come on over."

"Wait, what? How can that be? He just texted me and told me to stay the fuck away from him. How could he do that if he was riding on his bike?"

"Are you serious? The only way he could've done that is if he stopped at a light, but I doubt he'd have time to text you."

Then it dawned on me . . . what if it wasn't Ryley? Sighing, Gabriella seemed to be on the same page.

"How much do you want to bet Camden has his phone?" she stated. "I know how he works and I know he hates you for what you did to him. He's going to try whatever he can to come between you and his brother."

"Ugh, I truly despise him," I grumbled. "What am I going to do?"

"I don't know, but Ryley's walking in. I gotta go."

Grabbing my keys, I headed straight for the door. "I'm on my way.

By the time I got to the gym, I was drenched in sweat and I couldn't get my hands to stop shaking. I parked beside Ryley's bike and slowly got out of the car. Was it a mistake showing up at his gym? *Probably.* Was I going to go in there? *Hell yes.*

Keeping my head held high, I turned the corner and didn't hesitate when I entered the gym. My rapid breathing was all I could hear as the room shifted on its axis. It was like everything froze and the world stopped, except for me and Ryley. He didn't even look over at me and it was obvious he already knew I'd walked into the gym. His body stiffened.

The magnetic feeling I always felt when he was near pulled me to him. Out of the corner of my eye, Gabriella watched on in amazement, but I couldn't focus on anyone other than my fighter. I slowly approached him, biting my lip to keep it from trembling. He lifted his weights, one arm at a time, his muscles bulging with each curl.

Those arms used to hold me, but I was too stupid not to stay in their warmth and protection. "Ryley," I murmured softly. Either he didn't want to acknowledge me or he couldn't hear. Even my own voice sounded foreign to my ears. Moving closer, I stood in front of him and took a deep breath. "Ryley," I repeated. "Can we talk?"

Setting the weights down, he lowered his head and balled his hands into tight fists. His knuckles were torn wide open and all I wanted to do was touch him. Without making eye contact, he stood and towered over me, glancing around the room. He looked at everything, but me.

"Let's go," he demanded.

Before following him to the back, I looked at Gabriella who frowned and shook her head. This wasn't going to be good. I felt like I was being led to slaughter by the way everyone watched me with trepidation in their eyes. All I wanted was for Ryley to look at me and listen to what I had to say. However, with each step, it felt more and more like the end. Once we got to the back, Ryley opened the door to an empty office and turned on the light.

As soon as I walked in, he shut the door behind us and locked it. I swallowed hard as he stood there, head down, body coiled tighter than a snake's. I wanted to go to him and wrap my arms around him, but I was frozen. I wanted to hear him call me angel like he used to when we'd make love.

"I went to your house this morning. Your brother wasn't too happy with me. Did he tell you I came by?"

He stiffened and sighed. "No."

"I thought as much," I whispered. "I guess I can't blame him."

Panic started to set in and I could feel the blood rushing to my head. I felt nauseated and lightheaded, but I swallowed it back as hard as I could. "I'm so sorry, Ryley. I never wanted to hurt you. But you have to know, there's nothing going on between me and Colin."

He scoffed and leaned against the wall, looking at my feet. "It didn't look like that yesterday."

"I know what it must've looked like and I know you don't trust me after everything I did, but you have to believe me. All I want is a chance to prove it to you, to prove that—"

"To prove what?" he exploded, lifting his fiery gaze to mine for the first time. My breath instantly left my lungs and I faltered, tears welling in my eyes. "To prove that I can trust you? That you want to be with me? How the fuck do you expect me to do that?"

Shaking my head, I found the courage to move forward, tears falling down my cheeks. When I lifted my hands to his face, he turned his head, the connection gone. "No, that's not what I was going to say. I was going to say that I love you. That I'll do whatever it takes to prove it to you."

For a second it seemed as if he was listening, but then

he jerked his face out of my hold and moved away. "I think you're missing the point. You see, I don't want you back. I'm happy with the way things are."

"Really?" I choked. "So you get to screw whoever you want and party it up? Is that what makes you happy?"

Smirking, he shrugged his shoulders. "That's just the way my life is. You wouldn't even want me back if you knew the things I've done since you left."

"It doesn't matter," I shouted. "I know you still care about me, Ryley. Why else would you have wanted to find me in Aspen?"

He'd obviously had enough. Thundering to the door, he unlocked it and opened it wide, keeping his back to me. "I'm not going to lie and say I never cared for you. But that time doesn't exist anymore. It's over, Ashleigh."

And with those final words, he walked away. Tears clouded my vision and I clutched my stomach, envisioning the child I knew grew inside . . . his child. He was lying and one way or another I was going to make him face the truth. I could see it in his eyes that he still cared about me. I just needed to find a way for him to admit it.

Stalking after him, I found him in the ring, gloving up. Gabriella rushed up to me and put her arm around me, but I pulled away. "You're a liar, Ryley Jameson." He looked down at me, his face swirling with so many emotions. "Yeah, you heard me right," I sobbed, "but I'm here and I'm not backing down without a fight. I can promise you that."

Tightening up his gloves, he leaned over the rope and looked down at me. "And you will lose. Why don't you just give up?"

"Because . . . to me, you're worth fighting for." Wiping away my tears, I glanced around the gym at everyone's wide-eyed stares. I gave Ryley one last glance and turned on my heel, rushing to the door. I was going to be sick and the last thing I needed was to throw up in front of all of those people.

The second I got outside, I collapsed onto the ground, the asphalt digging into my knees.

"Oh, my God," Gabriella exclaimed, rushing to my side. "Are you okay?" She rubbed a hand soothingly down my back and helped me get to my feet.

Shaking my head, I held onto her hand and laid my head down on her shoulder. "No, Gabby, I'm not okay. There's something I need to finally tell you and I'm going to need your support."

"You don't have to worry about Ryley. I'm going to give him a piece of my mind when I go back inside."

Pulling back, I wiped the hair off my face. "That's not my only concern right now," I confessed.

Her eyes went wide when she spotted my hand held protectively over my stomach. "Holy shit, Ash. Are you serious? Have you been to a doctor?"

I shook my head. "No, but that's where I want your support. I need you to come with me. I can't do this alone."

Gabriella folded me back in her arms and held me tight. "Is it Ryley's?"

"I'm almost positive. He's the only one I had unprotected sex with. I won't know for sure until I find out how many weeks I am."

Letting me go, Gabriella held my arms. "You have to tell them, Ash. You need to tell Colin *and* Ryley. No more putting people in the dark, you hear me?"

Now that the truth was out, my tears flowed harder. The father of my child didn't want me and the other man in my life wanted me, but would most likely run far away once I told him I was pregnant with another man's child. I had no choice but to face my fears.

"I can't tell Ryley yet. It's not the right time. I'll tell Colin tonight though. I might as well get that fight out of the way." Round two was done, but at least I stood my ground. I didn't count it as a total loss, but it definitely wasn't a win either.

Ryley

"SO THAT'S THE famous Ashleigh that left you high and dry?" Megan asked, jumping into the ring. She had her gloves on and ready to go.

About three months ago, I had met her at a club, where I got into a fight with her boyfriend after he hit her. I guess it didn't help that he caught me about to fuck her. Anyway, I'd been teaching her self-defense techniques and luckily it saved her life when he'd tried to come after her again. Ever since then, we'd been really close friends.

"Yes, that was her," I snapped. "I'd appreciate it if we didn't talk about her during our lesson."

"Sorry, but that's not going to happen," Gabriella cut in angrily. She hopped up into the ring and smiled at Megan, smacking gloves with her. Gabby had been helping me teach Megan as well. "I just need a couple of minutes with him and then he's all yours."

"No problem. Just go easy on him." She winked at Gabby and then hopped out of the ring.

As soon as she was out, Gabriella attacked and punched me square in the jaw, catching me off guard.

"What the fuck?" I growled. "I guess that was for Ashleigh, huh?"

Getting into stance, Gabriella lifted her gloves and snarled, "You got that right. How could you be so mean to her? Don't get me wrong, I know she hurt you, but that's no reason to treat her like shit. She came home for you, jackass. I even have the text to prove it."

She swung again, but I dodged it. "Shit, Gabby, what do you expect me to do? Frolic back into her arms like a goddamn bitch? You're out of your fucking mind."

"She loves you, Ryley and I know you love her too. How long are you going to keep lying to yourself?"

After she swung again and missed, I grabbed her around the waist and took her down to the mat, pinning her beneath me. "I'm not lying to myself," I hissed low, so only she could hear. "Do you want to know the truth?"

"You still love her."

"And it fucking kills me. You may think I'm a cold-hearted bastard, but it ripped me apart to see her break down in front of me. I wanted to comfort her and tell her I loved her too, but I can't. You are the only one who knows how bad I fell for her. She left *me*, Gabriella. I can't go running back to her without making her fight for it. I have to know she's not going to leave again." Sliding off of her, I grabbed her hand and helped her to her feet.

"So you only treated her like shit for show? You humiliated her, Ryley."

"I didn't want to, but I have to see how far she's willing to go."

Glancing around the room, Gabriella approached me and released a heavy sigh. "I understand what you're doing, but whatever you do, don't make her suffer for long. Trust me, she's strong, but I'm worried about her. She's not . . . *well* right now."

"Is she okay?" I asked hesitantly.

Gabriella shrugged. "Not really, but she will be once she has you back. My only concern now is your brother. Do you have your phone with you?"

Now that I thought about it, I didn't remember putting it in my gym bag. "No, I must've left it at home."

"That's what I thought."

"Why do you ask?" I inquired.

"Well, not only did Captain Asshat refuse to let Ashleigh in to see you this morning, but I think he texted her through your phone. It wasn't a warm fuzzy one either."

Anger boiled in my veins. Lying to me about her visiting was one thing, but using my phone to mess with her was another. "I didn't know," I replied. "He lied to me about who was at the door this morning, but I had no clue he would text her and pretend it was me. I'll talk to him and tell him to back off."

"Good idea," she agreed. "Because if not, I'm going to handle it and it won't be pretty. I don't want him screwing around with my best friend."

Neither do I.

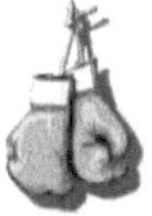

Camden never showed up at the gym to train, which was unusual since he'd never missed a session in his life. There were cars in the driveway when I pulled up . . . a lot of them. When I got inside, I found him by the pool with the same blonde chick from this morning, straddling his waist while she massaged his shoulders. Not to mention, a shit ton of other people lounging around, who happened to be none other than Kyle Andrews' groupies.

J.T. Michaelson caught my eye and I thundered straight over to him. He was one of Kyle's *best* friends, and any friend of his was an enemy of mine. "What the fuck do you think you're doing here?" I growled. Everyone grew silent as I towered over him sitting in the lounge chair with one of Camden's other girls fanning him. My body shook with rage. How could Camden cater to this douche bag?

Chuckling, J.T. stood and removed his sunglasses. "Your brother invited me," he replied flippantly. "Lighten up, we're just having a little bit of fun."

Fists tightening at my sides, I was ready to take him out. "Yeah, I know what your kind of fun is and I don't want anything to do with it. If *you,* and everyone else," I shouted, glaring at the horde of people loitering around, "don't get off my property, I'm going to personally escort you off. Now, get the fuck out!"

J.T. looked over at my brother, but my eyes never wavered from him. I was ready to kick his ass. In fact, I wanted to more than anything. "All right, you heard the man," my brother announced. "We'll continue this party at another time."

J.T. glared at me and snarled his lip before grabbing his things and stalking off with everyone behind him. I followed them out to make sure they all left and didn't touch anything in my house. Knowing Kyle's friends, they'd steal whatever they could get their hands on. As soon as they were all gone, I stormed back out to the pool. Camden still laid there on his lounge chair like nothing had happened.

"Do you want a massage brother? It looks like you need one," he teased, turning his head to face me.

"Are you fucking serious right now?" I snapped. "What the hell are you doing hanging out with Kyle's friends? I don't want them here, Cam. And if I see them again, nothing's going to stop me from beating the shit out of them."

Camden patted the blonde's thigh and she slid off so he could sit up. "Damn, bro, calm down. We were just having a little bit of fun. Now that Kyle's out of the picture, his friends were looking for a new leader. I guess I got the position. They love me."

Exasperated, I ran my hands roughly through my hair. I couldn't believe the shit I was hearing. "What the hell is wrong with you? First, you lie to me about who came by this morning. Then, you text Ashleigh using my phone. And now, you blow off practice to hang out with those cocksuckers. You're headed down the wrong path, fast."

Smile fading, Camden whipped off his sunglasses and stood, glaring straight at me. For years, it was like looking at a mirror when my brother was around. Now, I could barely tell who he was.

"You want to talk about heading down the wrong path? Okay, let's do this. What about you? The last thing you need to do is get caught up with that bitch again. Did you forget that she left you for someone else? I'm trying to *help* you, brother." His arms flew out to the sides. "You fucked her, she fucked you over . . . now move on."

"Where's my phone?" I asked, stressing each word.

Camden huffed and pointed toward the house. "It's in your room. I'm warning you, don't get involved with her."

At first, I thought maybe he was trying to protect me, but looking into his calculating blue eyes, that wasn't it at all. He had seriously turned into someone else. "And I'm warning you," I snarled, standing nose to nose with him. He didn't back down and I sure as hell wasn't going to either. "Stay out of my life and leave Ashleigh alone. I don't want to see or hear about you being anywhere near her. You got that?"

"So that's it. You're taking her back?" he asked, sounding disgusted.

"That's none of your business." Turning around, I stormed toward the house and yelled over my shoulder. "Just stay away from her!"

"You're a fucking idiot! Don't come crying to me when she fucks you over again."

Back then, I was an idiot because I let her go, knowing she still loved me. This time, I wasn't going to let that happen. If she truly wanted me back, I wasn't going to make it easy on her. *Until then, I'm not letting her in.*

Ashleigh

AS MUCH AS I wanted to put off finding out the truth, I knew I couldn't do it any longer. After leaving the gym, I stopped by the closest pharmacy and picked up a pregnancy test. I couldn't tell Colin before I had a definite answer. Maybe once he found out I was pregnant, it would give him the closure and the ability to move on.

Gabriella: Don't do the test without me! I want to be there.

Me: I won't. I'm just staring at it right now.

Me: I have to pee, so hurry.

Gabriella: Be there in 10.

I knew she had to finish her training, but I'd been sitting in our kitchen staring at the test. Even though my nerves were shot and I'd probably throw up everything I ate, I fixed a peanut butter sandwich and drank a bottle of water. So far, it all stayed down, but I was pretty sure it wouldn't be like that for long.

About ten minutes later, Gabriella opened the front door carrying a grocery bag filled with pints of Ben & Jerry's ice cream. When she noticed me looking at the bag, she smiled and shrugged her shoulders. "I figured we'd need it tonight. Ben and Jerry know how to make things so much better."

"I wish that were true in this case," I mumbled.

Opening the freezer, she started putting the pints away. "All right, babe, while I put away the ice cream go take a piss on the stick. I'll check it when you're done."

Holding the box in my hand, I started off down the hall toward my room. "Nothing like déjà vu, huh?"

Gabriella chuckled, "That's exactly what I was thinking."

Once I got into my room, I went straight to my bathroom and turned on the water. Even though I had to pee like crazy, there was nothing scarier than waiting on that little test to show the answer. Taking a deep breath, I took the cap off of the test and peed on it quickly before capping it and setting it on the counter. Keeping my eyes on the mirror, I washed my hands and opened the bathroom door. Gabriella was there waiting on me.

"Are you ready to find out?" she asked.

I was almost positive I already knew the answer. *Positive . . . oh, the irony.* When I nodded my head, she squeezed my arm and walked by me into the bathroom. This time, I didn't have Ryley to hold me in his arms as we waited. I was all alone sitting on my bed. After one long agonizing minute, I could see Gabriella in my bathroom with her hands on the counter looking down at the test.

"Gabby, what's wrong?" The second I heard her sniffling I had my answer. Gabriella never cried and when she turned to me with tears streaming down her cheeks, I closed my eyes and hung my head. I couldn't live in denial any longer . . . it was time to face the consequences.

Kneeling in front of me, Gabriella tilted up my chin and took my hands in hers. "You're going to get through this, Ash. I'm right here with you and I know Ryley will be too."

"How do you know? He walked away from me, Gabby. I don't think he's coming back."

She furrowed her brows. "You're not giving up on him, are you?"

"No," I stated adamantly. "He's not getting rid of me that fast."

Sighing in relief, Gabby helped me to my feet and folded me in her arms. "Good, because I know he'll come back. Just trust me and give him some time. Now let's call Colin and get this over with."

Nodding, I pulled away and grabbed my phone off the nightstand. Instead of texting, I dialed his number and waited on him to pick up. When his voice came on the line, I took a deep breath and cleared my throat. "Hey, Colin. Are you busy right now?"

"I just got through with baseball practice and about to head home. Are you okay? What's wrong? You don't sound good. I was worried you were coming down with something the other night."

"No, I'm not sick, but I'm also not okay. I need to tell you something in person, it's important."

"All right, I'll be there as fast as I can. I just need to go home and take a quick shower."

"Okay," I whispered, my throat closing tight. "See you soon." I hung up the phone and collapsed onto my bed. I honestly didn't know what was going to be harder, telling Ryley or telling Colin.

I didn't realize I had passed out, until I felt warm fingers brushing across my cheek. Instantly, I sat up and looked over at the clock. Thirty minutes had passed since my call to Colin and now he was with me, sitting on my bed. "I can't believe I fell asleep," I said, rubbing my eyes. "How long have you been here?"

Smirking, Colin smoothed the hair away from my face and moved closer. His blond hair was gelled in perfect spikes and he was wearing a light green button down and jeans, always so perfect. "Not long. I talked to Gabby for a few minutes before coming in here. I think her and Bradley are about to get something to eat. Do you want to go with them?"

Sitting up, I grabbed my pillow and clutched it to my chest. "I would, but I don't think it's a good idea right now. I need to tell you something and I'm not sure how you're going to take it."

His brows furrowed and he pursed his lips. "I know

what you're going to say and I'm fine with it. As much as you want to push me away I'm not going to let you. I love you, and I will wait on you for as long as necessary."

Shaking my head, I laughed once and then the tears started to flow. *Damn pregnancy hormones.* "If only it were that simple."

"Why isn't it?"

"Because I'm pregnant, Colin." *There, I finally said it.* Part of the weight lifted, but it was only a temporary relief considering I still had to tell Ryley. Colin's eyes went wide and he turned his head, clearly in shock.

When he finally faced me again, he looked down at my stomach which was covered by my pillow, realization dawning in his green eyes. "Is this why you left me? Because you knew you were pregnant?"

"No, but I had my speculations. I took a test when we were in Vegas and it came back negative."

"So that's what happened. I knew something was wrong, but you never told me. How far along are you?" I knew what he was truly asking.

"I don't know," I whispered. "I haven't been to the doctor yet. I just took the pregnancy test today. What I'm trying to say is—"

He held up his hand and pressed a finger to my lips. "Don't say it, Ash. Whatever you do, don't say it's his. I don't give a shit what you two did, but there's a possibility the baby could be mine as well."

Gently, I took his hand and held it in my lap. "I don't see how, Colin. You and I always used condoms."

His grip tightened. "So you're saying you and Ryley didn't?" I didn't even have to answer. He could see the stricken look on my face. "Goddammit, Ashleigh. What the fuck? Have you told him?"

"No, and I can't right now. I went to see him today and he's still angry at me from before. It's not the right time to tell him."

Angrily, he got to his feet and paced my room. "Why tell him at all? He's a fucking player for Christ's sake. He wouldn't know the first thing about taking care of you and the baby."

"He deserves to know."

His glare then turned to me, his green eyes blazing. "He doesn't deserve shit. *I'm* the one who deserves to be the father of that baby. *I'm* the one who loves you and would do anything for you."

"But what if the baby isn't yours? How would you feel then?" I asked, my heart ripping open with each second. More tears flowed down my cheeks and before I could wipe them away, Colin beat me to it, his hands warm as they brushed them away.

"I would feel the same as I do now. I'd love you. Even if the baby isn't mine, I would love it as my own. No matter what you think, there's still a chance the baby could be mine. We didn't exactly use condoms the entire time we made love, Ash. There's still a possibility."

He was right, we never started out using them; he would just put one on when he knew he was close. The possibility of him being the father was slim, but still there. "I'm going to call and make a doctor's appointment. They should be able to tell me how far along I am. As soon as we find that out, we'll have our answer."

"Until then," he murmured, caressing my cheeks. "Don't push me away. I want to be here for you. I know you still love me."

"I do love you, Colin, but I'm *in* love with Ryley. I'm not giving up on him. I know he still cares about me."

He huffed and closed his eyes. I hated having to tell him that, but I didn't want to give him false hope. Even if the baby was his, I still wouldn't love him the way I loved Ryley. I had no doubt the baby was Ryley's, but I knew I would have to prove it to Colin before he let me go. Opening his eyes, he let his hands drift down my face, then to his lap.

"I just want you to answer one question for me. I'll do whatever it takes to make you happy and to take care of the baby, even if it's not mine. But can you say the same for Ryley? You say he still cares about you, but what's going to happen if the baby happens to not be his? Will he stay with you knowing that the child you carry isn't his?"

And that was the question I was too afraid to find out the answer to. When I didn't reply, Colin sighed and pulled me into his arms; where I promptly broke down for the fiftieth time. I hated crying, and I had a feeling I was going to be doing a lot of it.

"I'm sorry, Ash, I didn't mean to upset you, but I wanted you to face the truth. I just don't want to see you get hurt."

"Then you might want to look the other way because my heart's already been ripped out."

Ashleigh

BRADLEY AND COLIN both stayed the night, with Colin taking up residence on the couch. After a couple of pints of ice cream and watching my favorite movie, *Pitch Perfect*, the night didn't turn out as badly as I expected. The main thing that sucked was that I threw up my ice cream, but if I were being honest with myself, it was probably because I ate two pints.

I spent the morning looking up available Marine Biology jobs in the area, but most of them I wouldn't be able to do pregnant. I wanted to be out in the field, doing research on marine mammals and sea life. Most of the job descriptions for this type of work required you to travel and live in extreme conditions. I couldn't do that. I only had one other option.

"What are you doing?" Colin asked, stretching his arms above his head. He was shirtless, with only his boxers on, and I knew he was doing it just to get a rise out of me. Even more so, it pained me to see the dragon that took up his entire back. I'd helped him design it.

Joining me at the bar, I slid my laptop over so he could see what I was looking at. "I need to find a job and this is all I could find. I can't work out in the field being pregnant. I probably could right now, but toward the end, there's just no way."

Colin furrowed his brows and slid my laptop back. "Why do you need to work at all? Once I start playing pro baseball next year, you won't ever have to work again. I told you I can take care of you."

"Whatever happens, I don't plan on having any man take care of me, Colin. I'm perfectly capable of taking care of myself."

Grabbing the bag of cinnamon raisin bagels, he pulled two out and put them in the toaster oven. It was what he used to do every morning we spent together. While they toasted, he fetched the cream cheese and orange juice out of the refrigerator and grabbed us two glasses. When he noticed me watching, he smiled and tapped me on the chin.

"Old habits die hard, I guess. And I know you can take care of yourself. I just didn't want you to stress about finding a job if there weren't any available."

My chest ached with how normal mine and Colin's lives used to be. He would do anything and everything for me, but it wasn't enough. I wanted the spark . . . the passion.

Once our bagels were done, Gabriella came running

out of her room with her gym bag across her shoulders. She grabbed a banana and raced for the door. "Hello and goodbye. I'm running late, but I'll see you later. We're having a girl's night tonight, so be ready."

"Where's Bradley going to be?" I asked.

She opened the door and repositioned her gym bag. "Get Colin to explain. I have to go before my brother kills me."

Turning to Colin, he laughed and shook his head. "We're leaving today for a baseball camp in Texas. We'll be gone until Sunday. I was going to tell you last night, but there were more important things to discuss."

"Your baseball is important. You'll be playing pro next year and traveling across the states. You should be happy about that."

Sighing, he threw away the rest of his bagel and left to grab his shirt and jeans off of the couch. "I am happy, but right now I'm more worried about you and the baby. Just let me know when you make the appointment, so I can go with you." After putting on his clothes, he walked over and pulled me to him, hugging me tight.

"I'll get an appointment scheduled. Have fun in Texas."

Letting me go, he grabbed his keys off of the counter and kissed me on the cheek. "I'll call to check up on you, okay?"

I nodded and watched him walk out the door. He deserved someone who loved him as much as he loved me. Picking up the phone, I dialed the number to my doctor's office and waited on them to pick up. I needed answers . . . and fast.

By the time Gabriella walked through the front door, I had just gotten off the phone with the principal at Stonewall Academy. They were impressed with my resume and wanted to schedule an interview for a teaching position. Setting my phone down, I looked at her over my shoulder and smiled.

Her eyes went wide. "Wow, I think that's the first smile I've seen on your face since you've been home. What's up?"

"Well, first off, I have a doctor's appointment scheduled in two weeks. It sucks, but I love my doctor down there and I refuse to go somewhere else. And second, I have an interview tomorrow."

She sat beside me and bumped me with her shoulder. "Well, at least you made the appointment. You'll just need to figure out when to tell Ryley."

Whenever he decides to talk to me again would be a start. "I'll figure that out when the time comes."

"So what's the interview for?" she asked.

"Well, it's not exactly what I want to do for a career, but since I can't exactly work out in the field with being pregnant and all, I opted for a teaching position. I think it'll be fun."

"Oh wow, that's great," she exclaimed. "And since it's still summer, you'll have the rest of the season off. I'm so happy for you. Maybe one day down the road we'll get a job exploring the ocean depths together. Now that is what I look forward to."

I laid my head on her shoulder. "Maybe one day," I murmured. "Right now, we have bigger plans."

"And part of those plans involve you coming with me to the fights on Saturday night. I have one against Jaden Eller. This time, it's not in Tyler's gym. It's going to be in the real spotlight. You have to be there for me."

And I'll most likely see Ryley again. She was thinking the same thing by the sly expression on her face. At least I wouldn't have to worry about Colin and Ryley crossing paths for the time being. That was the last thing I needed..

Ashleigh

FRIDAY CAME AND went, along with my interview, which I had to admit went amazingly well. Thankfully, I made it through the interview without getting sick and throwing up all over the principal's desk. I had a good feeling about it. Now, I was in the car with Gabriella as we headed on our way to the Sleep Train Arena in Sacramento. It was five hours away so we decided to book a hotel room, so we didn't have to drive back late tonight. I was focused on round three with Ryley, and this time, I wasn't going to let him walk away.

"Do you want to go to the party tonight?" Gabriella asked.

When I looked over at her, she smiled. Her midnight hair was sleek down her back and she wore a pink MMA

Pride T-shirt with a pair of denim shorts. My tank top, however, had *Team Gabriella* written on it in bold, pink letters. She also brought two with *Team Ryley* written across the chest, and told me that we were going to change into them before his fight. I didn't think it was a good idea, but saying no to Gabby wasn't exactly easy.

"I promise you'll have fun. I'll even let you be the designated driver. How does that sound?" she asked with a sly grin.

"Gee, thanks," I laughed, rolling my eyes. Pausing, I glanced out the window and my smile faded. "Do you think Ryley will be there?"

"I'm not sure, Ash. I haven't talked to him in two days. I saw him at the gym yesterday, but he kept to himself. He barely talked to Megan when we were working with her."

"Megan? I remember him talking about a Megan before. Is it the same girl?"

Gabriella nodded. "Yeah, it's the same one. Don't worry there's nothing going on between them. I've been helping Ryley teach her some self-defense moves. If Ryley hadn't taught her how to fight I don't know if she'd be alive right now. Her ex attacked her about a month ago."

"I remember," I claimed, thinking back to the day he'd received the phone call. We were on our way to his cabin when Megan's brother said she was in the hospital. I would never forget the tormented look on Ryley's face when he heard the news. It was then when I fell in love with him more.

"So anyway, I don't know what he's doing tonight. Have you tried calling him?"

"No," I replied, shaking my head. "I would rather

wait and talk to him in person. It's not like he'd answer the calls anyway."

We rode the rest of the way in silence, Gabriella was obviously trying to keep her mind focused before her fight with Jaden. Tonight would be the first time I'd actually get to watch her in action instead of seeing her through the television. I was so proud of her.

By the time we pulled up to the arena, there were many people lining up to get inside. I didn't see Ryley's car in the fighter's parking lot, but I saw Camden's. He was going to be a problem.

Gabriella followed my line of sight and growled. "Ryley wasn't too happy when he found out what Camden did. He said he was going to handle it. I told him if he didn't, I was going to kick his brother's ass. I know you could do it yourself, but you have to take care of that little one in there," she said, glancing down at my stomach. "I'm sure little Ryley would be more than happy to kick his uncle's ass."

The thought made me laugh and also made my chest tighten. I could just imagine having a little boy running around with my brown hair and Ryley's crystal blue eyes. He would be a heartbreaker just like his dad. Even if he didn't want me back, I would still have a part of him with me . . . our child.

"How do you know it's going to be a boy?" I asked, rubbing my still flat stomach.

Gabriella opened her car door and winked. "For some reason, I can see Ryley only making boys. Knowing your luck, you'll have twins. Double trouble. Let's just hope the other one isn't like Camden."

Chills fanned across my skin and I shivered. "No way

in hell. That's not going to happen," I claimed.

Once I got out of the car, we started toward the arena and went through the back door. I recognized a few of the faces from before; especially, one who smiled at Gabriella the moment she locked eyes with him. Quickly, she took my hand and pulled me along behind her. "Okay, we need to get out of here," she insisted awkwardly. Before turning the corner, she looked back once and blew out a nervous breath.

When we got to her room, she ushered me inside and shut the door. "Uh, do you mind telling me what's going on? Wasn't that Paxton Emerson?"

She groaned. "Yes, and he won't leave me alone." Setting her bag down, she opened it up and started pulling out her gear.

"Well, tell me if I'm wrong, but you don't look too upset with his attention. Is there something going on between you two?"

"No, there can't be," she exclaimed, slamming her things down on the table. "Can we just stop talking about him? I need to get ready and focus."

Something was going on, but she was right; I didn't want to pry and piss her off when she had an important fight coming up. Plus, I couldn't exactly be angry at her for keeping things from me, since I'd kept my life bottled up for the past few weeks. A few minutes later, her brother and coach, Matt Reynolds, walked through the door. Gabriella's agent, Garrett Wells, followed closely behind. He used to be Matt's agent until he retired from fighting—I had yet to be formally introduced to him.

Matt and Gabriella had the same color hair and eyes, and he was dressed in none other than a black 'Team Gabriella' T-shirt and jeans. I couldn't stop the snicker from escaping my lips.

He looked over at me and smiled when he realized what I was laughing at. "Yeah, I know," he grumbled. "I figured since she wore them for during my fights, it would only be fair to wear them to hers. I owe her that much, even if she does get on my nerves."

Gabriella punched him in the arm. "Hey, I'm right here. Why don't you be a good coach and tape up my hands?"

Garrett chuckled along with them and then sidled up beside me, adjusting his gray dress pants as he sat down. His shirt matched his blue eyes and his golden blond hair was combed and styled perfectly. Gabriella told me he wasn't much older than us, but he happened to be a little snobbish. I could see it in the arrogant way he smiled.

Extending his hand, he smiled and said, "I'm Garrett Wells, Gabriella's agent."

Returning the gesture, I shook his hand and grinned. "Ashleigh Warren. Very nice to meet you."

"Likewise. So are you excited about watching her fight? I haven't seen you here before, but she talks about you all the time."

"I've been in Aspen for a while and just flew in a couple days ago. Although, I *did* have the luxury of training with her one day, until I stepped out of line and left with a bloody nose." I hung my head dramatically.

"It was an accident," Gabriella shrieked.

We all chuckled, but then Garrett looked down at his watch. "All right, it's about time to go." His gaze then lifted to mine. "Are you ready? You're sitting with me tonight."

"Oh yeah, of course, let's go." Getting to my feet, I walked over to Gabriella and hugged her tight. "Good luck tonight. I can't wait to see you kick ass."

"Thanks, Ash. I'll see you out there. Afterward, we can come back in here and get something to eat before Ryley's fight. I have a strange feeling you're going to need all the energy you can get tonight."

She winked at me and nudged me toward Garrett who took my elbow and guided me to the door. What did she mean by that? I didn't have time to ask because I was being led down the hall. Garrett talked to me the entire time, but my attention strayed when I felt a presence watching me from behind. When I turned around, I only got one quick look at him before I disappeared around the corner. At least he knew I was there.

Ashleigh

GARRETT AND I took our seats just in time to watch Jaden Eller strut down the aisle and into the ring. She and Gabriella were about the same size, with the same long, dark hair and everything. Putting his arm across the back of my seat, Garrett leaned over toward me. “You know, it’s amazing how fast Gabriella’s learned to fight. Jaden’s been doing this for a couple of years and she doesn’t come close to the skills Gabby possesses.”

About that time, Gabby walked down the aisle with Matt beside her and caught my eye, winking at me. She was always confident, but I could see it in her more now. *I wish I could be like that.*

Hell, I couldn’t look at anything else; she was on fire wearing her red sports bra and black shorts. Once the bell rang, I moved to the edge of my seat, eyes wide. Jaden struck first, but Gabriella ducked and swung her leg low, sweeping Jaden off of her feet.

Instead of pouncing, Gabriella smiled and let Jaden get back up. Over in the corner, Matt rolled his eyes and shook his head. She could've ended it there, but she chose to toy with her prey. From what I heard, Jaden was a complete cunt. I saw how she provoked Gabriella in that video a while back ago. Now she was furious because she knew Gabriella was playing with her.

Snarling, she got back into position and Gabriella struck, landing a hard punch to Jaden's left cheek. Her head snapped to the side and before she could gain focus, Gabriella jabbed again and this time hit her right side. Jaden fell to her knees, and grabbed Gabby's legs, taking her down to the mat. They grappled and fists flew wildly in the air, but when Gabriella got behind Jaden and wrapped her legs around her like a pretzel, I knew it was all over.

Jaden tapped out and the bell rang. Gabriella won. Jumping to her feet, she ran around the ring with the biggest smile on her face. Looking at her, she didn't look like a hardcore MMA fighter. It was still strange to see how goofy she acted, yet still kicks major ass for a living.

"So where do you think her career will lead her?" I asked, looking over at Garrett.

He grinned. "If she keeps kicking ass, I'd say she could be the next women's Bantamweight champion. Not only is she a great fighter, but she's sexy as hell. I've had people contacting me about putting her in magazines and even the possibility of a movie deal. I haven't told her yet, but I thought I would surprise her tonight."

"Holy shit, that's amazing," I exclaimed. "She's going to flip out."

"That she is. Come on, let's go."

He helped me up and we trudged our way through the throngs of people to get to the back. Gabriella stood outside of her room while people took pictures of her and her brother together. When she saw us she rushed over and threw her arms around us both.

"Did you see me kick ass out there or what? I feel like I'm on air," she squealed.

Garrett nodded. "And it's only going to get better."

Since we had about two hours to spare, Gabriella and I left to get something to eat, much to my dismay. I didn't want to leave, knowing Ryley was so close by. It killed me not to be able to touch him or talk to him. Once we got back, Gabriella made me change into one of her 'Team Ryley' shirts even though I protested the whole time. She swore up and down that he'd like it. I had my doubts.

Now that it was time for his fight, we all went to our seats. As soon as we sat down, it was time for Ryley to make his entrance. Gabriella and I jumped to our feet and I screamed as loud as I could as the multi-colored lights flashed around the arena. The speakers blared to life with his fight song, except this time it was something different. Everything halted in my body when I heard the words of the song echoing in my ear. It was a message to me and I heard it loud and clear. The song was *One Step Closer* by Linkin Park. He was basically telling me to back off or he was going to break. That he needed room to breathe.

I thought maybe I was being paranoid, that it wasn't meant for me, but even Gabriella looked pale when she watched Ryley storm into the ring with his blue robe draped low over his eyes. Judging by the lyrics, it didn't bode well for me. My eyes burned, but I stood my ground and concentrated on staying strong, even though the song and his actions were basically a right hook to the jaw.

"Ashleigh, I'm so sorry," Gabby sighed. "He's taking this too far."

Squeezing her hand, I shook my head and forced a smile. "No, it's okay. He's hurt and lashing out at me. After the fight, I'm going to talk to him. If he truly doesn't want anything to do with me, then he'll have no problems saying it to my face."

"Are you sure you want to do that? You might want to be careful loading all of this stress on yourself," she commented, sneaking a quick glance at my stomach.

"I'll be fine." *I hope.*

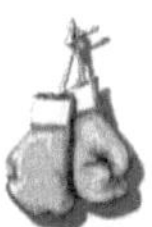

By the third round, Ryley still hadn't acknowledged me. Landon Baker was a tough striker, but Ryley lived up to his fighter name and went on a rampage. He was ruthless, yet held back just a bit to keep his opponent on his toes; he didn't want it to end. It wasn't until the last minute of the fight when everything snapped. Before the punch even connected, I knew it was going to be a knockout. The sound echoed through the arena, followed by the thud of Landon's body falling limp on the mat.

"And the winner by TKO is *Ryley . . . the Rampage . . . Jaaammmeeesssooonnn!*" The crowd went wild when Ryley's hand was lifted into the air. He smirked and circled the ring victoriously before jumping out and heading back up the aisle.

My heart was beating out of control, but it was now or never. I had to talk to him, even if it was the last time. "Gabby, I'm going back there," I announced, getting to my feet. "I have to talk to him."

"Okay, but I'm going with you. Let's go."

Gabriella and Garrett both followed behind, trying to keep up with my brisk pace. As soon as we got to the back, I didn't care what he was doing or who was in his room, so I turned the knob and slammed it wide open. Gabby gasped behind me and so did the woman who was in the room with Ryley. She jumped to her feet and clutched her chest, her brown hair covering her face when she bent down to pick up her phone.

"What the hell? You scared me," she exclaimed, lifting her head. Over my shoulder she saw Gabriella and her face softened.

"Megan, can you come out here with me?" Gabriella asked sweetly. "I think they need some private time."

So this girl was Megan. She was beautiful. I should've known that one of Ryley's close woman friends would be gorgeous. A knowing smile spread across Megan's face and she nodded. "Sure thing, girlfriend." She then turned to Ryley. "I'll meet you outside at the car."

Ryley nodded at her and then busied himself with taking off his gloves. He still hadn't looked at me. Once the door shut and everyone was gone, I didn't waste any time. "Ryley, please stop ignoring me. I need you to talk to me."

"I think I've said everything I need to say. I told you before you were wasting your time. Why can't you leave me alone? I don't want you."

"Then look at me and say it," I thundered. Charging over to him, I smacked his bag away, grabbing his face with my hands. "I love you, Ryley, and I need you to stop lying to me. Look me in the eyes and say the words. If you tell me you don't love me, I'll walk out that door and you'll never see me again." Tears blossomed in my eyes and all I could think about was the baby inside of my womb. "If letting you go is truly what you need, I'll do it."

Relentlessly, my heart pounded and tears fell down my cheeks. He stared at me and I could feel him leaning closer, his lips almost touching mine. Instead of kissing me, he took my hands and pulled them away from his face. Looking straight into my eyes, he sighed and shook his head. "I don't love you, Ashleigh. I never have and I never will."

My world shattered in that instant and everything came crashing down. I couldn't stand to look at him any longer, so I turned around and rushed out of the room, running as fast as I could. There were people everywhere, but they bolted out of my way when I went storming past. I had to get out of there, away from the humiliation and rejection. It was over. Shock was consuming me; I never really believed he'd say the words.

"Ashleigh, *stop*," Gabriella yelled. I was almost to the door but her grip on my arm forced me to halt. When I turned, her face fell and she pulled me into her arms. "Holy hell, what did he say to you?"

Holding onto her, I burst into tears and closed my eyes. "He looked me in the eyes . . ." I choked. "He looked me in the eyes and said he never loved me and he never will. I don't know what to do. This isn't happening. This just can't be happening."

"Shh . . . don't worry, Ash. It'll all be okay. I'll take you back to the hotel and you can rest. I'll handle everything from here."

There was nothing she could do. It was over.

Ryley

WHEN YOU THINK about words, you never really put it into context how strong they could actually be when spoken. I had gone too far and the second Ashleigh ran away from me, I regretted the harsh response. Hurting her was my goal . . . I didn't plan on breaking her. *Dammit.* I let my anger and pain get in the way. Before I could rush after her, Gabriella beat me to it and took off down the hall. How could I be so fucking stupid?

"Ryley, are you okay?" Megan asked, coming into my room. "What did you say to her?"

Grabbing my bag, I slung it over my shoulder and started for the door. "Something I shouldn't have. Let's go to the party and see if they show up. I have to find her."

Once outside, I texted Gabriella but she never responded or called back. That didn't surprise me, considering I just tore her best friend's heart in two. Hopefully, they would be at the party. It took ten agonizing minutes to get to the house and when we pulled up, there were cars everywhere, but I didn't see Gabriella's or Ashleigh's. *Fuck my life.*

"All right, Ry, I'm going inside. Are you going to wait out here for them?"

Holding my phone, I texted Gabriella again and nodded my head. "Yeah. I don't even know if they're going to show up."

"I have faith you'll find her. Good luck, and call me if you need anything."

Her heels clicked on the driveway as she walked away and I was left to myself. Ten minutes later, I was still sitting there in shock, staring into nothingness, when Gabriella sped down the street and squealed her tires coming to a stop in front of me.

She opened her car door and slammed it shut. "What the fuck is your problem? Do you have any idea what you just did?"

"I was angry, Gabby. What do you want me to say? I wanted her to feel the pain that I did when she left. I thought it would make me feel better."

She crossed her arms over her chest. "And did it?"

I lowered my head. "No. It made me feel worse."

"Good. Because she's a hot mess right now. She loves you, Ryley, but I don't know how much more she can handle. I'm pretty sure she's hit her limit."

"Where is she?" I asked solemnly.

Gabriella sighed and squeezed the bridge of her nose. "She's at the hotel bawling her eyes out. She doesn't know

I'm here."

"Take me to her," I commanded. "I have to tell her I'm sorry."

Her eyes went wide. "Does this mean you're giving in and forgetting your macho bullshit?"

"I'm done, Gabby. Keeping her away is only making it worse."

Reaching in her purse, she pulled out a room key and handed it to me. "Here's the key to our room, the number is on it. Go there and talk to her. I'll stay here to give you some time." Holding the key in my hand, I closed my eyes. *Please don't let it be too late.*

Ashleigh

I DON'T KNOW how long I cried, but it felt like an eternity. The pillow was stained from my tears and mascara. My chest ached, making my whole body sore. Gabriella had turned off all the lights and told me she would be right back, but she had yet to come back. I wanted to be alone anyway to wallow in my grief and despair. I was to blame for my own misery, but Ryley's words pierced straight through my soul. Not only did he rip my heart in two, but he took away all my hope.

The door to the hotel room opened and clicked shut, footsteps shuffling across the floor. My eyes were basically swollen shut from crying, but I heard the bedroom door open. I didn't want Gabriella feeling like she had to babysit me.

"Gabby, please go to the party," I whispered hoarsely. "You don't have to stay with me." The bed dipped low and a strong arm wrapped around my waist, pulling me in tight.

"No, she doesn't . . . but I do."

I froze and held in my gasp. Ryley's scent filled my senses and I couldn't tell if I was hallucinating or not. I touched his hands, they were real. I could feel his breath on my ear. It was all real. "Are you really here?" I cried, swallowing hard. "Please tell me it's not a dream."

Turning me over, his hands covered my cheeks. I tried to focus on him, but in the darkness, I couldn't really see much of anything. But I could feel him, and smell him.

"It's not a dream, angel." And then, the moment I had been waiting for finally came. His lips were warm as they closed over mine, and I willingly opened to him when he pushed his tongue inside. My whole body tingled and sparked to life under his touch. I felt alive again.

"Wait," I pleaded, quickly remembering the past hour. I moved away from him and turned the lamp on.

He squinted under the bright light and my breath hitched at the sight of him. There was no anger in his face, only sadness and regret. A small smile splayed across his face when he looked down at the *Team Ryley* printed on my T-shirt.

"Why are you here? You said you didn't love me anymore, that you never could."

He swallowed hard and lowered his head. "I know, and I wish I could take it back. It was a lie, angel. I've never stopped loving you, even after you left."

I closed my eyes and squeezed them hard, still not believing he was real. "Then why did you lie?" I glanced wearily over at him.

"Because I wanted you to feel the pain I felt when you left me. I wanted to see your heart break . . . maybe just to prove that it *could* be broken over me—that you really did still love me."

"But you didn't break it," I cried, "You ripped it apart."

He nodded. "And that's why I'm done. I can't hurt you anymore. I watched you walk away once, I refuse to let you go again." Closing the distance, he took my hand and pulled me to him. I laid down, facing him, memorizing every single line and angle of his face. His lips parted when I brushed my fingers across them, so soft. Following my lead, he brought his hands up and caressed my face, never taking his gaze off mine. I don't know how long we stared at each other, but it felt good to be in his arms again.

For the first time in over a month, I could breathe. Time stood still and even though I didn't want to miss a single moment, my eyes drifted shut and I succumbed to the peace he offered me. I wasn't going to let him go.

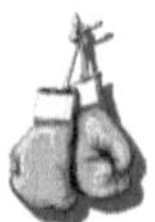

I don't know how long we were asleep, but when I woke up it was still dark outside and the light was on in the room. Ryley slept peacefully beside me, his arm tucked tightly around my waist. My heart hurt thinking about all of the nights I wasted when I could've been with him—not missing a single moment together. Gently, I trailed my fingers down his chest to the waistband of his jeans. He jerked with my touch, but his slow, deep breaths showed he was still asleep. I ran my hands over his groin and massaged his growing arousal, smiling when his eyes began to open.

"Now this is how I like to be woken up," he teased, his voice gruff with sleep.

I played with him more and his cock bulged thick and hard behind his jeans. Climbing on top of me, he pushed his groin against me and rocked his hips. *Holy hell, I wanted him to make love to me.* He brought his hands to my breasts and massaged them through my shirt while kissing along my collarbone. My breasts felt heavy, sensitive. I couldn't get enough.

"I missed you," I whispered. "There wasn't a day that went by when I didn't think about you." He moved against me more rapidly and the friction drove me insane. By the heated look in his eyes, he was close to losing control. I wasn't far from it either.

"I missed you too, angel." He trailed his fingers down my cheek, and neck, all the way down to the hem of my shirt. His visage darkened, expression serious. "If we do this there's no going back. I can't lose you again."

Gently, I took his face in my hands and caressed his jaw stubble with my thumbs. "I'm not going anywhere. I can promise you that." My lips lifted to his, sealing the promise I just made.

His fingers tightened on my breast and in one swift move my shirt was over my head and he had my bra undone, lowering his mouth to my nipple. He bit and sucked, rolling his tongue across my peak while I squirmed beneath him, wanting more. The tension grew with each touch and I could feel his control slipping. Abruptly, he slid away and took off his shirt and jeans, tossing them on the floor, exposing the hardness between his legs.

Opening my legs to make room for his body, he pressed his hips into me and unbuttoned my jeans. Without looking away, he lowered them down my legs, licking his lips. I shivered in anticipation, my clit throbbing relentlessly.

Gently, he pushed a finger inside and then another, stretching me. He smiled in delight when he licked the wetness off of his fingers. "Do I need to put on a . . ."

"No," I interrupted softly, wishing I could tell him the truth. "We'll be okay."

Placing his hand on my cheek, he lowered his lips to mine and settled his body between my legs. He pushed in just a little and circled his hips to spread my wetness on his cock. Once I stretched around him, he thrust all the way in, making me arch off the bed with a loud moan.

"Fuck, I missed this," he growled. I missed it too.

It couldn't have been more than a few minutes, but I wasn't able to hold out any longer. My orgasm felt like it exploded from the inside out, tearing me apart and putting me back together. I screamed with my release at the same time Ryley dug his fingers into my skin and spilled his come inside of me, his cock pulsing with the aftershocks. For a long moment, we laid there staring at each other—so many things left unsaid. But for now, it was enough just to be in his arms and to know that things were about to change.

Please God don't let me wake up and it all be a dream.

Ashleigh

WAKING UP, I laid in bed without opening my eyes. I took inventory of my body, noticing the small pains here and there. It was just confirmation that last night had really happened, and I smiled before stretching and rolling over. Ryley was beside me, his lips spreading into a smile when my gaze focused on him.

"I thought you'd never wake up," he teased, running his fingers down my bare arm. I shivered and curled into his chest, nuzzling my cheek against his skin.

"I could've sworn last night was just a dream. You have no idea how many nights I dreamt of us together, only to wake up and nothing."

"I had those nights too, angel. But right now, we need to get back home. Check out is in forty-five minutes." Lifting the sheets, he climbed out of bed, stark naked, and my insides clenched to have him again.

"Are you sure you don't want to stay in bed with me?" When he turned around, I pinched my nipples and rolled them between my fingers.

His cock instantly got hard and he groaned. "Fuck, you're going to kill me. But Gabriella's in the next room, I heard her talking to someone on the phone. I think she's worried about you."

Ryley went to the bathroom and brought me a robe. I slid it on while he put on his clothes. When he was done, he grabbed my hand and gave me a kiss. "I'm going to run to my room, take a shower, and change clothes. I'll be back down in a minute, okay? This should give you a little time to catch up with Gabby. She was pretty pissed at me last night."

"Yes, I was," she called out from the living room. Once my robe was tied, I opened the bedroom door and her eyes instantly found mine. She beamed when she saw Ryley and me together. "Hot damn, it's about time you two got your shit straight. I thought I was going to have to kick both your asses."

"His maybe," I said, pointing to Ryley.

He chuckled and wrapped his arm around my waist, kissing the side of my head. "What can I say? I'm a quirky son of a bitch, it's part of my charm. I'll be right back."

Gabriella stopped him before he could walk out the door. "Oh, and just so you know, Megan and I are riding back to California together. That way you and Ash can catch up. Judging by the level of your disheveled appearance, I don't think you got much talking done last night."

Ryley winked and smiled before closing the door,

leaving me to Gabriella's teasing. Except now that Ryley was gone, her smile faded and she handed me my phone.

"Colin has been calling you nonstop, Ash. He's starting to get on my nerves."

"What did you tell him?" I asked, dialing his number.

"I told him you were sleeping. Are you sure you can't move up the doctor's appointment? Until you find out for sure he's not the father, he's going to be hounding your ass. Not to mention he'll probably cause problems between you and Ryley once he finds out that you two are back together. It's going to be a shit storm."

Groaning, I hit the send button and waited on him to pick up. I loved him, but Gabriella was right. He wasn't going to leave me alone until I could prove that my child was Ryley's. I had no doubt the baby was Ryley's. I could feel it in my blood.

"Ash, thank God. Where the fuck have you been? I tried calling you last night and all morning," he snapped worriedly.

"Colin, I'm fine. I just got up and we're about to leave Sacramento and head home. How's camp going?"

"Actually, it's going pretty good. They say I'm one of the best pitchers they've seen in years. Which will be good for when the pro teams start looking for new players."

"That's great. You'll be able to travel and see new places. I think I'm jealous," I teased, hoping to break the tension.

"You'll be coming with me too, Ash. You and the baby. We can see it all together."

Hello tension. Back so soon? Sighing, I sat down on the couch while Gabriella stared at me, biting her lip. She knew the shit was about to hit the fan. "Colin, that's not going to happen," I murmured regretfully.

The line went silent, but then his angry voice came back over the line. "You're there with him, aren't you? That's why you went with Gabriella. It wasn't to see her, it was to see him."

"Why do you sound so shocked?" I countered. "I love him, Colin. The baby I'm carrying is his. I have no doubt about it."

He scoffed. "But you love me too. And as far as the baby goes, you can't determine that it's Ryley's because you *think* it is. Until your appointment, there's still a chance. I'm not letting you go."

"You don't have a choice," I replied sadly. "I choose him and it'll always be him."

"Things can change, Ash. I'll see you tomorrow." And with those last words, he hung up.

Throwing my phone on the couch, I hung my head and groaned. "What the fuck am I going to do, Gabby? He's not going to go down without a fight."

"Yeah, I could hear him through the phone. But I guess it's a good thing Ryley's not going to let you go either. It looks like you have a lot of talking to do on your way home. Are you going to tell him about the baby?"

"I can't. It's too soon. I'll tell him about Colin being in my life, but I can't just get back with him and dump something else in his lap."

Gabriella nodded. "I understand, but men don't think like we do. He might see it as deceitful when you told Colin and not him."

Throwing my hands in the air, I huffed and stalked into the bedroom. "Well, I was hoping Colin would see it as a sign that we weren't meant to be together. But *no*! Now he has this false hope that the baby is his. It completely backfired."

I had a few minutes to spare so I turned on the shower and waited for it to get warm while Gabriella came in and grabbed her toiletry bag. "It'll all work out in the end. I think you and Ryley are strong enough to handle it."

I hope so.

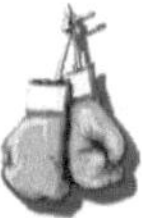

Now that we were on the road, we had a five hour drive ahead of us with just me, him, and the highway. There were so many questions I wanted to ask, I didn't know where to start. Granted, there were a lot of questions I really didn't want to know the answers to.

"How was it up in Aspen with your family? Did you get on your four wheeler a lot?"

The thought made me smile. It reminded me of the time we'd spent at his cabin, with all of the four wheeling and hiking. Alas, I didn't get on it for safety reasons. "No, I didn't. I mainly stayed at the hotel and worked. There wasn't much else to do. What about you?" I braced myself. I can only imagine the kind of shit he'd gotten into, or on top of.

Reaching for my hand, he brought it up to his lips and kissed my palm before clasping our fingers together in his lap. "I trained, day and night. It was the only thing that kept me from thinking about you."

"I'm sure there were other things that helped with

that," I mumbled, turning my attention to the window. Fucking a bunch of slutty hosebeasts came to mind.

He squeezed my hand to get my attention. Reluctantly, I glanced over at him, hoping my jealousy didn't show. Yes, I knew if he'd been intimate with other women, it was my own fault, but that thought didn't comfort me right now.

"I know what you're thinking, angel. And as much as I wanted to fuck away my problems, I didn't. I haven't slept with anyone since you."

Mouth gaping open, I stared at him, wide-eyed. "Are you serious? But you made it sound like you did."

"I'm not saying I was perfect during our month off, but I can honestly say I didn't fuck anyone during that time."

I held up my hand, halting him. "Okay, I don't want to know the details."

"Unfortunately, I know you can't say the same. What's up with you and Colin? I know what I saw at the airport and he didn't look at you like you were just a friend."

Closing my eyes, I laid my head back on the seat and took a deep breath. "I was going to bring this up. I knew you would want to know."

He scoffed, "Let me guess, he wants you back."

I looked over at him and nodded. "And he's not backing down. I talked to him this morning and told him you and I were back together. I don't know what else to do. I have to know that you're not going to let him get to you."

He gripped the steering wheel tight, his stare hardening on the road. "He'll be fine as long as he doesn't touch you. There's nothing he can do to get between us, unless you let him. You're not going to hang out with him are you? I know Gabby's messing around with his douchebag best friend."

"And that's going to be the problem. I'm not going to lie, it's going to be hard to avoid Colin; he's persistent. He also hates you, which will make him want to try harder."

Ryley snorted. "The feeling's mutual."

The tension in the car grew thicker by the minute. I could see it now, Colin was going to be a huge problem until I found out the baby wasn't his. I just couldn't explain all of this to Ryley. "On a brighter note, I applied for a new job. If I get it, I'll be teaching Biology, along with a couple of Marine Biology classes for advanced students."

His lip tilted up in a small smile and his eyes brightened. "That's fucking awesome. What made you decide to teach instead of actually doing the scientific research?"

"Well," I began, "if I went out into the field I'd have to travel a lot. I wasn't exactly ready for that quite yet."

He furrowed his brows and glanced at me quickly. "It's not because of me, is it? I don't want to ever keep you from your dreams."

Little did he know he wasn't keeping me from them . . . he was fulfilling them. "I admit your part of the reason. I just got you back and the last thing I want to do is leave for weeks and weeks at a time. Gabriella and I were going to travel together, but she chose her own dream of fighting. I lost my partner in crime. Besides, I think teaching high school will be fun."

"Oh hell," he groaned giving me a wink. "Now I'm going to have to worry about pubescent high school boys."

I laughed. "Oh, whatever. If they saw you, I don't think they'd go anywhere near me."

"I might need to come eat lunch with you then," he teased, but then turned serious. "And since we're talking about things coming between us, I want you to stay away from my brother. He's into some bad shit now and once he finds out about us I don't know what he'll do. I already warned him to stay away from you."

Camden was capable of anything, but I already knew to be on my guard. "Do you think he'll listen?"

Ryley scoffed, "Fuck no. He's most likely going to play mind games with you. Whatever he does or says just don't believe him. The only problem is, I can't avoid him."

"We'll be fine," I assured him. We actually had bigger concerns than his dumb ass brother. "You can always stay with me tonight instead of going home. That way you don't have to deal with him."

He flashed a sly smirk. "How can I say no to that offer? We still have a lot of making up to do."

Yes, we do.

Ashleigh

OUR MAKING UP took all night and into the morning; I was exhausted and I could barely walk. Being pregnant definitely had an effect on my body—my hormones were completely out of whack. Even though we made love numerous times, I still wanted more. Sadly, when I woke up, Ryley was gone. My alarm clock said it was ten-thirty. No wonder he was gone, he had to train. When I walked into the kitchen, there was a note from Gabriella.

Ash,

I'm sure you know that Ryley had to leave early. He didn't want to wake you. I fixed you some boiled eggs and bacon for breakfast. Make sure you eat. It's not much, but I figured the blander the better. I didn't want you getting sick when you came to the gym.

Now get your lazy ass here. Just because you have a bun in the oven doesn't mean you can slack off. Now you have even more reason to keep that tight ass in shape.

Love you,

~ Gabby.

And then it dawned on me. Ryley was going to be surrounded by beautiful women while I gained baby weight. Would he still find me attractive? The better question, was he still going to be around after he found out? I had to have faith that he would.

After throwing on some workout clothes, I found my eggs and bacon sitting in the microwave. I cracked and peeled both eggs, eating them along with four pieces of bacon, while I checked my emails. Once I put my dish in the dishwasher and washed up, I was ready to go. The gym wasn't too far away, so I cruised along in my little white Toyota Camry. Everything felt like it was going right for a change.

The feeling didn't last long. I groaned when I saw Camden's little sports car in the parking lot of the gym. *If he bothers me, maybe I'll throw up on him.* That would be funny as hell. Taking a deep breath, I opened my car door and got out, grabbing my gym bag out of the back seat. I packed a couple of snacks and some waters to hopefully help curb my nausea, if it decided to resurface. Honestly, I never knew when it would hit.

Just the other day I had run away from this place, upset because Ryley told me he didn't want me. It was hard to believe so many things could change in just a matter of a couple of days. As soon as I walked through the door, my eyes immediately found Ryley in the ring . . . with his brother. When he spotted me, he smiled. There was no warm welcome from his twin. He charged after Ryley and they went down on the mat.

"I guess he's not too happy to see you," Gabriella quipped, coming to my side. She shook her head and laughed, watching the guys grapple on the mat. "Eh, I wouldn't worry too much about Camden. He'll get over it."

"I have my doubts about that," I grumbled.

"So what did you think about my note? Pretty funny, huh?" She took my hand, leading me over to the stationary bikes and pointed at one.

Rolling my eyes, I set my bag down and got on the bike. "Yeah, it was funny, all right," I replied sarcastically. "It just reminded me I'm going to be a whale, while you and everyone else are going to stay hot as hell."

"Hey, pregnant girls are sexy. Ryley's not going to be able to keep his hands off of you. Now get to work. I'll keep you in shape." She got on the bike beside me and waved her hand for me to start.

Laughing, I flipped her off and pedaled. At least I was in the perfect spot to watch Ryley. By the sly look in Gabriella's eyes, I knew she put me there on purpose.

After thirty minutes of watching the boys butt heads, Camden threw his gloves on the mat and stalked out of the ring, straight for the door. The last time I saw him that angry was when I tied him to his bed and left him there. There was something different about him now, he was more volatile.

Ryley and his coach talked heatedly in the ring before his coach threw his hands in the air and stormed away.

With his hands on his hips, Ryley closed his eyes and hung his head. "What's going on?" I asked, turning my attention to Gabriella.

"The guys haven't really been getting along today. Camden found out that you and Ryley were back together so he's been an ass all morning."

"Did Ryley tell him?"

She shook her head, furrowing her brows. "No, I'm not sure who did. He just came in all pissed off."

Camden was jealous of Ryley and even admitted it to me that night I tied him to the bed. He did well at hiding it, but now I could see it all over his face. "Who do you think told him? I didn't think that many people knew."

"Word spreads fast in the MMA world," Gabriella admitted. "Megan or my brother might have said something to someone and it just got around. I wouldn't worry about it. Camden was going to find out eventually."

That's true. Now that I was drenched in sweat and my legs were on fire, I leaned back on the bike and watched Ryley take off his gloves and shove them in his bag. I hated seeing him upset over his brother, even if I didn't like the douche nugget. "I'm going over to Ryley," I said, picking up my bag.

Gabriella winked and continued to pump her legs on the bike. Before I could take another step, my phone started to ring. I dug around in my bag until I found it, and I didn't recognize the incoming number. I hated answering the phone when I didn't know who it was.

"Hello?" I answered.

"Good morning, Miss Warren, this is Principal Briggs at Stonewall Academy. How are you doing today?"

Eyes wide, I smiled and bit my lip. *Please tell me I*

got the job. Stonewall Academy was where I wanted to teach. It was in a great location and the campus was amazing. Even Principal Miranda Briggs seemed like a nice woman. She sort of reminded me of my mother.

"I'm doing great, just hopping off a bike at the gym. How are you?"

"Oh, I can't complain, dear. The summer has been amazing. It's hard to believe school starts in just a month. Time sure does fly by."

"Yes, it sure does," I agreed with a polite laugh.

"Which brings me to the reason I'm calling. I've had thirty people apply for this position, and out of all thirty, you were the one who stuck with me. I like your energy and passion. I think you'd be a good fit here. Are you still interested?"

"Of course," I exclaimed excitedly. "I would love to accept."

Ryley finally joined me and Gabriella and grinned when he saw my wide smile. I held up my finger, signaling I would tell him the good news in a minute. He looked over at Gabriella and she shrugged. I couldn't wait to tell them.

"I'm glad to hear it," Principal Briggs replied. "I'm going to mail you a packet which will include all of the paperwork I need you to fill out and so forth. You can either mail them back or drop them off at the school. I look forward to having you."

"Thank you so much, Principal Briggs. I'm really excited about being there."

As soon as we said our goodbyes I bounced over to Ryley and jumped in his arms. "I got the job," I squealed.

He swung me around and pressed his lips against

mine. I was all sweaty, but he didn't seem to care. "That's great, angel."

Gabriella jumped to her feet and bounced over to us. "You know what this means?" Ryley and I both looked at each other and then back to her, eyebrows raised. She rolled her eyes and slapped me on the arm. "It means we have a reason to celebrate. So Friday night, it's *on*. I would say we'd do it tonight, but my brother isn't going to be here until later. My nephew's been sick, so he's trying to help out." She winked at me and then started down toward the weight benches. "I'll get everything set up. All you have to do is be there, okay?"

"Okay," I agreed. "It better be good." Now that Ryley and I were alone, I wrapped my arms around his neck. "Is everything okay with you and Camden? I saw him storm off."

He sighed and buried his head in my neck, sending shivers across my skin when he kissed my flesh. "No, but it'll all work itself out. However, right now I don't want to talk about him. I think we need to do a little pre-celebration ourselves."

The need in his blue stare made me shiver in his arms. "What do you have in mind?" I asked, whispering the words across his lips.

"Follow me." Taking my hand, he led me away from the exercise machines and past the ring, toward the back. Thankfully he didn't take us to the room where he locked us in the other day. There were bad memories in that room.

Instead, I followed him to the end of a hallway where he ushered me inside a pitch black room. When he turned on the lights, I smiled as my reflection showed in the mirrors along each wall. It was the kind of room you'd see at a dance studio.

I watched his image in the mirror as he shut and locked the door, grinning devilishly as he stalked after me. "Celebrating, huh?"

He lifted his shirt over his head and dropped it to the floor. "All you have to do is hold on." Placing his hands on my waist, he turned me around so I faced the mirror with him at my back. I watched as his hands splayed across my stomach and then went under my shirt to my breasts, squeezing them. "Do you like watching me touch you?"

"Yes," I breathed, leaning back into him. He lifted my tank top and sports bra over my head and groaned when he saw my naked flesh in the mirror.

"I think I like watching it too." His fingers pinched my nipples and I jumped, earning a deep chuckle to rumble in his chest. Next he lowered his hands to the waistband of my shorts and slid them to the floor, along with my underwear. He kept his gaze on mine as he dropped his shorts to the ground and pressed his rigid cock against my ass. "Do you think you'll like watching me make love to you?"

My clit throbbed and I grew wet between my legs. "You have no idea."

Turning me around, he picked me up in his arms and I straddled his waist. Then he walked forward, until my back was against one of the mirrors. It was cold, but it instantly warmed up from the heat of my body. "Hold on tight, angel." He circled his cock along my opening and moaned when he could feel how soaked I was for him. Not wasting any time, he slammed into me and I cried out, leaning my head against the mirror.

He bent down and flicked his tongue across my nipple, biting at the same time he plunged deep. In the mirror, his muscles contracted with each thrust and his ass tightened. I loved watching him make love to me.

Bouncing me up and down, I held onto his shoulders as my sweaty skin made noises against the mirror. Burying his head in my hair, he breathed me in and held me tighter, his cock lengthening inside of me. He was close. "I'm going to come in you, angel."

On the verge of orgasm, I moaned and dug my nails into his back. "Yes," I whispered heatedly. I tightened my legs around his waist and rocked my hips against his, the perfect friction. The second he felt me tighten against his cock, he grunted with each thrust, pulsating inside of me. I cried out his name as my body exploded all around him. He trembled and jerked, slowing his pace until every single drop of him was released inside of me.

Breathing hard, he switched places with me and leaned his back against the mirror, lowering us down to the floor. He watched over my shoulder and he smiled, no doubt staring at my bare backside. "You are so fucking sexy," he admitted.

Holding me down tightly on top of him and using my ass as leverage, he rubbed me along his spent cock.

"Let me guess, you want to watch me make love to you now?" I smiled as I pushed my core into his growing arousal.

"You're going to have to work for it, babe. Are you up for the task?"

I raised my eyebrows and smirked. Lifting my hips, I maneuvered his slippery, semi-hard dick into me and sat down . . . feeling his come seep out of my body, coating my thighs. Thankfully, there were stacks of towels in the corner because we were going to need them. "You better believe it, stud. I think we need to celebrate twice."

By the time we got done in the mirror room and cleaned up, an hour had passed. I couldn't stop my face from blushing when we walked out into the gym and Gabriella spotted us. "It's about damn time you two got done," she teased. She then looked up at Ryley. "I don't know whether to be annoyed or impressed, big boy. By the way, Megan's here and she wants to talk to you. She's over in the corner talking to Carter."

I saw Megan at the fight so I knew what she looked like. Carter was short and bulky with shaved gray hair. I had seen him before because he used to be Matt Reynolds' coach. He gave up coaching when Matt retired.

When Megan saw us approach, she smiled and waved. "Hey, you two. I see things finally worked out." She leaned over and whispered in my ear. "Thank God, too. Don't let him fool you, he was miserable."

"I don't even want to know what you just said," he grumbled. "Anyway, Megan meet Ashleigh. Ashleigh this is Megan. So what did you want to talk about?"

Sadly, she smiled. "I'm moving to Las Vegas."

"Really? When did you decide that? You've never talked about it before."

"I know. Don't get me wrong, I love it here and I wouldn't have been able to get my life back on track without you. It's just, I kind of want a new change of scenery now that Alex is in jail. Besides, I have family in Vegas."

"Well, damn, I don't know what to say," Ryley replied.

Sheepishly, Megan shrugged and bit her lip. "Maybe

say that you'll miss me? Because I'm sure as hell going to miss all of you guys here." Ryley chuckled and I let go of his hand so he could give her a hug. A tear escaped the corner of her eye, but she brushed it away.

"Hell yeah, I'm going to miss you. Make sure you hit Tyler up when you get there. I'll let him know you're coming his way. Now that Kacey's starting up her restaurant, she's not working at his gym anymore. Maybe you could get a job there."

"That would be great, I might just do that. I don't leave for another week, but I'm probably going to be scarce while I pack up. I'll be in Vegas though for the title fight. You know I can't miss that." She kissed him on the cheek and then wrapped her arms around my neck. I returned the hug even though I barely knew her. Quietly, she murmured in my ear, "I'm sorry we didn't get time to get to know each other. Whatever you do, don't leave him again. He wasn't the same when you left."

"I won't. He's got me for life." Letting me go, she laughed away her tears and waved at us before walking out the door. I glanced up at Ryley, his expression melancholy. "I take it you two became good friends."

Carter patted Ryley on the shoulder and smiled at me before trudging off toward the exercising machines.

Ryley put his arm around me and held me close. "We did. She was kind of like a second Gabby to me. I confided in her about things."

"Like what, me?"

He smirked. "Yeah, you and how much I hated you. She knew it was all a lie and constantly badgered me about it. Hell, I couldn't even fool myself."

Neither could I. "So what are we going to do? Are

you done training for the day?"

Nodding, he reached down and grabbed our bags. "Yep, and now we're leaving. I need to run to my place and get some things. Do you mind if I stay with you to-night? I don't want you anywhere near my place with Camden there. Not until I can assure he's going to leave us alone."

I didn't want to be around him either. However, thoughts of Colin came to mind. It was Monday and he was supposed to come over. "What about Colin?" I in-quired. "He wants to see me today."

Ryley snorted. "The sooner he realizes it's over, the better. I'm not going to tell you who you can and can't see, but if the roles were reversed? How would you feel if I was hanging out with one of my ex's?"

Groaning, I followed him out to the parking lot and to my car. "I would hate it. And to answer your question, yes, you can stay with me tonight. You can stay however many nights you want. Just don't start a fight with Colin if he drops by. That's the last thing we need."

Ryley winked and opened my car door for me. "Oh, I'll behave, as long as he keeps his hands to himself. You might want to give him a friendly warning about that." He leaned in and kissed me, parting my lips with his tongue. I moaned into his mouth and melted. "Because these," he said, running his tongue over my lips, "are mine. I'm not going to share them with anyone."

When he pulled back, I glanced down at his. "The same goes for yours."

He winked at me again and started off toward his car. As much as I didn't want to hurt Colin, I had no choice. Ryley was right. The sooner he realized it was over, the better. It was still early in the day so at least I had time to get home, take a shower, and possibly take a nap. Regrettably, that didn't happen when a text came through, squashing my plans.

Colin: On my way over. Be there in fifteen.

I never thought the day would come when I didn't want him around. Today happened to be one of those days.

Ryley

MY BROTHER HAD pissed me off one too many times and if he didn't watch it, I was seriously going to kick his ass. He spent the whole morning being a dick and even more so when Ashleigh walked into the gym. Deep down I knew the problem didn't fully revolve around Ashleigh, but she was the spark.

Tension was already running high between us since the title fight was coming up in less than two weeks. Even Danny had mentioned today that it might be a good idea to split up practices so we could have our own space. Out of all of the years of training together, it was finally at the point where we had to fend for ourselves; we were divided.

When I pulled up to the house, I wasn't surprised to

see a shit ton of cars. I had a feeling I wasn't going to like what I was about to see. That was one of the reasons I was glad Ashleigh wasn't with me. Thankfully, I listened to my gut; especially when I opened the front door and the first thing I saw was J.T. Michaelson and one of his whores fucking on my couch. Rage burned in my gut as I thundered straight to the living room and tipped the couch over, knocking them both to the floor.

That was when I noticed they weren't the only people fucking in my house. It was like a goddamn porno and orgy all in one. "Camden, where the fuck are you at?"

Jumping to his feet, J.T. snarled at me, but I ignored him and rushed up the stairs to Camden's room. The door was locked, but it didn't take much to kick it in. In fact, the door flew off its hinges when I burst through.

"Well, hello brother," Camden greeted. He had two girls in bed with him and he looked high as a fucking kite.

"I want you out," I growled, clenching my hands tight. I wanted to hit him so fucking bad my whole body shook.

Camden guffawed. "What do you mean you want me out? I live here."

Actually, the house was all mine. Camden had his house in Malibu while I had this one. But once my father died I asked him to stay with me for a while. It was never supposed to be permanent. "Not anymore you don't. You're not welcome here anymore. If you're not out by tomorrow, I'll drag you out by force. It's your choice."

Turning on my heel, I headed straight for my room and packed a bag. As soon as Camden was gone, I was going to gut the whole fucking house to erase every trace of him.

"So it's come to this?" he snarled in my doorway. "You're *actually* choosing a girl over your own brother?"

Grabbing my bag, I slung it over my shoulder and pushed past him. "You're the one making me choose, dickhead. I can't even stand to look at you anymore."

I started down the stairs, but Camden wasn't done. "If she knew what you were really like, she wouldn't have anything to do with you. I can't believe you're giving up all of this for her."

Stopping by the door, I glared up at him and opened it. "I would give anything up for her, even you, if you force the issue. You better be gone tomorrow when I get back."

With those final words, I left.

Ashleigh

BEFORE GETTING TO my apartment, I made sure to send Gabriella a text message and pleaded with her to take a break and meet me at home. I breathed a sigh of relief when she said she would be right behind me. I knew Ryley would be coming over soon and the last thing I needed was for Colin to be here, without her to break the tension. If they got into a fight, there was nothing I could do to stop them.

When I pulled up, Colin was waiting by my front door, leaning over the banister. He smiled at me when I got out of the car. I was nervous as hell and when I reciprocated the smile, it didn't reach my eyes. Slowly, I walked up the three floors to my apartment, dread settling in the pit of my stomach.

"What's up, babe?" he asked, coming toward me. Nonchalantly, I stepped out of the way and unlocked the door, swinging it open. I didn't want to be mean, but I couldn't have him touching me.

"Nothing much. I just got done working out at the gym. Gabby wants to make sure I stay in shape. I definitely want to keep the weight gain at a manageable level."

He scoffed, "Seriously, Ash? Is that what you're worried about with Ryley? That you'll get fat and he won't find you attractive?"

After throwing my keys on the counter, I slid off my shoes and grabbed a banana. Noncommittally, I shrugged. "I don't know, maybe." Taking a seat at the bar, I unpeeled my banana and took a bite.

Colin sat beside me and bumped me in the shoulder, his green eyes warm as he looked at me. "You wouldn't have to worry about that with me, Ash. I'll love you no matter what, even if you gained fifty pounds with this baby. Why can't you see that with me, you wouldn't have to worry?"

"I honestly already know that, but it doesn't change anything. I'm going to be with Ryley, end of story. Why can't you understand that?" I countered.

His stare hardened. "Because I refuse to believe it. There was a time when we were inseparable, Ash. And then Ryley and his fucktard brother come into the picture. Don't forget you left him for me. Doesn't that say something?"

The banana I just ate felt like a brick in my stomach. "I did leave him for you, but it was a mistake. I was scared." I tried to look away, but he turned my chin to face him. Reluctantly, I looked into his eyes and my lips trembled.

His face was a mask of pain and I was the one who put it there. "If you could go back and change things, would you have never come to me?"

Before I could answer, Gabriella opened the door and her smile disappeared. "Oh, hey guys," she stammered awkwardly. "Sorry, Colin, I didn't know you were going to be here this early. What time did you and Bradley get back? I haven't talked to him yet."

Colin sighed and moved away, giving me some space. "We got in town about thirty minutes ago."

Shutting the door, she perked up and sidled into the kitchen. "Cool. I need to give him a call and tell him about the celebration this Friday. Has Ashleigh told you yet?"

She and Colin both turned their attention to me and I shook my head at her. Then to Colin, I put on a smile and said, "Do you remember the other morning when I told you I wanted to find a job?" He nodded. "Well, I went on an interview on Friday and they called me this morning. I'm going to be a teacher at Stonewall Academy."

His eyes lit up and he smiled. "Congratulations."

"And that's why we're celebrating," Gabriella chimed in. "I'm going to get reservations for all of us to go. Are you in?"

"Hell yeah, I wouldn't miss it. Who's all going?"

"Well, let's see," she started, counting on her fingers, "there's you, Bradley, me, my brother, Megan . . ."

"And Ryley," I finished.

Colin stiffened. "Why am I not surprised?" About that time, a knock sounded on the door. "Speak of the devil. Let me guess, that's him?" He got to his feet and towered over me, glaring at the door.

Sliding off the stool, I looked at the door and then back up to him. "Yes, and the last thing I want is trouble. Please don't start something, Colin."

When I answered the door, Ryley stepped in with his bag in hand and his stare immediately caught Colin's. Gabriella came around the bar and stood to my side, kind of in the middle of them. "He was just leaving," Gabby blurted, grabbing onto Colin's arm.

"Are you serious?" Colin growled, glaring at us both. "Is that what you want?"

Hesitantly, I nodded and leaned into Ryley who put his hands on my waist. "I think it's for the best," I whispered softly. "I'm sorry."

He stepped back like I'd slapped him in the face and jerked out of Gabriella's hold. "Fine, I'll go, but in the end you'll see who's there by your side. And I can assure you it won't be him," he said, pinning a lethal glare at Ryley.

Ryley tensed behind me, and I blocked his path before he could follow after Colin. "Let him go," I warned. I shut the door and leaned against it, releasing a heavy sigh.

"Yep, he's going to be a problem," Ryley pointed out.

Gabriella punched him in the arm. "Give the guy a break. He's upset that the love of his life left him. I'm sure you know what that feels like." He turned his glare to her and gritted his teeth. She lifted her brows, begging for him to reply . . . which he didn't. She had a point.

"Okay, I'll cut the guy some slack. He can't be any worse than my brother. I just kicked him out of the house."

"What? Oh my God, what happened?" Gabriella and I both stared wide-eyed at each other and then back to him.

I pulled him over to the couch and sat down, while Gabriella sat across from us. "Well, I go home to grab some clothes and he he's having a fucking porno party. There were people everywhere."

"You mean like having sex?" I gasped. For some reason that didn't exactly shock me coming from Camden.

He nodded and pinched the bridge of his nose. "Yeah, and what's worse, he's hanging around with all of Kyle's friends. So I kicked down his bedroom door and told him to get out. He has until tomorrow, or I'm going to take every single belonging of his and burn them. Hell, after what was going down today, it might be best to get the center for diseases involved, and then burn the whole fucking place to the ground."

"Is this the type of stuff you guys did all the time?" I asked.

"Fuck no, not like that. I mean, I might have done some crazy shit before you, but I didn't do stuff like that while we were broken up."

Thank God.

"All right, you two, it's been fun with all the drama," Gabriella remarked sarcastically, "but I need to head back. I'll see you both tonight some time."

"Have fun . . . and thank you."

She kissed me on the head and ruffled Ryley's hair. "What are best friends for?"

As soon as she walked out, Ryley put his arm around my shoulders and pulled me close. "I think we need some time away. Do you want to head to the beach? We can eat at that Italian restaurant you loved so much."

That night was one of the best dates I'd ever had. I was upset because Colin hadn't returned my calls, so Gabriella called Ryley to cheer me up. We ended up laying out on the beach and then eating at this amazing restaurant with the best lasagna. I missed it while I was in Aspen.

"Have you been back there since I left?" I asked, laying my head on his shoulder.

"No, but I have to admit, they have the best stuffed shells."

Even though I was tired and felt like I could sleep all day and night, I didn't want to miss these special moments with Ryley. Lifting my head, I smiled up at him and grabbed his hand. "Let's go."

Colin

RYLEY JAMESON. I hated that bastard with every fiber of my being. He could have any woman he wanted and it had to be something of mine. Hell, I could have anyone I wanted, but I chose *her*. I was a pretty good guy and would do anything for her, yet she wanted a man who would most likely cheat on her the first second he got. And now, to top off this clusterfuck, she was pregnant. If I could only get her to see that I would give her everything that cocksucker couldn't.

"Would you like another one?" the bartender asked, shoving his floppy brown hair out of his eyes. If I was him, I'd cut that Bieber shit right off.

I looked down at my empty glass and chuckled. "Sure, why not?" *It's not like I have anything better to do.*

The girl I love was most likely in bed right this moment, fucking another man. The bartender passed me a rum and coke, trying his best not to look pityingly at me.

I was at a bar, drinking by myself. How lame could you be? Pretty fucking lame, obviously. As soon as I left Ashleigh's apartment I came straight to our favorite bar when we were in college. Now we'd graduated, and everything was screwed to hell. I'd do anything to turn back time.

I knew I wasn't the baby's father. I wasn't stupid or naïve to think I was. It was just the only way I could think of to make Ashleigh see that I was better for her. There was still time.

"Well, look who's sitting all by himself," a voice interrupted my pity party.

Glancing up from my drink, I found none other than Camden Jameson sitting down on the stool next to me.

"Oh, but wait, that's right you *are* all by yourself now that your girlfriend left you for someone else. I know that has to piss you off," he taunted.

After tossing back my drink, I glared over at him and his two friends who sat down on the other side of him. "What do you want, cocksucker?"

Camden laughed and waved his hand in the air to get the bartender's attention. Almost immediately, the guy came back, recognizing him. "Hey man, what'll it be?"

"Uh, let's see," he started, pursing his lips, "how about another round for my friend here and a double shot of whiskey on the rocks for me."

The bartender nodded. "Coming right up. By the way, I saw your fight last weekend. Good stuff, man."

Camden smirked and I wished to hell I could punch

the shit out of him. "Thanks, dude. Only one more to go before the title fight." Then he turned to me. "Which I plan on winning."

"And how do you plan to do that?" I stammered. Damn, those drinks were strong.

He smiled and patted me on the back. "With your help, no doubt."

"Touch me again and you're the one who's going to need help," I spat.

Camden chuckled and lifted his hands in the air. "Okay, okay. I won't touch you again. I think we got off on the wrong foot. I have a way I can help you with Ashleigh."

I sneered. "Why do you care about helping me with Ashleigh? She's with your brother now."

"Yeah, and I want to remedy that quick and in a hurry. I'm sorry to say this, but I don't like the bitch. Bottom line, I don't want to see her with my brother."

Even though it killed me when she told me she touched that fucker, it was still pretty epic what she did to him. I smiled as the bartender passed me another rum and coke. "Yeah, I heard about that. Must suck for you."

His smile faded and he turned his head, tossing back his whiskey. "So do you want me to help you or not? Either way, I'm getting those two apart. But if you want to drown your sorrows be my guest. I don't like to waste my time on pathetic pussies." He laid a few high bills on the counter and pushed off the stool, getting to his feet. "Come on, guys. We're wasting our time here."

Goddammit, what the hell am I doing? Closing my eyes, I swayed a bit, as I envisioned Ashleigh with Ryley. I didn't want them together, but I was going to need help. I guess I'd need to cross over to the dark side.

"Wait," I called. Out of the corner of my eye, I watched Camden stop and turn around. A leer spread across his face, and I knew I had sealed my fate. "What did you have in mind?"

Ashleigh

THANKFULLY, OUR DATE went perfectly. We ate dinner and as soon as we got back, I was so exhausted I passed right out. However, right at this moment, it'd all caught up to me. Gabriella knocked on the bathroom door and opened it a crack to peek inside. She found me sitting on the cold tile floor with my arms around the toilet. Morning sickness was no joke.

"Ash, are you okay?" she asked, sliding through the door. Ryley had already left to go to the gym, so at least I didn't have to worry about explaining to him why I was sick.

Groaning, I sat up and ran my hands through my stringy hair, fingers getting stuck in intermittent knots. I really needed to take a shower. "Yeah, I'm fine. I usually start feeling better as the day goes by. It'll pass. I just feel so tired all of the time and my boobs hurt like hell."

"The joys of being pregnant," she replied flippantly. "Why don't you take the day off and rest. Keeping up with Ryley can't be easy."

Getting to my feet, I chuckled and shut the toilet lid so I could sit on it. "You got that right. Are you getting ready to leave?"

"Yep, in about twenty minutes. I can toast you up a bagel if you want. Although it might be kind of hard to find them with all the seashells lying around."

Grinning, I ran my hands over my face and laughed. "I think I went a little overboard picking them out yesterday. My intention was to make something special for the baby. One of my first real dates with Ryley was at the beach, so I figured it'd be something we could all treasure."

"Oh, Ash, that's a great idea. I'd love to help."

My stomach growled and my hand immediately went to my abdomen. "That would be awesome. I think I might take you up on the offer of a bagel though. I'm just going to take a shower and I'll be right out."

"You got it. My niece needs to eat and get strong."

"I thought you said it was going to be a boy?" I countered.

"I did, but then I got to thinking. Ryley desperately needs a little girl to wrap him around her finger."

The thought made me smile. "That would be something. In my mind though all I can see is a boy, one that looks exactly like him."

"In that case, you're going to have some trouble when he gets older. Imagine a miniature Ryley."

Smiling, she shut the door and left me to my thoughts. I didn't care if it was a girl or boy, as long as they were healthy. There was no way I could keep the pregnancy from Ryley much longer, not when a bump started to show. I just had to pray he'd understand why I didn't want to tell him right away.

After showering quickly, I threw my hair up in a towel and put on a pair of black yoga pants and a pink T-shirt. When I walked into the kitchen, Gabriella had my bagel ready, with a glass of orange juice sitting beside it. She was nowhere to be seen, but the door was wide open. Grabbing my bagel, I took a bite and was about to shut the door when Gabriella sauntered in holding our mail. She flipped through the stack and held out a large brown envelope.

"It's addressed to you, but there's nothing on it other than your name. It was sticking out of our box like someone tried to jam it in there."

Taking it from her, I ran my hands over it to get an idea of what was inside; it felt like a disc. Almost instantly my skin prickled and crawled, chill bumps fanning across my body. I had a feeling I would regret opening the package, the bad juju was just rolling off of it in waves. Ripping open the envelope, I took a deep breath before reaching inside. I was right, it was a disc with *Watch me* written on it in bold black letters.

"What the hell? Really?" Gabriella snorted disgustedly, snatching the disc out of my hand. She held it up, her eyes blazing. "This is the same type of shit Kyle pulled on my brother's wife. What do you want to bet this is all Camden?"

"I don't have to bet," I replied, taking it from her.

"He's taken Kyle's place, so it doesn't surprise me that he's resorted to similar antics. Obviously, he wants Ryley and me to stay apart."

I slipped the disc into the DVD player and turned on the TV. Gabriella stormed over and turned it off, blocking my view. "Please tell me you're not going to watch it. It's all a ploy to mess with you. It's going to be nothing but lies."

"And you're trying to tell me you wouldn't sneak and watch it behind my back? You're just as curious as me. Admit it."

Huffing, she stared me down and then rolled her eyes, sliding away from the television. "Fine, I'm curious. Just turn it on before I change my mind."

She sat down on the couch while I grabbed the remote off of coffee table and took a seat beside of her, my hands shaking as I hit the play button. The video came to life and at first it was fuzzy and dark, but then it cleared up. It was loud with strobe lights all around, like the person was in a club. Then that's when I saw what I was supposed to see. It was Ryley, dancing with a horde of women, touching them.

"Can we stop watching this?" Gabriella snapped. "You and Ryley were broken up. Yes, he went out and messed around, but it's not like he cheated on you." I knew that, but it still made my heart hurt. I couldn't blame him for the things he did, although it still didn't make it easy to watch.

"I guess I just like the torture," I grumbled, leaning my head on my hand. "Is Camden constantly going to try and come between us?" There was no need for Gabby to reply. The answer was a simple . . . yes.

The video suddenly switched scenes to another club atmosphere and this time Ryley was kissing the dark haired girl he was dancing with. There were different videos of different scenes all depicting the same shit, Ryley kissing multiple girls and feeling them up. I lost count after a while. Unfortunately, the videos steadily kept getting worse. The next one had escalated to something more. It was in the gym locker room, where another dark haired woman was on her knees in the shower, sucking him off.

Gabriella gasped and hung her head. “Fucking shit, Ash, this is insane. You don’t need to be watching this.”

Turning my head, I closed my eyes and felt the bile rise up in my throat. “Do you know any of these people?” I asked.

“I know the girl in the shower,” she admitted. “She’s a regular at the gym.”

When I glanced at the video again, Ryley and that same girl were in a different room, doing the same thing. He was with her more than once. “He told me he didn’t have sex with anyone, Gabby,” I choked. “It appears that was all a lie.”

Gabriella reached over and took my hand in hers, squeezing it tight. “Well, maybe he didn’t actually have sex with them. There’s nothing in the video showing him doing that.” She grabbed the remote control and turned off the television.

I watched the screen go black and wished I could erase the images out of my mind. “It just hurts knowing he was with all of those women. When I left him, I had a feeling he would go back to the way he was.”

Letting her hand go, I stood and marched to the kitchen to wrap up my bagel. I had to get out of there for a while. My hair was still up in a towel, but I didn't care. I flung it off and ran my hands through my wet tresses, not caring that I looked like shit.

"What are you doing?" Gabriella asked, following behind me.

I drank my glass of orange juice and snatched a bottle of water out of the refrigerator. "I'm leaving. I need to clear my head and I can't do it here. I just want to be alone for a while." Sliding my bagel and water into my purse, I grabbed my car keys and started for the door.

"Where are you going? Do you want me to come with you? I don't want you alone when you're this upset." She chased after me, down all three flights of stairs, and before I could get into my car, she gripped my shoulder and turned me around. "Please don't leave like this," she pleaded.

Sighing, I placed my hand over hers. "I'll be fine, Gabby. Your brother would kill me if I made you miss a practice. I'll be back later, I promise."

"And Ryley? What about him?"

I unlocked my door and slid in. "I don't know, but after today I think it's time to come clean . . . both of us."

Shutting my door, I started my car and sped out of the parking lot, only to have my silence interrupted by the incessant ringing of my phone. I huffed and put in my earpiece, knowing it was going to be Gabriella scolding me for letting the video get the best of me. "I don't want to talk about it, Gabby. What did you not understand about me wanting time alone to think?"

"Uh . . . maybe because I'm not Gabby," Colin replied. "What's going on?"

Great, the last thing I need is to hear him mouth off

about Ryley. "I don't really want to talk about it, Colin."

"Is it Ryley? What did he do?"

Gritting my teeth, I kept my eyes on the road and stayed silent. I wasn't going to talk to him about it.

"Okay, I get it, you don't want to tell me. All I'm saying is, you knew he was going to be a problem."

"Colin," I growled, gripping the steering wheel with brutal force.

He sighed. "I'm sorry. I shouldn't have said that. Listen, I got some good news this morning. I think I have the perfect place for you to get away to."

"Oh yeah? And where would that be?"

"New York, baby. I know you've been dying to go there. I got a call this morning from one of the scouts saying they want me. They're flying me up this afternoon and I want you to come with me. We can go anywhere and do whatever you want. This would be the perfect chance for you to clear your head."

I'd dreamed of going to New York for so long a part of me was excited about the thought. "Colin, it sounds great . . . but I can't go. It's not the right time. I would be running away again, when really, I need to stay and face my problems. I'm happy for you though. I wish I could go, except there's something I need to do."

I could hear the disappointment in his voice when he spoke. "All right, I understand. I'll be back on Friday for your celebration dinner. Take care of yourself, babe."

"Don't worry about me, I will. Be careful while you're out there."

"Will do. I love you, and will see you soon."

"Okay, see you later." I wished I could tell him I loved him too and have it not lead him on. I did love him, but not in the way he wanted. He waited on the line for a moment, but then sighed and hung up. My guilt consumed me. There was only one place I wanted to go, where I knew I could think clearly. Hopefully, this time away would be what I needed.

Ryley

AFTER LEAVING ASHLEIGH sound asleep in her bed, I came in early to the gym so I could get done sooner. Danny helped me with my first round of training and then left for lunch, while I stayed behind to work more. I was giving my brother until the afternoon to have his shit out of my house. He hadn't been into the gym yet, which didn't surprise me one bit.

"Do you want to spar with a real partner today?" Matt asked, sidling up to the ring. He lifted his dark brows and smiled, waiting on an answer. Gabriella hadn't shown up yet, which was kind of odd since she was always on time. Her brother would make her pay for it though.

"How can I refuse?" I replied. "Just make sure you go easy on me. I'm not as big as you."

Matt chuckled and opened his gym bag, pulling out his gloves. "Don't worry, you'll be fine. I've been watching you the past few weeks. You're technique has really gotten better."

He jumped into the ring and smacked his fists together, getting into stance. "What you lack is a real partner. I haven't seen your brother much lately. Where's he been?"

"That's what I'd like to know," Danny interrupted, throwing down his gym bag. "He called and basically said I was fired. I wonder if he was being serious?"

Matt jabbed left and I went right, swinging around to powerhouse kick him in the head. I didn't want to think about my brother, other than hoping he was packing his shit up and moving out of my house.

"Honestly, I'd say good riddance, Danny. I don't give a shit where he's at or what he's doing, as long as he moves the fuck out of my house. I'm done being his keeper." Matt's eyes went wide in disbelief, and Danny huffed, pinching the bridge of his nose.

"I can't believe this," Danny grumbled. "That boy is fucking up. Your dad would have a heart attack if he was still alive."

The thought of my dad made me falter and Matt advantageously punched me right in the jaw, knocking me back. *Fuck, that hurt.*

"You lack focus, Jameson," Matt chastised. "I know you're having issues with Camden, but you need to put all of that out of your mind. You can fight with anger, but if you don't have the focus, you'll make a wrong move. Take lessons from my fight with Kyle. He almost had me down because I was angry with him. Once I was able to clear my head, I fucked his shit up." Danny jumped into the ring and he nodded at him, then fist bumped me.

"I'll work on it, Reynolds. Thanks for the help."

"No problem. I just wish Gabby would get here. I swear that girl never shows up on time for anything."

"I resent that." Gabriella stormed in, her lips pursed.

Matt chuckled and met her on the floor, while Danny slid on his gloves. Now that Camden wouldn't be my sparring partner anymore, I had to go against him. Gabriella talked heatedly to Matt and glanced up at me, a solemn expression taking over her face. Something was wrong. When Matt nodded at her, she climbed into the ring.

"Danny, do you mind if I talk to Ryley? It's kind of important."

Furrowing his brows, he looked at her and then at me. "Yeah, fine. He deserves a break after working so hard this morning."

Gabriella watched him until he was out of earshot.

"What's going on, Gabby? I don't like the look on your face."

She crossed her arms over her chest and nodded. "Yeah, well, that might be because you're not going to like what I'm about to tell you."

"Fucking shit," I grumbled. "Just tell me and get it over with."

"Okay, but I'm not going to sugarcoat it," she began. Taking a step closer, she looked around the room before leaning in. "Your brother sent Ash a video and it wasn't good. She's taken off, and I don't know where she went."

"What do you mean she took off? And what kind of video are you talking about?"

"I'm talking about live footage of Deep Throat Natalie sucking your cock in the locker room. Also included, numerous videos of you dry humping a shit ton of women. Ashleigh told me you said you didn't mess around with anyone while you two were broken up. Why would you lie about that? Now she knows you lied to her."

"Goddammit," I hissed, ripping off my gloves. "I didn't lie to her, Gabby. Yeah, I messed around with more than a few, but I never slept with any of them. That wasn't a lie. But what was I supposed to do? Give her details on how I let other women suck my dick?"

Gabriella sighed, uncrossing her arms. "No, I don't think she would've wanted to know the details. It just hurt her to see you with other women. Be glad I turned off the TV before she could watch the rest."

Danny watched me shove my gloves into my gym bag and nodded. He knew I wasn't going to stay. "The *rest*? What more could there have been?"

"Oh, believe me, there was a lot more, but I'm assuming it wasn't you, since you just confirmed you didn't screw anyone else . . . it must've been Camden. He was in your room, fucking three women, Ryley. The room was dark, but I could still see three women and you, I mean Camden. Whatever, the girls were even moaning your name."

"You have got to be fucking kidding me," I exclaimed. Grabbing my bag, I slung it over my shoulders and jumped out of the ring. I bolted out of the front door and Gabby stopped me with a hand on my arm. Breathing hard, I didn't turn around, but I listened.

"What are you going to do? Ashleigh left, and I have no clue what she's thinking. She wouldn't talk to me."

That was what I worried about the most. If I watched a video of another man touching her, I'd be out of my mind with rage. I needed to find her, but first . . .

Gabriella let my arm go and I finally turned around to face her. "Right now, I'm going to go to my house and make sure every trace of my brother is gone. And then, I'm going to go look for Ashleigh. However long it takes, I'm going to find her."

She nodded, her attitude melancholy. "Good luck, Ryley. I don't know what it is about you two, but you have a lot to work through. I guess love is never easy."

Not in my life it's not. Turning on my heel, I ran to my car and sped out of the parking lot. Camden better pray he was not at my house. *If he is, I don't care about the consequences . . . I'm going to break his fucking face.*

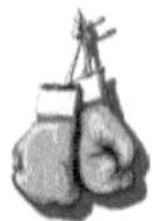

By the time I got to my house, there were no cars in the driveway and the house looked vacant. Even when I opened the garage, Camden's cars and motorcycle were all gone. Did he actually leave? I figured he would make a big scene. When I got inside, I marched straight up to his room and slammed open his door . . . everything was gone. There was no trace of him at all. The rest of the furniture in the house was all mine and it was all still in place. However, when I got to my room, it wasn't how I left it.

My bed was unmade, the sheets in disarray, with a note left on top of my deep blue comforter. It was folded over once with my name written on the outside in Camden's handwriting.

My dearest brother,

One day you'll thank me. By the way, your bed is a lot more comfortable than mine. I had fun in it last night.

~ Cam

Gritting my teeth, I crunched the note in my hand. I was going to fucking kill him. Throwing the letter in the trash, I ripped the sheets off my bed and opened my balcony door, throwing them over. Washing them wouldn't be able to wipe away the memory of my brother fucking his whores all over them. They needed to be burned.

My fingers shook with rage as I dialed his number. I knew he wouldn't pick up, but it didn't stop me from leaving him a message. "You motherfucker," I hissed. "What the hell is wrong with you? I don't know what you think you're doing, but it's going to stop *now*. You can hide and ignore me all you want, but come time for the title fight, it's on. I'm not going to hold back and I sure as fuck am not going to let you ruin things between me and Ashleigh."

Ending the call, I squeezed my phone in my hand. Now where could she be? Taking a deep breath, I dialed her number. I dialed again when she didn't pick up, and still nothing.

Me: Please answer the phone, angel. I need to talk to you.

Me: Where are you?

I waited for her to text or call back, but she never did. She could be anywhere. Pacing along the floor in my room, I racked my brain, trying to think of where she could be. Then, my eyes landed on something displayed on my dresser. Walking over, I picked it up and grasped it in my hand. I had a feeling I knew exactly where she was. Now, I just had to hope she'd listen to me.

As fast as I could go, I sped down the highway to our beach. It was the longest hour of my life. Once I got there, I saw her car in the parking lot and breathed a sigh of relief. Quickly, I rushed out and stopped at the top of the staircase leading down to the sand. My eyes instantly found her sitting on a towel with her staring straight out at the ocean.

Slowly coming up behind her, I stopped and just stood there, watching the way her chocolate brown hair blew in the wind. I had so much to say, but I didn't know where to begin.

"It's over, Ryley," she spoke without even turning around. "The lies, the secrets . . . I'm done with them."

"What are you saying exactly?" I asked, wishing like hell I could hit something. I wasn't going to let it end—not like that.

She turned her head and the tears falling down her cheeks reflected the sun. "It's just what I said . . . I'm done."

Colin

WHEN I WATCHED Ashleigh run out of her apartment, I knew she'd watched the video. Hell, I was the one who shoved it in her mailbox. My plan didn't go quite the way I wanted it to, but by the look on her face when she sped away, I knew it was going to be over between her and that douche bag. Unluckily, I couldn't watch it all play out since I was on my way to New York, alone. I had hoped she wanted to come with me.

"So how did it go?" Camden asked, answering the phone.

"I think it worked. She looked pissed as fuck when she left."

He chuckled. "Yeah, and I know my brother definitely is, judging by the message he left me. I'm going to keep a low profile until the fight this weekend. I need you to be my eyes and ears."

"Will do. I'm heading to New York for the next two days, but I don't think we have anything to worry about."

"Let's hope not. If I have to step it up, I will."

The thought made my hackles rise. I didn't want him messing with her more than he already had. She wasn't in the condition to handle the stress. "Look, you're not going to do anything, unless I approve it. The video was fine and it'll do the job. I don't want you anywhere near Ashleigh, you got that?"

"Hey, you're the one who agreed to all of this. You want your girl, right? Well then sit back and let me handle it. She'll be yours soon."

The only problem was, secrets never stayed hidden for long. If she were to find out I had any part in this, she'd hate me. But it was too late. I had to keep going and hope she would never learn the truth. She was mine . . . and I wasn't going to let her go.

Ashleigh

RYLEY DROPPED TO his knees. "Please don't say it's over, angel. Gabby told me about the video. I know it looks like I lied to you, but I swear I didn't."

The way he said it broke my heart. I didn't mean we were over. "Ryley, no, I didn't mean it that way," I exclaimed quickly, turning my body to face him.

He pulled me into his arms, his expression wild. "Thank fucking God. You have no idea how bad I want to kill my brother right now. I did some stupid things after you left, but I stand true to my word. I never slept with any of those women. You have to trust me, angel. Don't let my brother tear us apart."

I breathed him in and let him hold me, the visions of those women plaguing my mind. "He's not going to tear us apart. I'm not going to let him. I just don't know how much more of this I can take. What's going to happen next, when he finds out his ploy didn't work?"

Ryley sat back and took my face in his hands. "I don't know, but whatever it is, we just have to stick together. If he sends another video, we'll break it apart and laugh in his fucking face. Just promise me you won't let him get to you. I'm already going to beat the ever-living shit out of him when we fight for the title. That will be my revenge." He kissed me on the lips and touched his forehead to mine. "Promise me, angel."

Placing my hands on top of his, I nodded my head. "I promise. But now there's something I need to tell you." He let me go and sat beside me on the towel, keeping his attention on me. My hands started to shake so I busied them in the sand, looking out at the horizon.

"What's wrong?" he asked softly.

I shrugged and laughed through my tears. "I don't even know where to begin. I'm scared to tell you because I'm afraid you'll hate me."

"I could never hate you, Ashleigh. Even when you left, I wanted to hate you but I couldn't. I don't think it's possible. You have to have faith in me. I know that might be hard to do, considering my past, but I love you."

"And I love you too. I understand your reasoning for not telling me about your exploits with girls. With that being said, I'm hoping you understand why I didn't tell you about the following . . . I didn't keep you in the dark for malicious reasons or anything like that. I did it because I wanted to wait until the right time."

He froze, his eyes widening with uncertainty.

Taking a deep breath, I let it out slowly and focused

on my hands. I was too afraid to look at him. "I'm pregnant, Ryley. We're going to have a baby."

His breath hitched and I was preparing for him to storm away. But then, his hands gently grasped my face and his lips touched mine. "Holy fuck, this is insane—our lives will be altered forever," he murmured. "I don't know whether to be happy or angry right now. Is this why you left Colin?" He pulled back, but kept his hands on my face.

"Yes," I whispered. "Deep down, I knew I was pregnant. I was in love with you but I knew it was too late, you had moved on. I didn't know what else to do but leave and pretend everything was okay. Staying away only made it worse for me. That's why I had to come back and make things right."

I stared at him, trying to decipher his expression. So many emotions swirled through his crystal blue eyes. At least he hadn't stormed off. Taking this as a good sign, I continued. "For the last month, I didn't know for sure if I was pregnant or not. I was too afraid to take a test. I took one just a week ago and confirmed my suspicion. Please tell me you understand," I begged. "I didn't want to tell you and have you be with me out of obligation. I had to know you still loved me for me."

"And what if I didn't?" he countered. "Would you have told me then?"

The tears ran hot down my cheeks because I honestly didn't know the answer to that question. "I don't know, Ryley. I'm sure I would have approached you at some point."

"Does Colin know?"

Swallowing hard, I nodded once and hung my head. "Yes, which is why he won't leave me alone. I originally told him in hopes he would give up on me, but instead, it fueled him even more. He's determined the baby is his. I know it's not."

Without looking at him, I could feel his tension crushing me, smothering me. "How do you know it's not?" he asked in a low, cautious voice.

I opened my eyes and took his hand, placing it over my heart. "Contrary to what you might think, I didn't run into his arms and fuck him as soon as I left you. There's a time difference there. I go the doctor next week to find out when I'm due. If you want to come with me, you can, but I understand if you don't."

My stomach was in knots. I just gave him an out and if he took it, my heart would split in two. He released a heavy sigh and got to his feet. I was about to burst into tears and then his hands grasped under my arms and lifted me up. Eyes wide, I bit my lip to keep it from trembling.

"I'm not going anywhere, angel. Whatever happens with the baby, I'm going to be by your side every step of the way." Wrapping his arms around my waist, he looked down at me and smiled. "In fact, I have a few extra rooms in my house we need to figure out what to do with."

"Is Camden gone?" I asked. "Because I refuse to let my baby live anywhere with him."

"Correction . . . our baby. And yes, he's gone. He moved everything out today."

Lifting up on my tiptoes, I stared into his gorgeous blue eyes. "So what are you saying?"

He trailed his fingers up and down my back and smiled. "I want you to move in with me. I know it's early, but it's bound to happen anyway when the baby comes. Besides, I like the idea of having you to myself every single day."

It was crazy, but I didn't have to think twice. "I must seriously be insane. When do you want me to move in?" I didn't want to leave Gabriella, but he was right, it was going to happen eventually.

"Today, angel. I want you there now. Besides, I'm going to need your help picking out the furniture. We can go to your apartment and get some of your things if you want."

"I can't believe we're doing this," I remarked excitedly, letting him go to pick up my towel. He grabbed my bag and shoes while I dusted off. "How did you know I would be here anyway?" We started up the beach toward the steps leading to the parking lot. Our secrets were out and I felt amazingly light and free.

Putting his arm around my shoulders, he dug in his pocket and pulled out the small sand dollar I'd given him when we walked along the beach together almost two months ago. "I saw this and knew."

Smiling, I took it out of his hand. "You kept it all of this time?"

He took it back and put it in his pocket. "Believe me, there was a time I wanted to throw it away, but I couldn't let it go. Let's just say, I liked the torture of seeing it every day. Now let's go get your things and tell Gabriella. She was worried about you."

When I got in the car and we started on our way, I was on air. I couldn't get the smile off of my face if I wanted to. Hopefully, Gabriella would understand why I was leaving. Dialing her number, it didn't take long for her to pick up, her voice full of concern.

"Ashleigh, where the hell are you? Are you okay?"

"Yeah, I'm fine. Ryley found me."

"You didn't break up with him did you? If you did, I'm seriously going to kick your ass. He was so upset when I told him."

I chuckled. "No, we didn't break up, but there's something I need to tell you. What would you say if I moved out?"

"Moved out?" she gasped. "Why do you want to do that?"

I looked at Ryley following behind me in his car, his head bobbing to music. He looked so happy. My heart swelled with the thought of being with him and having a family together. "Ryley asked me to move in with him and I said yes. He wants me to move in with him today so we can be together . . . us and the baby."

"Holy fucking shit, you told him? What did he say? I mean obviously he's happy since he wants you to move in with him," she squealed excitedly.

"He is, and I was so afraid he would be pissed. Now that Camden moved out, it'll be just me and him. I want to do this, Gabby. I'm ready for this next step."

"Well then do it, girl. I'm happy for you. I'll be perfectly fine on my own. I'll be home in just a little bit, so don't leave before I get there."

"I won't," I laughed. "I have to pack up all of my clothes. Soon, none of them are going to fit, so we'll need to go shopping."

"I'm always down for that. Have you told Colin yet?"

"No," I replied sadly. "I'll tell him on Friday when he gets back from New York. He called me this morning and told me about them wanting him on the team out there. I don't want him upset right now."

“He’s going to be pissed when he finds out, Ash. I hope you and Ryley are ready for that.”

I hope we are too.

Ashleigh

ONCE RYLEY AND I got to the apartment, I packed up all of my clothes and had them all ready to load up by the time Gabriella came home. She was sweaty from working out, but she dashed through the front door straight to me, folding me in a big hug.

"I'm going to miss you." When she pulled back, she glared over at Ryley and pointed. "You better take care of my girl . . . both of them."

Ryley lifted his brows and laughed. "So we're having a girl now?"

"Gabby seems to think so," I explained. "Or at least she keeps changing her mind. I keep telling her it's a boy. Either way, I'll be happy as long as the baby's healthy. I can just see a little tyke running around with his father's bright blue eyes."

"Oh hell," he chuckled. "If we have a boy, we're going to be in for one hell of a ride." Holding out his arm, he pulled Gabriella into his side and squeezed. "Are you sure you don't mind me taking her away from you?"

Smiling, she kissed him on the cheek. "Oh, I mind, but I'm glad to see you both happy. I'll be more than fine, I promise."

"All right, well I'm going to start loading the car while you say your goodbyes. If you don't mind, I'm going to have someone come here tomorrow and load up the rest of Ashleigh's things. Is that okay?"

She nodded. "It's fine with me. I'll just get some baby furniture to fill up the empty space, so that Aunt Gabby can babysit her little niece."

"You are too much," I giggled. Then to Ryley, I looked at him and bent down to grab one of my bags. "Do you want help?"

He smacked my hand and shook his head. "Hell no, I don't want you falling down the stairs trying to carry your heavy ass bags. I'll get them."

He disappeared out the door and as soon as he was out of earshot, both Gabriella and I laughed. "He's going to be one overprotective ass, isn't he?"

Gabriella nodded. "Yes, he is, but he loves you. That's all that matters."

After we dropped off my bags and my car at his house, we decided to go shopping. His bed sheets were in the driveway when we pulled up and he regretfully told me about the part of the video I missed. We were going to put them in the fire pit by the pool and have a bonfire tonight. Needless to say, he wanted me to pick out a new bed-spread and sheets. Even when I picked out a set that had pink flamingos on it, he smiled and let me put the set in the cart. We walked around for about thirty more minutes, until I couldn't hold a straight face anymore. I burst out laughing and stood there while everyone in the store turned to look at us.

"Come on, let's put them back," I chuckled, bumping him in the side.

"Thank fucking God," he exclaimed. We walked back to the section where we got the flamingo sheets and he put them back. "Don't get me wrong, if that's what you wanted, I would live with it, but damn those sheets were ugly."

"Yes, they were. I was only doing it to get a rise out of you." There was a bedspread set I really liked, so I walked over and picked it up. "What do you think about this one? I like the different shades of blue and green."

Ryley took it from me and put it in the cart. "Much better."

We walked around the store until we finally got to the baby furniture. Instinctively, I rubbed a hand over my stomach and smiled. I didn't know how long I had, but in a few months I would have a baby in my arms with Ryley by my side. It was too good to be true.

"Do you think we should go ahead and buy a crib?" Ryley asked, looking at the various options.

I knew better than to get ahead of myself. "It's probably not a good idea," I murmured low.

He furrowed his brows and looked over at me. "Why do you say that? We're going to need one eventually, right?"

I ran my hands over the dark cherry sleigh-style crib and frowned. "There are a lot of things that can go wrong in the first trimester, Ryley. I would hate to have the nursery done and then something happens to the baby."

A pained expression crossed his face and he tensed. "I never thought about that. You've been taking care of yourself, right?"

"Of course," I claimed wholeheartedly. "I haven't had any alcohol since before we went to Vegas, when I had my first inkling I was pregnant. I didn't want to take the chance."

He put his arm around me and kissed the side of my head. "Then we'll be fine. My girls are strong."

Rolling my eyes, I smacked him in the arm. "Not you too. I told you we're having a boy. You and Gabby are going to drive me insane."

We walked up to the register and Ryley paid for the new bedroom set, smirking at me. "What can I say? I see us having a little girl with dark brown curls and green eyes. I'm going to have fun scaring off her boyfriends."

"No, you won't. She'll have you wrapped around her finger," I teased.

Ryley leaned over and placed his lips against mine, holding me close. "Just like her momma."

25

Ashleigh

AFTER THE DAY Ryley and I had, I couldn't believe how exhausted I was when we got back from shopping. I watched him start the load of bed sheets in the washer before navigating his way around the kitchen to cook us dinner. I was in heaven. We ate dinner on the back deck and then afterward, I went exploring in his house—our house—while he got the fire ready in the pit.

"I can't believe you're actually burning those sheets," I announced, shutting the patio door.

He tossed the last pillowcase onto the pile and the flames grew higher. "I'm not going to miss them." When he turned around, his eyes went wide as he regarded the length of my body with hunger. Since we were going to spend time by the pool, I'd put on one of my bikinis. "Hot damn," he exclaimed. "You look so fucking sexy right now."

It was strange because when I looked in the mirror, I could tell my flat stomach was starting to bulge just a tiny bit. "Do you think you'll be saying that when I get bigger?" I asked nervously.

He sensed my hesitation and came to my side, placing his hand on my stomach. "Are you serious? You're not going to be able to keep me off of you." Biting his lip, he glanced over at the pool and then back to me. "So what do you say? You want to relive that fateful night?"

I smiled and ran my hand over his growing cock. "What do you think?"

After lowering his shorts to the ground, he reached behind me and untied my top, letting it fall to the ground before untying my bottoms.

"You don't regret what we did, do you?"

"No," he answered seriously. "When we were in Vegas, there was a part of me that wanted you to be pregnant. After you took the test and I held you in my arms, I didn't want to let you go. I knew as soon as it came back negative you'd be gone again. Do *you* regret it?"

I shook my head and kissed his chest, trailing my lips up to his neck. "No," I murmured in his ear. "The only thing I regret is leaving when I was too afraid to stay. That is something I'll never forgive myself for doing."

Lifting me in his arms, I wrapped my legs around his waist and he carried me into the pool. "Well, we don't have to worry about that anymore. You're here and you're mine. That time doesn't exist to me now."

The water was warm as he lowered us into it and held onto me tight. When his lips found mine, I lost myself in his touch and opened for him, letting him claim me. Fisting my hands in his hair, I clutched him tighter when he circled his cock around my opening, pushing in just a bit. My skin broke out in chills as he lowered his lips to my neck on down to one of my nipples, pulling it with his teeth. I yelped and his deep chuckle vibrated all the way to my clit. He pushed in a little more until he was fully inside, lifting me up and down by my hips.

Backing me against the wall, he thrust harder and deeper, grunting in my ear. He grabbed my breast and squeezed, holding onto the back of my neck to keep me from rising up. "Fuck, this feels good," he growled. "And now I can come inside you anytime I want."

"Yes," I moaned, tilting my head back.

Lowering his face to my neck, he kissed me gently. "I could get used to his."

"Good, because I'm not going anywhere, Ryley. I'm always going to be right here."

Friday had finally come, which meant Colin was going to be back from New York. The fairytale life I'd had with Ryley the past couple of days was going to disappear. I couldn't sleep, even though it was still dark outside. Instead, I sat on the floor surrounded by a horde of seashells in the empty bedroom that would soon be my son or daughter's. For the past two hours, I'd made small crafts and hung them up on the walls—even making seashell candles to decorate the dressers. At least an ocean theme is something that would go great for a girl or a boy.

"What are you doing?" Ryley asked, shielding his eyes from the light. Wearing only his boxers, he sat down on the floor with me and handed me a couple of seashells so I could slide them down the wire. "How long have you been up? It looks like you've been busy."

I shrugged, scrutinizing the project in my hands. It was going to be beautiful once I finished. "I couldn't sleep," I confessed. "There's too much going on in my mind."

"Like what, angel?" he asked, tucking a strand of hair behind my ear.

"Like Colin, for instance. He comes back today and he has no clue that I live with you now. I just don't want to hurt him. Not to mention, he's not going to leave me alone until we find out everything from the doctor."

"Well, there's nothing he can do about it. Does he think if the child is his that you'll choose him?"

Sighing, I set my shells down and looked up at him. "He knows I want to do what's right for the baby. But what he doesn't realize is that I have to do what's right for me as well. I would never be with someone just because we share a child. That was my fear with you and why I didn't tell you at the beginning. I didn't want you thinking I was using the baby as leverage to get you back."

"I never would've thought that, angel," he murmured softly. "You're not the kind of person to do something so devious. That's why I fell in love with you. You saw through all of my faults and loved me for who I was. I've never had that before." He smiled and then looked down at my last project. "So what is that exactly?"

Grinning from ear to ear, I held it up by the top and let the seashells dangle down, all sparkly from the glitter I spread across them. "It's a mobile to hang over the crib so the baby can look up at it," I said, gently rocking it so the seashells clattered together. "I figured we could also get something that plays music too. I know babies like music."

"Do you think I'll be a good father?" he asked in all seriousness.

Furrowing my brows, I glanced up at him. "Do you not think you will be?"

"I don't know," he admitted, shrugging his shoulders. "I want to be, but I don't know the first thing about taking care of a baby."

What he didn't know was, I had the same fear. I didn't know the first thing about how to change diapers, or what the baby was going to want each time it cried. "Ryley, listen. You have nothing to worry about. You're going to be a great daddy. Your child is going to love you for just being there for him. I have a lot to learn too. We can do this together."

Ryley got to his feet and helped me up. "Yes we can, and right now we need to go to bed. Stop worrying about Colin or the things we can't change. He's not going to come between us."

"Usually, it's me who looks on the bright side. Since when did the roles switch?"

Lifting me in his arms, he chuckled and carried me to our bedroom, setting me down on the bed. "It's probably the baby hormones making you crazy. Don't worry, you'll be back to normal in a few months."

"I highly doubt that," I laughed. "We're going to have a miniature Ryley running around. There is nothing normal about that."

But I was going to love him . . . or her. Whichever one I was blessed to have.

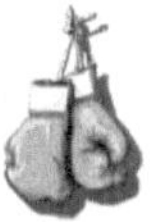

Later in the day, Colin called to tell me his plane had been delayed, but he would meet us all at the restaurant. It sucked because now I couldn't tell him beforehand. The place Gabriella reserved for us was one of my favorites. It was just a normal pub that had the best grilled salmon I ever tasted, along with a killer black bean cake. Thank God my nausea wasn't bad today.

When we got to the restaurant, everyone was there except Colin. Gabriella ran up to me and flung her arms around my neck. "You are absolutely glowing," she squealed. Then she leaned into my ear. "I bet that's because you have Ryley tucking you in every night, huh?"

"I do more than *tucking*," Ryley teased, walking past with a wink and a slap to my rear.

Gabriella giggled and rolled her eyes before turning back to me. "So have you talked to Colin? Bradley just told me he's on his way."

"Great," I murmured sarcastically. "Nothing like a brawl in a pub." I looked over at the table and everyone sitting there. Ryley took a seat beside Matt, while Megan sat across from them. Bradley was the only one who looked uncomfortable and that was because he hated Ryley.

Gabriella glanced over her shoulder and sighed. "Well, let's just hope nothing like that happens. Because I know Bradley would be more than happy to jump in and help Colin out."

"All right," I groaned. "I'm going to run to the bathroom really quick. I have to pee all the time and it's only going to get worse."

"Okay, well I'll just enjoy a glass of wine for you since you can't drink." She laughed and walked away.

Trudging into the bathroom, I was thankful there was a stall open. Once I was done and out in the hall, I looked down into my purse to grab my phone when a set of hands grasped my shoulders and pushed me back down the darkened hallway.

"What the—?" I started but then stopped once I glanced up. It was Colin with his mouth set in a firm line. He was very angry.

"You know, I thought I was going to come home and tell you my good news and that everything would be just the way it was."

"Did you make the team?" I asked, eyes wide. I was excited for him, but it didn't matter at this point.

"I did, but instead of celebrating with you, I get here and see him."

"Colin, don't start. Look, I'm happy you made the team. It'll be a wonderful opportunity for you. But what made you think Ryley wouldn't be here? I'm with him now."

His nostrils flared and for the first time in my life I'd never seen him so upset, not even when he told me he got arrested for getting into a fight with Camden out in Vegas two months ago. "Yeah, and the last time we spoke I assumed it was over."

"No," I gasped. "I was angry, but we worked it out. In fact, there's something I need to tell you." His eyes went wide. "I moved in with him, Colin. I didn't want to tell you like this, but I figured it would be better hearing it from me and not someone else."

"What if the baby's mine?" he snapped. "I'm not going to let you and *my* child live with that fucker."

"You don't have a choice," Ryley thundered behind us. I froze but I couldn't see him over Colin's shoulder. "And the baby's not yours," he added.

Tensing, Colin's grip tightened on my shoulders, but then he let go and turned around. "There's still a chance. You're not the only one who's been with her."

Ryley snarled and moved forward, but I jumped in his way, placing a hand on his chest. I glared at both guys and then settled on Colin. "I'm sorry this isn't what you wanted, but you're going to have to get over it."

"We'll see about that." Abruptly, he took my hand and pulled me to him, closing his lips over mine in a bruising kiss. It startled me, but then everything moved in slow motion as I was ripped away and he was on the floor with a busted lip.

"Holy fuck," I gasped, clutching my stomach. "What the hell just happened?"

Ryley's body shook with rage, but he stepped back and didn't make another move. Colin jumped to his feet quickly and licked the blood off of his lip. "I'm warning you, Ash. Once he finds out that baby isn't his, he's going to leave you."

Ryley growled, "Do you want a broken nose to go with the busted lip? I'd be happy to take this outside."

Colin stood to his full height and sneered, "You're not worth it and she'll realize that sooner or later. You don't know her like I do. I've spent almost every single day of the last three years with her."

Putting his arm around my waist, Ryley pulled me in close. "I may not know her as well as you do, but I'm going to have the rest of my life to remedy that. And the *only* reason I'm allowing you to walk away right now, is because I remember what it was like to lose her."

Colin stumbled back a step and looked gutted. "This isn't over." With those final words, he stalked past us and out the door.

My heart hurt for him, but he was being so damn stubborn it made me want to hate him. *I wish he would let me go.* I kept my attention on the door, wondering if he was going to come back, but he never did.

"Are you ready to go sit down with everyone?" Ryley asked softly, rubbing my shoulders. I hadn't even looked up at him since Colin kissed me.

"Yeah, I'm ready. I can't believe what just happened."

"Tell me about it. It took all I had not to hit him sooner, but when he kissed you I couldn't hold back. There was no fucking way. I'm sorry if I ruined the night for you." Taking my hand, he guided me out into the restaurant toward our table. By the looks on their faces, they had an idea of what just went down. Even Bradley wasn't at the table anymore.

"You didn't ruin my night, Ryley. If anything you make them all better. I'm sure you'll figure out a way to make it up to me." By the sly grin on his face I knew exactly how he was going to do that.

Colin

BRADLEY RACED OUT of the restaurant shouting my name, but I kept going. I had to get away from there . . . from her. The video didn't work like I thought it would. Obviously, Ashleigh didn't care that he fucked around with a shit ton of women. Grabbing my phone, I punched in Camden's number.

"What's up, fucker?" he answered.

I slammed my car into gear and sped out of the parking lot. "We need to talk. Can you meet me?"

The line went silent, but then he came back on. "It didn't work?"

"No, it fucking didn't," I hissed.

"Okay, meet me at the bar in an hour. It's time for Plan B."

We hung up and I headed straight for the bar. My jaw throbbed from where Ryley punched me, but at least I got to kiss Ashleigh right in front of him. I had to accentuate the fact he wasn't the only one who could touch her.

When I got to the bar, I walked straight on in and ordered two rum and cokes. I tossed one back and then the other, feeling the fire spread its way through my body. What other kind of plan could Camden come up with? It was obvious nothing was going to separate them.

By the time the hour was up, Camden waltzed in and took a seat beside of me, whistling when he saw my busted lip. "My brother?" he asked, looking at my mouth.

I huffed and rolled my eyes. "The one and only. Apparently, he didn't like me kissing his girl." But I wasn't the only one who had been beaten. Camden's eye was bruised and he had scabbed over cuts on his arms. "I'd say you didn't have a good week either by the looks of you," I added.

Camden slapped me on the back and chuckled. "That's what you call *real* fighting, not just some busted lip. But don't worry, Ashleigh will be yours soon. I just need to come up with another plan."

"I don't think there's anything you can do," I scoffed. "They're determined to stay together—she's even moving in with the asshat. However, I honestly don't see him sticking around if we find out the baby's mine."

"Baby? What the fuck are you talking about?" Camden stormed, getting in my face. "Please tell me you're fucking joking. Is it yours or his?"

I waved the bartender over and shook my glass, but before I could guzzle down my refilled drink, Camden angrily slid it to the side.

"You're not drinking anything else until I get to the bottom of this. When did you find out she was pregnant? Does my brother know?"

"Goddamn, slow it down with all the questions," I snapped. "I found out last week. She said she wasn't going to tell Ryley until we got the tests done, but it looks like she told him while I was in New York. Ryley and I had a little argument over it tonight."

"When does she go to the doctor?" he asked.

"She goes next Thursday. We'll find out everything then."

For a few minutes, Camden stared off into the distance until a devilish smile spread across his lips.

"I don't see how any of this is funny," I snarled.

"Do you think you're the father of the baby? I mean, like deep down do you believe you are?" he asked seriously.

"Fuck if I know. The chances are slim."

Camden rolled his eyes. "That's not what I asked. What I want to know is, if this baby happens to be my brother's, are you willing to claim it as yours if it meant getting your girl back?"

I stared over at him. What was he up to? "If it meant getting her back, I'd do just about anything."

"Even botching the test results?" he asked.

"What? Like at the doctor's office?" That shit only happened in movies and stupid ass soap operas.

Camden's eyes lit up. "Yep."

"How do you plan on doing that?" I inquired incredulously. It was ridiculous, but if he could do it . . .

"Let's just say, I know the right people. All I need to know is where the appointment's at and you'll be all set.

The baby will be yours and my brother's life won't be ruined." He stared at me with wide, excited eyes until I finally broke down and gave him the information he needed. Guilt consumed me, but I would do just about anything to keep hold of Ashleigh. In the end, she would see I was better—that I would stick by her.

Camden slid my drink over and I tossed it back, feeling the anger boil through my veins. I wanted to go back to that restaurant and beat the shit out of Ryley for taking her away from me. Yes, I took her away from him first, but I deserve her. He doesn't.

"Looks like you got some pent up aggression over there," Camden teased. "Do you want to do something about it? I'm sure we can find you a guy who looks just like Ryley to fight."

"What the fuck are you talking about?"

Camden leaned in and lifted a brow mischievously. "I'm talking about a fight, twinkle toes. None of this pansy ass fighting you're used to, but something real, where you can make people bleed. Are you interested? Although, I have to warn you this is real shit. Once you go there's no going back. Because if you speak a word of it to anyone, they will hunt you down and put a bullet in your head."

I glanced at his arms and then up to his face. "Is that where you got all of that?"

He winked. "You should see the other guy. So are you in or not? I think your girl likes the bad boys. Why don't you show everybody what you're made of? I'm sure there's going to be lots of women wanting to fuck you after tonight."

"I don't give a shit about fucking other women," I stormed. "The fighting sounds pretty interesting though.

What do I have to do?"

Camden threw a couple hundred dollar bills on the bar and put his arm around my shoulders. "Come with me and find out. You're switching to the dark side now. I hope you're ready for this."

I was more than ready.

Ryley

IT WAS SATURDAY night and we were at Staples Center, where I'd be competing in the last fight before the title match next weekend in Las Vegas. The announcer just called out my brother's name and the crowd went wild. If I went out there to watch his fight, I know I'd find myself trying to jump up in there and kick his ass myself. My coach thought it would be best if I didn't watch it.

"I can't believe he did that to you," Danny growled low, wrapping my hands. "Your father would have beat the shit out of him. The only thing I can think of is his jealousy over you. I've seen it for the past couple of years."

"Jealousy or not, he still shouldn't be doing this."

"I agree, but at least everything else is going great.

You haven't told your family about the baby yet have you? I talked to your mother the other day and she didn't mention it."

I glanced over at Ashleigh who was sitting in the corner looking at baby magazines. I hadn't noticed it before, but her *Team Ryley* tank top started to fit a little snug around her waist. It was barely noticeable, but I could see the change. I loved it.

"After Vegas I'm taking her to the mountains to meet my family. I'm going to ask if she wants to stay up there for a while during my down time."

"I heard that," she said, smiling down at the magazine. "I think it's a great idea. Hopefully, your mom won't hate me; especially, after I introduce myself as 'hey, I'm your son's girlfriend and you're going to be a grandma.'"

Danny laughed. "It's not going to be like that. She'll be thrilled to see one of her son's heading in the right direction."

My mom used to give me hell at every family gathering because I would never have a girlfriend to bring. For the longest time she thought my brother and I were gay, but it was just we had *too* many women to even consider bringing one around.

About that time, Gabriella burst through the door, breathing hard and wearing her royal blue tank top with my name on it. She didn't have a fight tonight so she decided to sit in the arena and watch everyone else's, including my brother's.

"Okay, so your brother just won by knocking Tate on his ass," she informed us, holding a hand over her chest. Well, it was confirmed . . . I was going to be fighting him for the title. I knew it was going to be between me and him, but there was something Gabriella wasn't saying. I could see it in her face.

"What's going on, Gabby? Spill it."

Ashleigh came to my side and wrapped her arm around my waist, keeping her focus on Gabriella. She had us all concerned.

"To be honest, I don't know exactly," she answered truthfully. "Have you seen your brother at all recently?"

I shook my head. "No."

"Well, he looks rough—like I'm talking lash marks and scars all over his body. It's really weird . . . and when I watched J.T. fight, he had similar markings on him as well. I've seen this before, a long time ago. It's not good, Ryley."

No, it wasn't and I had a pretty good idea of what was going on.

Ashleigh stared up at me, her brows furrowed in confusion. "What is she talking about?"

It'd been over a year since I'd heard of anything going on in the underground fighting scene. The last bust was in Vegas because there were MMA fighters showing up dead. Ever since then things had been quiet, until now. And if Gabriella's assumptions were correct, it meant my brother was involved.

"Are you sure that's what it looks like?"

She nodded. "I'm positive. I've been around it before and know what to look for. Even Matt confirmed it when he saw."

"Fuck," I hissed.

Danny passed me my gloves and nodded toward the door. "It's time to go, son. If your brother is involved in that shit, there's nothing you can do for him. You have to let it go and let him fall."

Ashleigh squeezed my arm. "Ryley? Tell me."

"Do it quick," Danny advised. "We have to go."

Sighing, I looked down at her. "For years there's been illegal underground fighting. Sometimes it's just normal fighting and sometimes it's with weapons and so forth. Last year, there were a bunch of MMA fighters showing up dead. The ringleader got busted and everyone involved was thrown in jail. Now, it looks like someone else is starting it back up."

"And you think you're brother's involved?" she asked, wide-eyed.

"If what Gabby says is true, then yes." Danny opened the door and waved for us to move. "All right, angel, I have to go. Wish me luck."

She kissed me on the lips and pushed me toward the door. "Good luck. Go kick some ass."

She and Gabriella took off while I followed Danny. Now that Gabriella told me about Camden, I wanted to see it for myself. By the time we got to the back curtain, they had already called out Mark Bailey to the ring.

"All right, son, just focus on the fight and nothing else," Danny commanded, pulling my hood over my head.

Through the curtains I could see the multi-colored lights charge into action and shower over the crowd. Then the announcer's voice blared over the speakers, "Ladies and gentlemen, I am proud to announce our next fight for the evening. The winner of this fight will continue on to Las Vegas, Nevada, for the chance to be the Middleweight title champion. Let's give it up for *Ryley . . . The Rampage . . . Jaaammmeeesssooonnn.*"

My song echoed throughout the arena, signaling it

was time to go. Taking a deep breath, I rolled my shoulders and stormed through the curtain, keeping my attention on the ring down front. Mark was ready, bouncing on his heels, but I wasn't worried. I knew I could take him. Ashleigh and Gabriella waved as I entered the ring, both on their feet and dancing to my song. I winked at my angel and slid off my robe, handing it to Danny.

"Let's get ready to *rrrrruuuummmmbbbbllllleeee*!" the announcer shouted into the microphone. The crowd screamed and chanted, ready for the fight. I loved hearing them shout my name. Mark and I joined each other in the center of the ring and bumped gloves before getting into stance.

Ding, ding, ding. The fight was on.

Ashleigh

IT WAS THE second round and Ryley was dominating. I thought Camden would be around to watch it, but I never saw him. I was kind of glad because if I saw him, I'd want to slap the shit out of him for the video. People were screaming left and right for Ryley and I couldn't help but smile with pride. He was amazing, but better yet . . . he was mine.

"Let me guess, you're going to go home and make him tap out," Gabriella giggled. "I swear the whole time he's been up there you look like you're about to fucking orgasm."

Ever since I became pregnant my body has been super-sensitive. Just the slightest touch to my clit made me horny. Not to mention every time I looked at Ryley I wanted him to tackle me to the floor and just fuck me. I'm not talking make love to me . . . I wanted him to all out fuck me.

"It's because I probably could," I replied, biting my lip. "And I want him to make *me* tap out. Not the other way around."

"Damn, girl. I guess there's no partying with you guys tonight. I'll probably just go back to the apartment."

"Where's Bradley? Is he not going to come over?"

She scrunched her nose and shrugged. "He could, I guess, but I'm not really in the mood. I love spending time with him, but after that shit went down with Colin and Ryley he's basically asking me to choose between them. He doesn't think that I should be friends with Ryley *and* Colin."

"That's not fair," I stormed. "He can't make you choose."

"Exactly, and if he does, I'm not going to have a choice. I will always choose Ryley over Colin. And in choosing you guys, I forfeit him. It's a sacrifice I'm willing to make."

"Oh, Gabby, I had no idea he was being that hard on you. It looks like you need to take a break from him or something."

She took a deep breath and nodded. "You're probably right. I need to be with someone who makes me feel like you feel when you're with Ryley. I've never had that, even when I was with Tyler."

"You'll find it, Gabby. I bet he's around here somewhere." She stiffened at my words and cleared her throat awkwardly. "Are you okay?" I asked, patting her on the back.

"Hey ladies," a voice called out.

Immediately, I turned and focused on the gorgeous dark-haired, green-eyed man who sat beside me. I'd seen him before . . . Paxton Emerson, the new Light Heavy-weight champion.

"Um, hi," I replied. I remembered seeing him at a party the night I met Ryley and his brother. Last I heard, he wasn't exactly part of the good crowd.

"What do you want Pax?" Gabriella asked, crossing her arms over her chest.

I leaned back in my chair so they could talk.

"I was going to see if you would go to the party with me tonight. I don't see your boyfriend here, so I thought I would ask."

She tilted her chin up defiantly. "No, thanks. I have plans."

Paxton sighed and shook his head, his eyes narrowed. "Are you seriously going to be this way? Haven't I proved to you that I've changed?"

"Whoa, I think I need to catch up," I interrupted excitedly. The tension in the air was palpable, with full blown sexual tension. I could feel it pouring off of both of them. "I'm Ashleigh," I announced, holding out my hand.

Smirking, he shook my hand. "Pax. I guess Gabby didn't tell you about me?"

She scoffed. "It's Gabriella, Pax. Only my friends can call me Gabby."

His smile disappeared and he got to his feet. "Well, then I guess you can call me Paxton. Only my friends call me Pax."

My mouth dropped open and I watched wide-eyed as he stalked off, never once looking back. "Holy hell, what was that all about? Why were you such a bitch to him?"

Gabriella wouldn't look at me. "You know why, Ash. He used to be friends with Kyle. I hate anyone who's ever associated with that turdburger."

"Oh, Gabby, even you don't believe that horse shit. I could feel the intensity between you two. Is there something you need to tell me?"

"Come on, Ryley," Gabriella yelled, getting to her feet. "I think we need to concentrate on your boyfriend right now."

She didn't need to twist my arm. Jumping to my feet, I cheered for Ryley. However, I couldn't help but watch Gabriella out of the corner of my eye. Her eye twitched and she bit her lip, a clear sign that she was flustered. I guess I wasn't the only one who ran away from love. Up in the ring, Ryley had knocked Mark down to the mat and there were only twenty seconds left to go in this round. He straddled Mark's waist and pummeled him, fists flying. Over and over he punched, until Mark's body went limp and he was pulled off. The crowd went wild and I screamed, jumping up and down.

Giggling, I turned to Gabriella. "That was so freaking hot."

"Uh-oh, sweaty guy coming your way," she exclaimed, nodding toward the ring.

By the time I looked back, Ryley had already jumped out and scooped me up into his arms, placing a hard kiss upon my lips. "Now everyone will know that you're mine," he stated proudly. Setting me down, he took my hand and led me up to the ring. My heart sped out of control as the cameras landed on us and the announcer held up Ryley's hand in victory.

I squeezed his hand and he pulled me closer, just as a young woman with bright blonde hair and huge tits about to pop out of her low cut silky top, came up to him with a big smile on her face. There was too much interest in those beady eyes of hers. I knew her name was Sarah Wilder and she was a spokesperson for one of the sports channels who covered the UFC fights.

"So Ryley, how does it feel to know you're going to compete against your brother next weekend for the title?" she asked.

Ryley didn't falter, he smiled and leaned toward the microphone. "We knew the time would come when we'd have to compete against each other. It's what we've trained for."

She moved a little closer and stuck her chest out, almost brushing him with her breasts. *So help me God she better back off.* "Well, I talked to your brother earlier and he made it sound like he's going to take you out. I do believe those are fighting words. It doesn't look like the Twins of Terror are causing havoc anymore."

Ryley chuckled and put his arm around my waist. "All good things must come to an end. But I have a lot to celebrate tonight. Not only will I be competing for the title, but I just found out that I'm going to be a father."

Most of the crowd cheered, but I heard a few disgruntled shouts from some of the women in the crowd. That was to be expected, since he was a highly sought out bachelor. *Not anymore.* Even Big Tittie Sarah had a frown on her face and faltered for a second. A sly smile spread across my lips when she glared down at me.

"I guess a congratulations is in order, you two." Abruptly, she turned around to the camera and plastered on a fake smile. "And there you have it. Make sure to stay tuned next Saturday night for the Middleweight title fight between Ryley Jameson and his very own identical twin brother, Camden Jameson. It's sure to be a good one." Once the camera was shut off, she hopped out of the ring, followed by her crew.

"I don't think she liked me very much," I pointed out.

Ryley snorted and led me out of the ring. "It's probably because I turned her down. That woman's fucked more people than I have. Camden, on the other hand, had his fun with her."

I gagged. "Ugh . . . I swear I could vomit just thinking about him. I can't wait for next week."

His smile vanished. "Me too, angel."

Danny met us outside of the ring, beaming. "Now *that* was one hell of a fight, son. Do you want to go out and celebrate?"

Ryley pursed his lips and shrugged.

"I know there's a party," I suggested. "Paxton asked Gabby to go with him. We could always go there."

"I swear that boy doesn't know when to give up." Ryley chuckled. "But honestly, I think I'm tired of the bullshit parties."

Danny clapped him on the shoulder, smiling with pride. "I never thought I'd hear that come out of your mouth. I couldn't agree with you more. Well, you two have a good night and Ryley," he said, staring at him, "I'll see you bright and early on Monday morning. Take tomorrow off."

Ryley nodded and watched Danny saunter away. "I'm sure I can think of plenty of things to do tomorrow on my day off."

I bit my lip and grew wet just thinking about it.

"All right, angel, let's get home. We can do our own partying by ourselves."

"Sounds good to me."

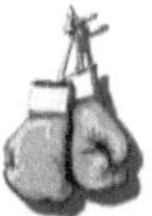

When we got in the car, my stomach started to cramp. I couldn't tell if it was because I was hungry or if I was having abdominal pains. Ryley reached over and placed his hand on my stomach, rubbing in smooth circles. "Are you okay?"

"Just some cramps, but they seem to be going away. It must be your touch making me feel better." It just so happened, all I could think about was having him inside me. Taking his hand, I lowered it down to the waistband of my jeans. His brows lifted and he smirked. I really wanted to bite him, sink my teeth into him and ravish him. Next, I unbuttoned my jeans and slid his hand underneath my thong so he could feel how wet I was.

"Damn, woman, you've turned into a horny freak. I think I like it."

He pushed a finger inside and I gasped, opening my legs further. "I swear it's insane," I admitted. "When you're in the ring fighting, it turns me on. The way you're aggression takes over and your eyes turn wild. You used to be like that when we were together. Why aren't you now?"

His face grew serious when he turned to stare at me. "I *want* to fuck you like that, angel. Don't ever doubt that for a second. I'm just afraid of hurting you and the baby."

"You're not going to hurt me or the baby, Ryley. I promise. You have nothing to worry about."

We finally pulled into the driveway and he slid his finger out, bringing it to his mouth. Moaning, he sucked my wetness off and unbuckled his seat belt. "If you want it hard, I'll give it to you. But then, you need to do something for me." He got out of the car and I followed.

"What do you want me to do?"

Once inside, he led me up the stairs to our room and roughly lifted my tank top, biting my nipple through my bra. Then, he lowered my jeans and thong to the floor and backed me up against the bed. "Lie down and spread your legs," he commanded, eyes blazing.

Reaching behind my back, I unclasped my bra and let it fall before sliding back on the bed and opening for him. A deep growl rumbled in his chest right before he grabbed my thighs and buried his face between my legs.

My head fell back and I moaned out my pleasure as his tongue licked and penetrated me. It was mind-blowing and completely orgasmic. I don't think I'd ever been this turned on in all my life; pregnancy was doing a number on my libido. Gripping a handful of his hair, I held him to me as I ground my center into his face. I was literally fucking myself with his face, and was ridiculously close to climaxing.

Ryley chose then to back away, his breath tickling me when he chuckled.

"What are you doing? Torturing me?" I pouted, rubbing my legs together, searching for the friction I needed.

Licking his lips and wiping his face on his shirt sleeve, he smiled down at me and covered me with his body. His cock strained against his jeans, and he pushed it into me. "I like watching you squirm. Now, here's what I want you to do when I leave."

Eyes wide, I gasped, "You're leaving? Where are you going?"

He placed a finger to my lips, smirking devilishly. "I'm just going to the store and getting something for you. I have a strange feeling you're going to want it after I'm done with you." I tried to speak, but he pressed down harder on my lips. "No talking . . . just listen and do as I say."

Chills spread across my skin and I grew even wetter. "Yes, tell me what you want me to do," I begged, pushing myself into his arousal. Holy fuck I wanted him.

"When I leave I want you to get in the shower and touch yourself. Only when I get back do I want you to finish. I want to see you come by your own hand. If you do this for me, I'll fuck you as hard as you want."

My chest rose and fell with ragged breaths. He was torturing me and I fucking loved it. Biting my lip, I slid my fingers down my chest to that aching spot between my legs. "Then you better hurry because I'm not going to last long." I inserted a finger inside and his eyes darkened. Only when I pulled my finger out did it break the trance.

"Now who's the evil one?" he pointed out. Adjusting himself, he leaned over and kissed me on the lips, pinching one of my nipples. "Get ready for me, angel. I'll be back in a few."

Then, just like that he disappeared out of the room and out the front door downstairs. Through the window I watched him leave and smiled. If he wanted a show he was going to get one.

Ashleigh

THE SHOWER WATER heated up quickly and by the time I got inside its blanket of warmth, I was already trembling with the need to release. I didn't know how long he was going to be so I held off touching myself and let the water run over my head. I wouldn't last long once I started. A few minutes later, I heard footsteps on the hardwood floor in his room and the sound of the door shutting. It was show time.

When his silhouette came into view through the foggy glass door, I slowly slid a hand between my legs and let the other grab a breast. "Is this what you wanted?" I asked, resting my foot on the tiled seat. He probably couldn't see much with the steam, but he would get the picture. Lifting his shirt over his head, he threw it on the sink and then lowered his pants enough for his cock to pop out. The next thing he did completely caught me off guard . . . he started stroking himself. It was so fucking hot.

"Oh Ryley," I moaned, inserting a finger inside. "I can just imagine you fucking me right now. This feels so damn good."

I watched him pump harder and that spurred me on. Using one hand to hold me up, I backed up and bent over, so my ass was pressed against the glass. I wanted to give him a clear view.

Ryley grunted and mumbled something about coming.

"Oh shit, I'm so close," I cried. Moving my hand to my breast, I pinched my nipple hard and screamed out my release, my body shaking. Gently, I circled my clit with my palm until the aftershocks wore off. I could hear his hand working his length fast and steady, so I looked behind me while keeping bent over. I caught him just in time, pulling hard as he came. He leaned against the bathroom counter, catching his breath.

Breathing hard, I placed my hands against the shower wall and closed my eyes. "I can't believe we just did that."

Two seconds later, the shower door opened and Ryley stepped in, his skin warm against my back. Smiling to myself, I leaned back into him. He brought his hands up to my breasts and squeezed while lowering his lips to my neck. Then when he dropped one hand to the inside of my thigh and pushed a finger inside, I grew liquid in his arms.

Completely resting into him, I reached up to touch his face and immediately froze. Something wasn't right. His cheeks were stubbly, and they weren't like that when he left. My eyes popped open and I panicked because it only took one look at the arms wrapped around me to know that it definitely wasn't Ryley behind me.

His free hand slammed down over my mouth before I could scream. "There's no reason for that, sweetheart," he taunted in my ear. "I just wanted to say that I enjoyed the show." He pulled his finger out and smacked my center with a few pats. "It's a shame you had to open your eyes."

Without even thinking, I bit down on his hand and elbowed him in the side when he faltered. "Get the fuck away from me," I screamed, stumbling my way out of the shower. I grabbed the first towel I could see and wrapped it around my shaking body. It felt like I was in a bad dream I couldn't escape from.

Camden chuckled and stepped out of the shower. "I guess this is payback for what you did to me in Malibu. Sucks, doesn't it?"

"I can't believe you would do this," I hissed. "You're completely fucked up."

His smile disappeared and his lip curled. "You want to know what's fucked up? That baby of yours. You're going to ruin Ryley's life by saying it's his. We all know how you left him and fucked your other boyfriend."

"You don't know shit," I thundered. "I know it's Ryley's, you bastard. He's happy that we're having a baby."

Camden smirked and put on his clothes. "Yeah, well, he's not going to be too happy when he finds out it's not his." He looked in the mirror and ran his hands through his wet hair like nothing was amiss. "Have a good night, whore. Have fun explaining to my brother about our little tryst."

As soon as he disappeared, I fell to my knees and

burst into tears. *This couldn't be happening to me.* My skin felt dirty and I felt violated and disgusting. I should've known that it wasn't Ryley in there with me. *What is he going to say when I tell him what I did?* The tile was cold against my skin, but I didn't have the strength to move, other than the sobs that shook my body. I don't know how long I laid there before pain radiated through every nerve ending of my midsection. The cramps I had before were nothing compared to what they felt like now.

"No, no, no," I cried, clutching my stomach. "This can't be happening."

Thunderous footsteps raced along the floor downstairs and then soon Ryley was in the bathroom. "Ashleigh, what's wrong?" he asked, panicking. Bending over, he lifted me in his arms and carried me to the bed. I couldn't see through the tears and I didn't want to. I was worried about our baby, and I didn't want to look in his eyes when I told him what just happened.

"The baby," I sobbed. "I think something's wrong."

His face paled, but he quickly wrapped me in a blanket and carried me downstairs. I didn't care that I was naked underneath as long as we got to the hospital and made sure the baby was okay. Opening the car door, he gently set me inside and slammed it shut, rushing over to his side.

I had never seen Ryley so torn up as we were headed to the hospital. Tears glistened in his eyes and hit the steering wheel a few times along the way. It broke my heart and in that moment, I knew for a fact that he loved our baby—he wanted it.

"This is all my fault," he muttered angrily. "I bet you fell in the shower, didn't you?" He put his hand over my stomach and pressed harder on the gas. "We're almost there. Keep strong for me."

"Ryley, *no*," I cried. "It wasn't like that and it sure as hell wasn't your fault." My stomach tightened again and I doubled over. "I was having cramps since we left the arena. Also, I had an incident with your brother. He came into the house."

The silence in the car was deafening. I was so afraid to tell him. When I finally had the courage to look at him, his knuckles were white and the expression on his face was a mixture of rage and agony. "What did he do?" he growled.

"Please don't make me tell you right now," I pleaded. "I just want to focus on making sure our baby is okay."

Clenching his jaw, he rubbed my stomach and then grasped my hand. "And once we find out the baby's okay, you're going to tell me everything that fucker did."

Taking a deep breath, I nodded and turned my head toward the window. Tears streamed down my cheeks, but I never made a sound. I had to believe everything was going to be okay.

Ryley

EVERY SECOND ASHLEIGH spent in the hospital bed, all I could think about was wondering what my brother did to her. She didn't want to talk about it, but I was on the verge of a fucking meltdown if she didn't speak soon. I was two seconds away from hunting him down. She was asked a bunch of questions by the nurse but we had yet to speak to a doctor. What the fuck was taking so long? We had no clue what was going on.

Ashleigh had been texting back and forth for a few minutes and as soon as she put down her phone, she sighed and looked over at me, her expression guarded. I could tell she was trying to stay strong by the way she bit her lip to keep it from trembling.

"Who are you texting?" I asked. I really wanted to

demand she tell me what happened but I didn't want to upset her more.

"I sent Gabriella a message and told her we were here. She's on her way."

That wasn't the only person she talked to. "What about Colin?"

Turning her head, she nodded. "I know you don't want to see him, but this way when they do the tests, he'll know we're not lying when we tell him the baby is yours."

The last thing I wanted was to see that fucker and to deal with my brother. Regrettably, I had no choice. Getting to my feet, I walked over to the window and peered out, even though I wasn't exactly looking at anything. Nothing could be worse than hearing the next words that came out of her mouth. I already knew it was going to be bad.

"I'm so sorry," Ashleigh cried. "I thought he was you when he came into the bathroom."

Closing my eyes, I squeezed them shut and fisted my hands on the windowsill. "Keep going, Ashleigh."

I didn't want to imagine him touching her in ways only I had the privilege of touching her, but I had a feeling it was going to get much worse. "Can you come over here so that I don't have to talk so loud? It's not exactly easy for me to say this," she murmured low.

Turning around, I blew out an angry breath and took a seat in the chair beside her bed, clasping her hand in mine. "I'm sorry, I didn't realize. I'm just a little upset right now." Upset couldn't begin to cover it.

"I know," she choked. "And like I said, I was doing what you asked me to do. When I saw you come into the bathroom, I . . ."

I squeezed her hand and hung my head. "You don't

have to give me details. The thought of Camden watching you infuriates the fuck out of me."

She nodded and licked her lips, averting her gaze. "Well, after that he came into the shower, but I didn't turn around. I just leaned back into him. I never thought in a million years it could be Camden instead of you. He—he touched me in places." She hiccupped and shook her head. "Anyway, when I opened my eyes and reached up to touch his face, that's when I realized."

"Did he . . . rape you?" I could barely get the words out I was shaking so hard.

"No," she stated quickly. "I don't think that was his intention. It was payback for what I did to him in Malibu. And to also make sure I knew I was ruining your life."

"What a fucking joke," I grumbled. "The last thing you need to do is believe anything that comes out of his mouth."

"Trust me, I don't. I just can't believe he did what he did. I feel so ashamed."

"You have nothing to be ashamed of. I'm the one who didn't think about the fact he still had keys. First thing tomorrow morning, I'm getting every single lock changed in the house. That fucker isn't going to be able to come in anytime he wants."

"Do you think it was just coincidence that he happened to come in when you weren't there? Or do you think he was watching the house?"

I honestly had no clue, but I had a guess. With me wanting to kick his ass, he would know better than to pull that shit with me around. "He was probably watching the house. What a cocksucker."

About that time, Gabriella burst through the door, her

eyes on fire. She was pissed. "So help me God if Camden showed up at that party I was going to kick his fucking teeth in."

"Did you meet Paxton there?" Ashleigh asked.

Gabriella rolled her eyes. "I'm not here to talk about him. I'm here to be with you. When do you see the doctor?"

"That's what I'd like to know," I grumbled.

"Guys, calm down. The pain isn't as bad and I'm not bleeding so that's a good thing. If I was, I'm sure they would be doing a lot more."

Colin came skidding through the door and went straight to her, not even acknowledging me or Gabriella. But then his face turned hard and he glared at me. "What did you do? Surely you upset her about something."

Ashleigh's eyes went wide and she squeezed my hand before I could fully get out of my seat. "Don't," she murmured quickly.

Colin fumed, his fists clenched and ready for a fight. I was ready to give him one.

"It wasn't Ryley's fault. It was Camden's," Ashleigh exclaimed, drawing his attention away from me.

Colin's eyes went wide and he paled. That was when I got a good look at his face underneath the green baseball cap. His right eye was black and blue, and he had scratches up and down his neck. Even his knuckles were split open. Ashleigh finally noticed it too.

"Colin, what happened to you? Why do you look like that?"

He ignored her question and countered with one of his own. "What did Camden do to you?"

She looked down at her hands and sighed. "Ryley, do

you mind if I talk to Colin alone for a minute? I don't want you to have to hear it again."

I didn't want to hear it again, but I didn't want to leave her either. However, Gabriella took my arm and pulled, leaving me no choice. "We'll be right outside, Ash. Come on, Ryley."

Huffing, I followed her out the door and rested my back against the wall. "How did Camden get so fucked up?" I asked, more to myself than anyone.

Gabriella smoothed her hand down my arm and leaned against me. "I don't know. It's crazy how he went downhill so fast. It's like he's a whole different person now. Jealousy will make you do stupid things."

"What the hell is he jealous about? We look the same and do the same shit. I'm no different from him."

"And that's where you're wrong," she stated. "You've always been different. Even when you and Camden used to tag team and play your women, you still had a good heart. If I asked you for ten thousand dollars, I know you'd give it to me in a heartbeat. He's greedier, he wouldn't."

I snorted and bumped her with my shoulder. "You obviously don't know me. You'd have to work for that shit on a corner somewhere. I wouldn't give you the money either." She glared up at me and pursed her lips when I smirked. "You know I'm kidding."

Looking over my shoulder at the door, she bit her lip and moved closer. "It looks like Colin got a little roughed up? You didn't do that, did you?"

I wished it was me who did it. "No, I haven't seen the fucker since the restaurant."

Colin chose that time to walk out, his body tense. He

looked straight at Gabriella and nodded toward the room. "She wants you."

Gabriella started in and I followed until Colin placed a hand on my shoulder. "You better get your hand off of me right fucking now," I growled. "I'm not in the mood for your shit tonight."

"And I'm not in the mood for Camden's, so you better listen to what I'm about to tell you." Taking off his hat, he huffed and ran his hands through his hair. "She's going to hate me when she finds out."

I waved him on. "Keep talking, I don't have all fucking night."

"When do you think the doctor will be in to do the tests?" he asked.

"Hopefully, sometime soon. That way you'll see that I'm the father and leave her the fuck alone."

Sighing, he leaned his head against the wall. "I already know you're the father, Ryley. I just wanted her to see that I was better for her than you. I held on to as much hope as I could, but it's obvious she's always going to pick you."

I stared at him in shock. Was he serious? "So what are you saying? That you're going to leave us alone?"

"It's not going to matter anyway once she knows the truth. It'll all be over."

"Will you just get to it?" I hissed impatiently. "I don't exactly want to stand out here shooting the shit with you. If you have another point, get to it."

"Does Camden know you're here?"

"Not that I know of."

"I don't think it matters anyway, since we're not at her doctor's office. But Camden was going to get someone to tamper with the results of the tests to make it look like the baby was mine."

Slamming my hand into his throat, I shoved his head against the wall. He didn't even fight me. "So you're saying that he was going to make sure I thought the baby was yours? To what . . . get me away from Ashleigh?"

He swallowed hard, but I squeezed even harder. "Yes," he choked, grabbing my wrists. "I—I thought she would . . . want me back if she knew the baby was mine."

Before letting him go, I knocked his head against the wall one more time and crossed the hall. If I didn't get away from him, I was going to do some serious damage. Gabriella rushed out, eyes wide. "Guys, what in the hell is going on?"

Colin put his hat back on and stood up straighter. "It's nothing. I was just leaving."

"You're not going anywhere," I hissed. "*I'm* not going to be the one to tell Ashleigh what you did. You're going to do that yourself."

"Oh, fucking shit," Gabriella grumbled, heading back into the room. "Why do things always have to be so complicated?"

Colin looked like he wanted to bolt, but I blocked his path and pointed to the room. Ashleigh deserved to hear the truth and it was going to be from his own mouth. The video was one thing, but Camden crossed the line when he broke into my house, when he touched the mother of my child, and now this . . . trying to sabotage the test results. I was seriously going to fucking kill him. *I may not even wait until the fight.*

Ashleigh

COLIN WALKED IN looking worse than before.

"You guys weren't fighting were you?" I scolded.

Ryley followed in behind him and came straight over to me, his muscles tense. "Maybe a little," he confessed. "But it was for a good reason. Care to explain, Colin?"

Gabriella moved out of Colin's way, so he could come to my other side. His green eyes looked down at me with angst and sadness. I could even feel it in his touch when he grabbed my hand. The last time he looked like that was when I broke up with him. "Ashleigh, there's something I need to tell you and you're not going to like it."

Ryley nodded and held my other hand. From the look on Gabriella's face, she had no clue what was going on.

"I love you, Ashleigh. I've loved you for a long time now. When you told me you were pregnant, I went a little nuts and thought I could get you back. But now I see that's not going to happen."

"I'm sorry," I murmured sadly. "I can't help the way I feel. I hope you know I didn't mean to hurt you, or lead you on after I broke things off."

He nodded his head and looked away. "I know that now, but I did something stupid."

"What?" My heart sped rapidly out of control and I began to feel sick. Whatever it was, it wasn't good. I was afraid to find out and even more so when I heard his next words.

"I had no idea Camden was going to do what he did. If I'd known, I would've never agreed to help him."

Jerking my hand away, I glared at him, eyes wide. "You can't be serious? What do you mean you've been helping him? What have you done?"

Sheepishly, he glanced over at Ryley and Gabriella. "The video for starters," he confessed. "Camden thought it would work. When he finished putting it together, I was the one who put it in your mailbox. After you stormed out, I figured you and Ryley would be over and you'd come back to me."

"You watched me leave?" I gasped. "How could you do that to me?"

He looked over at Ryley, but Ryley stayed quiet and kept his eyes only on me. "I wanted you back, Ashleigh. I didn't care how it happened, I just wanted you to know that I was better than him. He's not going to love you the way I do."

Now it was Ryley's turn to snap. "I don't think what

you have is love, asshole. It's more like obsession. If you really loved her, you wouldn't have agreed to Camden's next plot."

Colin tensed and closed his eyes, but I smacked his hand to get his attention. "Look at me, Colin. What's he talking about?"

He opened his eyes and tears fell down his cheeks. I'd never seen him cry. "Camden told me he could make something happen, and by being the obsessive asshole that I am, I agreed," he said, glaring at Ryley then turning to me. "I told him about the baby and how it could be mine. But who was I kidding, I knew it was a long shot. I just wanted to believe I still had a chance. Except, when you and Ryley started getting close, I became desperate."

"Desperate, my ass," Gabriella snapped. "You made a deal with the fucking devil. Please tell me Bradley didn't know about this. Because if he did, I'm going to wrap his balls around his neck and choke him."

Quickly, he turned to her, holding up his hands. "No, I swear he didn't know. Bradley has no idea about any of this."

Breathing a sigh of relief, she closed her eyes and stepped back. "Keep going, Colin," I interrupted impatiently. "What was Camden going to do next?"

Then tension pouring off of Ryley was enough to charge the air, it scared the shit out of me. When Colin's head lifted, his dread felt like a tightly wrapped blanket surrounding me, suffocating me. "Camden was going to get someone to change the baby's test results to make it look like the child was mine."

As soon as he said it, the monitors around me went on alert. The sound echoed throughout the room and it was loud—annoyingly loud—but the pounding in my ears was louder. Ryley got to his feet and grabbed my face, trying to turn my sight away from the man who deceived me. "Calm down, angel," he ordered soothingly. "You need to breathe." I fought against his grasp and kept my piercing glare on Colin's.

My heart sped out of control and I could feel the anxiety welling up in my chest. How could Colin do that? I didn't even recognize him anymore. "How could you?" I cried, gritting my teeth. When he tried to touch me, I smacked his hand away and roughly swiped my eyes with my palms. I couldn't see through the rage and tears.

"I'm so fucking sorry, Ashleigh. I'd do anything to take it all back."

About that time, a nurse in pink scrubs barged into the room and rushed straight over to the machines. "My heavens, what in blazes is going on in here? You can't be getting upset like this, Miss Warren. If the gentlemen can't keep it together I'm going to have to request they leave. The doctor is about to come in and examine you and we don't need you upset." She turned around and glared at both of the men.

"No, I'm okay," I replied, taking a deep breath. "One of them was just leaving." My attention fell onto Colin and his face fell.

"What about the baby?" he asked.

"It doesn't matter—" I stopped in mid-sentence. The nurse was fixing the machine, and I really didn't want her or the whole floor hearing our personal business. "I don't want to look at you anymore, please leave."

The nurse kept her head down and bustled out of the room.

"You can't keep me away, Ash. What if it *is* mine?"

Anger boiled through my veins, and thankfully, Ryley was on the other side of the bed or he would've punched the shit out of him. When he tried to step around Gabriella, she blocked his path. "Colin, I want you to leave," I growled venomously. "It's over, all of it. I don't want to see or talk to you right now. If you don't leave this second, I'm going to get security up here and throw you out."

"Or better yet, I'd be happy to do it," Ryley thundered.

Colin stared down at me in complete and utter despair.

"I'll have Gabby text you when we find out the baby belongs to Ryley. That way, you'll have your confirmation."

Nodding, he backed away toward the door. "I love you, Ashleigh."

I averted my head and looked down at the floor. There was no way I could love him after what he did. I didn't want to think about what would've happened if Camden succeeded in changing the results. It would have affected not only us, but the baby as well. The door opened and he looked at me one more time before shutting the door. He was gone and I never wanted to see him again.

"I seriously can't believe this shit," Gabriella exclaimed.

Ryley bent down and brushed the hair off my face. "Are you okay?"

I latched onto his hand and held it to my cheek. "No, but hopefully, I will be soon."

The door opened and I was afraid it was going to be Colin again. Thankfully, it wasn't. "Good evening," a voice called out.

Ryley moved back, giving me full view of the lady at the foot of my bed. She was a middle-aged woman with auburn hair, dressed in green scrubs and a white lab coat. Hopefully, she was the doctor. I couldn't see her name tag clearly.

"Good evening," I replied back.

She came around to the side of the bed and held out her hand, a genuine smile splayed across her face. "I'm Dr. Clarice Morgan. I'll be the one taking care of you tonight."

"Ashleigh," I said, taking her hand. "Nice to meet you."

"Likewise. Although, I hate we have to meet on these terms." She then shook Ryley's and Gabriella's hands before immersing herself in my chart. "It says here you haven't seen your gynecologist yet, but your urine results confirm you are indeed pregnant."

I nodded. "Yes. I had an appointment to see my doctor in Aspen, but then I came back here and had to cancel. I've been trying to take care of myself though."

Dr. Morgan smiled and set the chart down on the table. "Have you had any more pains since you've been here?"

"It comes and goes, but it intensifies when I'm upset."

"I see." She moved closer but then glanced over at Gabriella and Ryley, then back to me. "I'm going to do your exam now. You're more than welcome to have your guests stay."

"Actually," Gabriella interrupted. "I'm going to step outside. I think this time needs to be with just them." She smiled at me and nodded toward the door. "I'm just out here."

After she disappeared and shut the door, the doctor proceeded. "All right, Miss Warren, if you wouldn't mind moving down as far as you can for me, please." At the edge of the bed, she pulled out the stirrups and my gut clenched. I hated those things. I'd heard that by the time you deliver a baby, you're used to airing your hoo-ha to every stranger donning a white coat, but I wasn't there yet.

I scooted down to the edge and put my feet in the holders. Dr. Morgan stayed by my side and lifted the hospital gown above my stomach and placed her hands on me. It hurt when she pressed down, but it wasn't bad. My muscles were tight, tender. As soon as she was done, she strolled over to the sink and washed her hands before putting on a pair of gloves. Standing between my legs, she squirted the lubricating jelly on her fingers and gently inserted them. Tensing, I looked up at Ryley and he reassured me by giving a small smile. Once she was done feeling around, she removed her gloves and lowered my gown.

"The good thing is, you're not bleeding. If you ever have pains with bleeding, you need to call immediately. So far, everything looks normal. We're going to do an ultrasound to make sure though." She opened my chart and started jotting down notes. "From what I could tell, it looks like you're around eight weeks along."

Eight weeks? If that was correct . . . Ryley was definitely the father. Breathing a sigh of relief, I relaxed and grinned up at him. I could tell he was relieved too. "So when would my due date be?" I asked.

She pulled out some kind of chart from her pocket and studied it. "Well, let's just see now. It looks like you'll be due on February the seventh, but the ultrasound will confirm."

I gasped and so did Ryley. "Are you serious?" he asked.

It was his birthday. Needless to say, it was Camden's as well, but I didn't give a shit about that. What I did care about was that our child could be born on the same day Ryley came into the world.

Dr. Morgan chuckled, "Let me guess, it's your birthday?" He beamed and nodded his head. "It's crazy how that happens sometimes." She stared down at me and grew serious. "I'm going to give you a prescription for prenatal vitamins. Make sure you take one every day.

"Also, these pains you're having seem to be just your typical pregnancy pains. When mothers get stressed, sometimes the pain increases, especially now that your body is stretching and expanding to accommodate your little one. Try to minimize the stress. I can't tell you enough how important that is. Stay away from your triggers. We need to make sure it doesn't happen again."

"It won't," I replied.

"Good." Grabbing my file, she smiled at us both and stopped by the door. "I'll be back after the ultrasound to answer any more questions you might have. I'll let Karen know you're ready." When she left it was like the entire burden had been lifted off my shoulders. It was an amazing feeling.

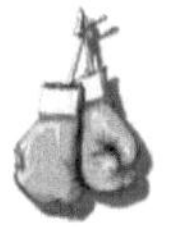

Karen ended up being a short, rotund lady with the funniest laugh I'd ever heard. When she saw Ryley, she immediately blushed and couldn't stop talking to him. It ended up being that she recognized him because her son watched UFC fights all of the time.

"My son will never believe I met you," she giggled. The ultrasound machine was ready and I silently groaned when she whipped out a wand that looked like a long, freaking penis. She even rolled what looked to be a condom down over it.

"All right, sweetheart, this might be a bit uncomfortable and cold, but at least you get to see your little one for the first time." The monitor sprung to life and I winced when she slid the wand inside me. It didn't hurt, but it felt odd being probed by a woman with Ryley in the room. His focus was just on the screen. However, I had no clue what the hell I was looking at.

Karen turned the monitor up and I shrieked when I heard the rapid beating sound. "Oh my God . . . is that?"

She chuckled and nodded. "Yes it is, sweetie. That's your baby's heartbeat."

Tears sprung to my eyes and my lips trembled. Even Ryley appeared teary-eyed, but I could tell he held them back.

"Let's see if we can get you some pictures of your little peanut," she said. Tilting the wand this way and that, she stopped and pressed a button at various times.

It wasn't until she gasped that my body froze and Ryley tensed. "What's wrong?" I asked quickly.

Karen's eyes went wide and so did her lips, her face beaming. "Oh, dear me, nothing's wrong at all. It looks to me like you have not one, but *two* little peanuts in there.

Look." She pointed at the screen and right there, in clear sight, she pointed out the babies snuggled side by side.

"Twins," I whispered.

Karen winked up at Ryley. "It looks like it runs in the family. Congratulations, you two."

I was in shock. Two? I wasn't sure I was ready for one, but now there were two? It was surreal. After Karen printed off our pictures and handed them to Ryley, she left the room.

He stared at them in silence. I watched him through the tears in my eyes, until he set the pictures down and leaned over me, brushing my tears away with the pads of this thumbs. His eyes were heated, but also full of torment . . . rage.

"Angel, I don't know what to say or what to do. I'm so goddamned furious with my brother for trying to take all of this away from me. I'd give anything to hunt him down right now. If we'd lost our babies because of him . . ."

"Shh," I whispered, bringing him down to my lips. "The babies are fine. I'm pissed off too, but you'll get your chance to make him pay. And since I don't need you getting carted off to jail right now, I'd prefer you save it for the ring."

He lowered his forehead to mine and breathed me in. "I love you so fucking much, you know that?"

"Yes, and I love you too."

"As soon as we get out of here, we're going back to my house and packing up our shit. I'm not staying there. We need to leave or I'm going to go after him and there's no telling what I'd do. It goes against my nature not to protect . . . I failed to protect you."

"No, you didn't," I murmured. "We didn't know your brother was going to do what he did. You can't blame yourself."

I could see his internal struggle. He didn't want to leave, but he felt he had no choice. He wanted to go after his brother, but stayed to take care of me. In a way I wanted him to go after Camden and just beat the shit out of him for what he did. But in the long run, what would that accomplish? Camden would still be the same..

Ashleigh

I WAS EXHAUSTED by the time we rushed to Ryley's house and packed a week's worth of clothing. Thankfully, he decided to drive the four hours it took to get to his cabin in the Sierra Nevada Mountains. If not, I would've fallen asleep at the wheel since it was so late at night. It didn't shock me when I woke up in his bed with the sun shining through the window. It was already eleven o'clock in the morning. *Holy hell, I can't believe I slept so long.* We were in his cabin and it felt more like home to me than anywhere else I'd ever been. Even his home in Los Angeles didn't feel like a true home. Maybe it was because Camden made me feel violated there.

I heard him moving around downstairs, so I got out of bed and changed into a pair of yoga pants and one of my favorite USC T-shirts. The smell of bacon and eggs wafted up the stairs and my stomach growled. I was so hungry.

"I'm sorry I slept the morning away," I called as I was halfway down the stairs. "You should've woken me up." When I turned the corner to the kitchen, I gasped. There was someone in the kitchen, but it definitely wasn't Ryley. "Oh my God, I'm sorry. I thought you were Ryley."

The old lady turned to me and chuckled before spooning a helping of eggs and a couple of pieces of bacon onto a plate. Her hair was as white as snow and pulled back in a low ponytail. She reminded me so much of my grandmother back home. Even though her skin was wrinkled with time, she was still beautiful—almost angelic.

"No worries, dear. He's actually outside in the garage. He spent all morning working out in there. The poor boy has a lot on his mind."

That he does.

She pointed to the table and set the plate down, along with a fork and a glass of orange juice. I sat down and took a deep breath. The food smelled amazing.

"I have homemade biscuits in the oven. They should be done soon." Taking a seat across from me, she smiled and reached for her coffee. "I guess I should introduce myself . . . I'm Ryley's grandmother, but you can call me Mamaw. That's what he calls me. I should also mention that we all heard about what happened.

"Ryley called us this morning and told us you were here in town, so that's why I thought I'd come by and visit. His mother will be stopping by this afternoon. We're all excited about the grandbabies though."

"Oh wow, so I guess he *did* tell you everything," I

remarked, scooping a forkful of eggs into my mouth.

Laughing, she drank the rest of her coffee and got up when the timer went off on the stove. She pulled out the biscuits and put one on a plate with a spoonful of butter. "Yes, dear, he tells me everything. I remember the day he came up here and sat on the porch all day . . . even when it began down pouring." After handing me the plate, she sat back down and frowned. "I had never seen him quite so upset. He wouldn't talk about it, but I finally coerced it out of him. I'm glad you two found your way back to each other. I was growing rather tired of his bachelor ways."

My heart constricted and it took all the strength I had to swallow my eggs. I could only imagine what day that was. But what was even crazier was I used to do the same thing in Aspen. I would sit on the back deck and stare off into the distance, letting my mind wander. Even when it rained, I could imagine I was back here, making love outside. Sometimes I could even feel him touching me.

"Trust me, Mamaw. It was hard on me too. I should've never left him."

"Well, child, you can't worry about that now. You're here and that's all that matters. My concern now is making sure Ryley doesn't kill his brother. I don't want him doing something he'll regret later. I can see it eating away at him and it's not good. If he keeps his anger bottled up, he's going to blow."

"It's a good thing he'll get to release it at the title fight. What can I do until then?"

Before she could answer, Ryley marched into the house, breathing hard and sweaty. The conversation was over, but it only took one look to know he was a ticking time bomb. The energy around him crackled like fire and it made my skin prickle. He kept it together pretty well in the hospital, but now everything had changed. He had a new focus . . . revenge.

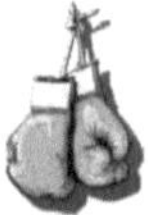

For the rest of the day, I watched him from the back deck as he pummeled his punching bag and worked his body to exhaustion. Even then, he didn't stop. I didn't know if I should try to talk to him or leave him be. I was about to go down when the sound of car doors slamming shut echoed in the air. Ryley obviously couldn't hear from the incessant pounding of the bag.

By the time I made it inside, I looked out one of the windows and saw it was Danny, along with a woman. Almost instantly, I knew who she was. The bright blue eyes and blonde hair gave her away.

Before they came up the steps, I opened the door wide. "Hey, Danny. I didn't know you were coming."

He got up the stairs first and folded me in a hug. "Ryley's going to need me this week. Where's he at?"

When he let me go, my smile faltered. "He's out back, absolutely murdering the punching bag. He hasn't stopped all day."

Danny groaned and hung his head. "All right, I'll go out there. I hate it when he gets like that." Reaching behind him, he took the woman's elbow and helped her up the last couple of steps. The way he looked at her was a little more than friendly. *Ryley never mentioned Danny and his mother were seeing each other.*

"Ashleigh, this is Ryley's mother, Terry. Terry, this is Ashleigh. I'm going to leave you two to get acquainted while I deal with Mr. Rage."

Terry lifted her brows and crossed her arms. "Now don't be too hard on him, Danny. He's going through a lot right now. I can't imagine what he must be feeling."

"He'll be fine," he retorted. "He's just angry."

Once Danny left, I stepped aside so Terry could enter. Her eyes grew misty when she looked around. "You'll have to excuse the waterworks, it's just been so long since I've been here. I had hoped Ryley would move up here one day. We all miss him." She glanced back at me and smiled.

"I wondered the same thing when he first brought me here. It's so much better than Los Angeles. I guess with Danny and his brother being back there, he felt like that was where he needed to be."

I wanted to go back outside and she followed me to the porch, taking a seat beside me. "I *know* it was because of Camden," she confessed. "After their father died, they were inseparable. Now with things being cross between them I don't know what's going to happen."

"Neither do I," I murmured regretfully. From where we sat, we had a good view of Danny and Ryley inside the garage, as the double doors were open.

"I'm glad I finally got to meet you, Ashleigh. I wish it was under better circumstances. Although, I am happy to hear I'm going to be a grandmother and that my little grandbabies are okay."

Instinctively, I ran my hand over my stomach and grinned. "If they're anything like their father, they'll be okay. He's strong."

Terry giggled. "Well, so are you, darling. If you can put up with one of my boys, I'd say you're a saint." Her gaze landed on Danny and she smiled, but not before catching me looking at her.

"Does Ryley know about you and Danny?" I asked boldly.

Sighing, she looked down at her hands and shook her head. "Is it that obvious?"

"To me it is, but I look for that kind of stuff. I don't think men are that perceptive. Do you not want Ryley to know?"

"It's not that exactly," she said, meeting my stare. "It's just, Danny was their father's best friend. I wouldn't want them to think ill of me for being with someone other than their father. Danny's been there for me and the boys. He loves them. It tore him apart when Camden let him go."

"Yeah, well, Camden has a knack for hurting people," I grumbled.

"Maybe once the fight is over, I'll tell Ryley what's going on. Right now he needs to concentrate on his fight and winning the title. And I do hope Ryley teaches Camden a lesson. It's unforgiveable what he did to you both."

We watched Ryley for another hour before his mother had to get up and walk away. She didn't have to worry about Ryley teaching Camden a lesson. There would be no mercy shown.

Ashleigh

TERRY HAD MADE a lasagna and put it in the oven before she and Danny left. It was closing in on seven o'clock and Ryley still hadn't said one word to me. I didn't know how long he planned on staying outside, but I wasn't going to let him do it alone. Taking a deep breath, I quietly walked down the patio stairs and tiptoed across the walkway to his garage.

When I peered through the doorway, Ryley was seated on his weight bench with his head in his hands. In that moment, my heart tore wide open. Men really were from Mars—they handled things so much different than women. However, I didn't want him to shut me out. Maybe that wasn't what he was doing, but I needed him.

His body glistened with sweat and his hair was

drenched. It didn't stop me from running my hands down his arms and getting to my knees in front of him.

"What are you doing out here?" he asked. Lifting his head, he stared down at me, his eyes tired.

"You've been out here all day. I've missed you."

Sighing, he looked down at his wrapped hands. "I'm trying, angel. Every time I close my eyes or my mind wanders, I can see him touching you. It's driving me in-fucking-sane."

I flipped his hand over and gently started undoing the tape. "I know this is hard for you, but don't let your desire for vengeance come between us. I'm here and I'll give you your space, but don't forget that I need you too."

Once I had his hands free, he touched the side of my head and stroked my temple with his thumb. "I'm sorry. What can I do to make it up to you?"

With a sly smile, I licked my lips and ran my hands over his groin. His cock jumped at my touch. "If you want to stay in here all day and work yourself ragged, that's fine. Do what you have to do to get ready for the fight. But once that sun disappears, I want you to spend the energy you have left with me. Make love to me, fuck me, do whatever the hell you want. I just want you to be with me."

Eyes darkening, he gripped my arms and lifted me to my feet. He wasted no time in ripping off my pants and tearing off my shirt, then getting to his feet and doing the same with his own. Once he sat back down on the weight bench, he grabbed my ass and made me sit on his lap, his dick nestled between my legs.

"I don't think you know what you're asking of me, angel. I'm pissed off and angry, but I'm also fucking turned on. It's a lethal combination and the last thing I want to do is hurt or scare you."

"Oh, I don't know . . . I think I'm ready for what you got," I teased, playfully squeezing the bulging tip of his cock.

Jerking into my hand, he tilted my body back and roughly closed his lips over a nipple, sucking hard. The stubble on his chin started to rub me raw. When he bit down, I cried out and rocked my hips against his length.

His fingers dug into my hips as he lifted me up and slammed me down. Once he was fully seated within me, he lifted me up and pushed me down onto him over and over. My movements weren't my own. I was in his control and I fucking loved it. Even with me on top, he dominated and took what he wanted. Fisting his hands in my hair, he tilted my head back and bit my neck, marking me.

"Oh, yes. Ryley . . ."

His low rumble of satisfaction vibrated down to my core. I was so close to orgasm I could barely think straight. Over and over he dropped me down on his cock with punishing force. He licked and sucked my nipples, pulling them with his teeth. Wrapping an arm around his neck, I arched my back to give him better access. Reaching behind my ass, I cupped his balls, massaging them.

"Holy fuck, I'm going to come," he growled, shortening his thrusts. Grunting, he pulled my body into his and dropped his head down to watch where we were connected.

Screaming with pleasure, I sat down on him as far as I could go and pressed down on his taint with my finger. He groaned and squeezed me tight, but I kept my finger pushing down on him as I rode wave after wave of my release.

It all intensified when I felt him blast inside of me. I loved the feel of his cock pulsating. Catching my breath, I let my head fall to his shoulder while his fingers loosened on my waist.

"Now that's what I'm talking about," I marveled.

Brushing my hair to the side, he gently kissed my neck and wrapped his arms around my waist. "Just remember, angel. You asked for it. Every day at sundown, I'm going to find you and take you in any way I please. There's no turning back."

I pulled his bottom lip between my teeth and moaned. "I'm counting on it."

Ashleigh

Five Days Later

TOMORROW RYLEY WOULD fight his brother. None of us knew if Camden was aware I had gone to the hospital after the incident, or that I was definitely pregnant with his brother's twins. He'd disappeared without a trace. I half expected him to show up at the cabin, but nothing—no sign from him or any of his friends.

I could smell the approaching rain and thunder rumbled in the distance. The sky over the mountains began to fill up with gray clouds. This time, I wouldn't be alone during the storm. When I left to go to Aspen, I dreaded the rain. It brought back too many memories. Now, I welcomed it.

"What's wrong?" Ryley asked, sitting down beside

me. Brows furrowed, he watched me cautiously as he handed me a cup of hot chocolate. Even though it wasn't cold outside, I craved the chocolaty goodness.

Forcing a smile, I held the cup in my hand and looked down into it. If I lied, he'd be able to tell in a heartbeat. Why was I such a terrible liar?

"Thank you for this," I replied, lifting my cup. "I was just thinking."

My mind hadn't totally been on the fight with Camden, but in helping him find some level of peace. For the past five days, Ryley had manhandled me into submission, literally making me tap out. He hadn't lied when he said he was going to take me any way he wanted. He needed the release and I was happy to give it to him—even if it provided just a small shred of bliss underneath all of the hostility. Looking at him now, he appeared relaxed, but it only lasted for so long before his thoughts plagued him once again. I was ready for the fight to be over.

"What have you been thinking about?" His piercing blue eyes bore into mine, like he was searching for something.

I blew on my hot chocolate and took a sip. "You. The fight. Our babies. This rain. Sex in the rain. You name it, it's been on my mind. Mostly, I don't have a good feeling about tomorrow, Ryley. My gut is telling me something bad is going to happen."

Sitting back in his chair, a small smile splayed across his face. "You have nothing to worry about, angel. I'm not going to let anyone near you, and you sure as hell are *not* going to be alone at any point in time."

I loved how he was so protective. He was a true alpha male, fighting for what he wanted in life. However, even alphas weren't invincible. "I'm not worried about me," I confessed. "I'm worried about you."

Chuckling, he leaned over and slid his hand up my thigh. "Trust me, the only person who needs to be worried is my brother. I'm ready to end this too and I'm not giving up until he's down." Thunder rumbled again overhead and we both looked up at the sky, a raindrop falling onto my cheek. "There's something I want to talk to you about," he murmured, pulling my chin to face him.

Once I focused on him, he let go of my chin and slid his fingers down my neck making me shiver. "What is it?" I whispered breathlessly.

"You like it here, don't you? Up here . . . at the cabin."

"Of course, it's amazing," I stated wholeheartedly. "If we could live here, I would. Why do you ask?" More rain started to fall, but it didn't faze us. I was used to sitting in it, hoping it would take away the pain.

Ryley helped me to my feet and put his arms around my waist, the droplets of water soaking through our clothes. "Because I think we should live up here. I don't want our kids growing up in Los Angeles. We both grew up in the mountains and there's so much more to offer them here."

"What about your training? Everything you have is in L.A.," I stated incredulously. "Not to mention I start a new job next month." Was he serious? Would he leave it all, for a quiet life hidden away?

Brushing the wet hair off my face, he leaned down and kissed me gently, lingering with just his lips pressed to mine. When he pulled back, he held onto my face and looked deep into my eyes. "I would leave it all for you, angel. Besides, I told Danny last night about this. He mentioned moving up this way too. The point is, nothing out there compares to the life I want here, with you," he said, glancing around him. "You can get a job out here if you want, but you know you don't have to."

A sly smile spread across his face. "Besides, once February comes we're not going to have any more alone time for a while. But if we move here, I'm sure my mother would be happy to babysit." We both laughed, and then he turned serious. "Would it really be so bad to spend all of our time together, getting to know each other?"

"No, but I want to contribute, Ryley. I want to provide something to this instead of it all being on you."

"You will be contributing. You're going to be the mother of my children. That in itself is going to be the hardest job of all. Well, that, and keeping up with me. I'm probably going to have to start paying you to put up with me."

Sliding his hands down my neck, he kept his eyes on me while he unbuttoned my shirt, one button at a time. Once all were undone, he brushed it open, exposing my bare breasts. I didn't even bother with a bra today since no one had been by. Ryley seemed excited by my lack of clothes.

"I think I like you not wearing a bra," he murmured gruffly. Once out of my wet shirt, it flopped to the deck with a smack. Ryley's breath fanned across my heated skin as he lowered his lips to my neck and trailed them down to my breasts. I almost buckled in his arms, but he got down on one of his knees, and held me firm with his arms wrapped around me.

My clit throbbed with need, especially when Ryley

set me down on his bended knee and rocked me against him as he pulled my nipple between his teeth, biting gently.

Unbuttoning my jeans, I slid off of him and had to work my way out of them since they were wet. Ryley got to his feet, doing the same, and then pulled me back to him, both of us glistening with rain on our bare skin. I wrapped my hand around his cock.

Closing his eyes, he moaned and bit my lip, thrusting his tongue inside. I melted in his arms, but all too soon he moved away, my hand sliding off of his length. "Give me one second," he remarked with a wink of his eye. Just inside by the patio door was the sleeping bag we used the last time we were out in the rain.

"You had this planned, didn't you? You sneaky little bastard."

Smiling, he spread the sleeping bag out and grabbed my hand. "When the clouds rolled in, I knew I couldn't pass up the chance. But at least you won't get splinters in your ass." Which had been my concern when we did it two months ago, right in the very same spot.

Gently, he lowered me down and covered me with his body, shielding me from the pouring rain. Taking my hands, he held them over my head and clasped his own with mine. Holding them tight, he opened my legs with his knee and settled in, slowly thrusting inside.

For the past few days he hadn't touched me this softly, or so gently. I loved the wild and dangerous side of him, but I was beginning to think I loved the gentler side of him more.

His lips brushed across my skin and my breasts so smoothly as he pushed in slow, deep. As soon as he let my hands go, I wrapped my arms around his neck and stared into his eyes. The last time we did this very same thing, he'd demanded I keep my attention on him. Right now, I didn't want to look at anything else.

"I love you so fucking much," he murmured.

Wrapping my legs around his waist, I rocked my hips slowly against his and held on tight, trying to keep him deep. He groaned in my ear as my insides clenched. When I let my climax take me, my body trembled. It came from the very depths of my soul, from the part of me that absolutely yearned for the man inside of me. He too let go and filled me with his release, breathing heavy in my ear. Never had I felt so connected or loved by anyone in my life than in that moment. Ryley was mine and I was never letting him go again.

"I love you too," I whispered.

I don't know how long we laid out there, staring at each other with him still inside of me, but when the rain stopped, it was like everything went back to normal. It was almost like I'd been in a trance. I missed the rain already. Slowly, Ryley pulled out of me and got to his feet, lifting me up in his arms.

"As much as I would enjoy making love to you all night, we have plans." He carried me inside, straight up the stairs to the bathroom.

When he set me down, I got a good look at him, all tattoos and muscles with his semi-hard cock protruding from between his legs. "Oh, yeah? What are we . . . I mean, um, what are we doing?" *Holy hell, get it together.* If he ever wanted to get me flustered all he'd have to do is get naked. The boy was seriously sex on a stick—or, I guess the more accurate term would be sex *with* a stick. I giggled at my thoughts.

He turned on the shower water and looked back at me with a smirk. "Well, my mother kind of told everyone in my family about you, and the babies. They want to meet the woman who tamed the beast."

"Judging by the last few days, I wouldn't go saying your *tame*," I laughed. "But it would be nice to meet your family. Hopefully soon, I can take you to meet mine."

He gestured for me to get in the shower, and then followed behind. "Do you think they'll like me?"

Turning around, I leaned up on my tiptoes and folded my arms around his neck. "My mother will love you. My father on the other hand, is old fashioned. Once he finds out I'm pregnant, he'll demand a wedding. Don't worry, though. He'll soften up as soon as he finds out how wonderful you are."

He stared down at me. "Is that what you want? To get married before we have the babies?"

Was it? We hadn't been together long and I knew we had so many things to learn about one another. "I want us to do what's right, Ryley. Getting married just because we're pregnant is the one thing I wanted to avoid. As much as the thought thrills me to no end, I want to make sure we're ready. Right now, we have other things to focus on."

Grinning mischievously, he pressed his cock against my stomach. Leave it to him to turn something serious into humor. "It thrills you, huh? How about I show you what thrills me?"

Turning around, I splayed my hands against the shower wall and arched my back, spreading my legs. "Be my guest."

Ashleigh

Fight Night

THE GATHERING WITH his family was amazing. It made me miss my own. Ryley's grandfather was the best of all with his smoky gray hair and beard. I could sense how they all wanted Ryley back. I never would've imagined that he of all people, was a family guy. He amazed me and I was positive there was a lot about him I didn't know. I couldn't wait to spend the rest of my life figuring him out.

Instead of driving eight hours to Las Vegas, we opted to fly. As soon as we got on the plane, I passed out and didn't wake up until Ryley tapped me on the nose.

"It's time, angel. Come on."

Rubbing my eyes, I yawned and unbuckled my belt.

"Are we renting a car?"

He shook his head and smiled. "No, I actually have someone meeting us here."

After helping me up, he reached overhead and grabbed our bags, which thankfully had fit up there. I jammed as much as I could in my carry-on so we wouldn't have to check our bags. The last thing I wanted was for it to get lost.

As soon as we got off the plane, we started toward the exit. I didn't even have to ask who was picking us up because I saw him straight ahead . . . Tyler Rushing. "What up, fucker?" Ryley called.

Tyler guffawed and they bumped fists. "Nothing much, man. Just coming by to pick up your sorry ass." He looked over at me and smiled. "It's good to see you again, Ashleigh. I hope you're not mad at me."

He looked the same as he did the last time I saw him, closely shaved blond hair and gray eyes. Crossing my arms, I pursed my lips before breaking into a grin. "I should be, but I'm not. If you didn't tell Ryley, I doubt we'd be together right now. So, in other words, thank you."

He winked. "You're welcome. Kacey's out in the car waiting on us. We'll drop you off at the hotel so you can both get ready for tonight." As far as I was aware, no one knew about the incident with Camden, except Gabriella and Colin. Ryley could barely keep his anger in check when the subject would come up, so I tried to keep from talking about it. His control hung on the edge, but he did good keeping calm.

"We appreciate it," Ryley insisted, throwing his arm across my shoulders. "My baby's momma probably needs to relax just a bit before the festivities begin."

"Oh, dear Lord, don't call me that," I laughed, smacking his arm. "I can't stand it."

When we got outside, Tyler led us to his shiny, black truck where Kacey stood waiting on us. Her golden blonde hair was pulled back off her shoulders, and she was dressed in a pink tank top and shorts. She waved when she saw us and I waved back. I didn't know if she'd like me or not, being that I was Gabriella's best friend.

"Hello Ashleigh, I'm Kacey," she said, extending her hand. "Congratulations on the baby."

Before I could reply, Ryley chuckled and hugged her. "I think you mean *babies*. We're having twins."

"Oh, hell," Tyler joked. "Why didn't you tell me?" He opened the back door to his truck and Ryley slid our bags inside, his jaw firm.

"I would have, but things have been a little fucked up the past week. All I can say is that I'm ready to get tonight over with."

"Have you talked to your brother?" Tyler asked.

Ryley helped me into the truck and glanced quickly up at me. "No, I haven't spoken to him in a while. From what I hear, no one has heard from him."

"Hmm . . . that's strange. I wonder what the fuck he's doing?"

Ryley hopped into the back with me and leaned down toward my ear. "That's what I'd like to know."

Ashleigh

TIME SEEMED TO fly by. When we got to the hotel, I only had enough time to take a quick shower and get dressed before it was time to go. It just so happened I had a royal blue tank top with *Team Ryley* on it, thanks to Gabriella. She sent a text saying she was going to meet us at the arena, since we were going to be riding over there with Tyler and Kacey. Hopefully, it wouldn't be too weird sitting with them all. I couldn't abandon Gabriella just because Tyler and Kacey were my escorts.

Ryley was quiet the entire time on the way to the arena. Tyler understood and didn't bother him. He needed time to get his mind focused. No doubt about it, he was ready. My only concern was of him letting his anger and vengeance cloud his judgment. By the time we got to the arena, the whole place buzzed with excitement. I wanted to be excited, but I couldn't shake the feeling of unease creeping up my spine.

Danny met us by the door as soon as we entered the arena, while Tyler and Kacey left to get their seats. "It's a madhouse here tonight," he exclaimed. "All everyone's talking about is the fight against your brother." He led us down the hallway until we got to Ryley's room. He too wore a royal blue shirt with Ryley's name. What would be amazing is if the whole crowd had shirts like that to show their support.

"It's going to be a bloody one," Ryley growled. "But it'll be a good show." I sat in the corner and pulled out my phone so I could surf the internet while he got ready. He didn't know I was listening when he spoke next. "I'm going to have Ashleigh walk out with us. I don't want her walking anywhere alone."

Danny returned the quiet gesture. "Do you think someone will try to do something to her?"

Surely, Camden wouldn't be stupid enough to do that.

"I don't know," Ryley whispered, "but I'm not taking any chances. Tyler will be there to sit with her once she takes her seat."

"Knock, knock," Gabriella chimed, opening the door. "Can I come in?"

"Um . . . it looks like you're already in," I said, turning off my phone. Sure enough, she was wearing one of her Ryley shirts with her dark hair pulled high into a ponytail.

She opened the door wide and strolled in. "You about ready to go get our seats?" she asked.

"Actually," Ryley began, tightening up his gloves,

"she's going out there with me. I don't want anyone messing with her."

She scoffed. "And you think someone's going to mess with her while she's with me? I *do* know how to kick some major ass, Ryley. No worries though, I'll just walk out there with you too. You'll have your whole crew there, including your mini me's," she said pointing at my stomach.

With the mood Ryley had been in, I expected him to blast on her, but he actually smirked. "And how can I say no to that?"

Gabriella scrunched her nose and shrugged. "You can't. But anyway, it's almost time. That's why I came to get Ash." She came to my side and bumped me in the shoulder, noticing my tension. "It'll be okay," she whispered in my ear. "Ryley's going to handle this the way he needs to. Camden deserves to get his ass kicked."

"All right, let's get our champion in place," Danny advised.

After Ryley put on his blue robe, we walked out of the room and made our way to the arena. My heart sped out of control because I knew at any moment we were going to see Camden, most likely with a sneer on his face. Thankfully, when we got to the entryway, Camden was nowhere to be seen.

"Do you know who's being called out first?" I asked, whispering to Gabriella.

Her eyes darted around, most likely searching for Camden. "I think they're calling Ryley first. I'm hoping they do it soon, before Cam shows up back here. We don't need Ryley jumping ahead of himself and getting disqualified."

No, we don't. Which is what I was afraid would happen if they don't hurry the fuck up and call Ryley's name. Gabriella and I hung back just a bit to give Ryley some room, but when he turned around and pulled me into his arms, I gasped.

"Promise me that whatever you see tonight it won't scare you away from me. This fight will be different from any other you've ever seen." His song started to play, but he grabbed my face, his eyes wild. "Promise me," he ordered.

Swallowing hard, I nodded my head. "I promise."

He kissed me long and hard and rested his forehead to mine, before Danny came to his side.

"It's time to go, son."

About that time, the announcer's voice boomed over the speakers. "Ladies and gentlemen, it is with great pleasure to introduce tonight's Middleweight fighters. We all know them as the Twins of Terror. Brothers, competing for the Middleweight Championship title. Let's first hear it for *Ryley . . . The Rampage . . . Jaaammmeeesssooonnn!*"

Ryley breathed me in and then turned on his heel, lifting the hood of his robe. It was almost like everything moved in slow motion after that. The curtain opened, the music blared, and we walked out. The crowd screamed and shouted, but I couldn't hear any of it. All I could hear was the pounding of my heart as I walked behind him to the ring. The announcer with his slicked back gray hair and suit, smiled wide as Ryley approached, knowing this was going to be the fight of the night.

Please let this be over quick.

Ryley

THE CROWD CHEERED and shouted, but I didn't care about the fame or the title tonight. In fact, the title was worthless to me right now. I only wanted to make sure Camden suffered. If I won the title in doing that, so be it. Ashleigh and Gabriella took their seats while I bounced on my feet, waiting for them to call my jackass brother out.

"Don't lose focus, Ryley," Danny instructed, taking my robe. "Do not let your anger get the best of you. This is an important fight in your career and I don't want to see you blow it over something stupid."

"I'm not," I snapped, glaring at the curtain. "I'm ready to get this shit started."

"And now," the announcer called, "let's get this party started. Are you ready for it? Let's hear it for *Camden* . . .

The Bone Crusher . . . Jaaammmeeesssooonnn!"

His song blared over the speakers, but all I focused on was my anger. My brother had fucked with me one too many times. There came a point in time where it was enough. He couldn't use excuses anymore. He was seriously one fucked up human being. No one made him that way . . . he became that way on his own.

All right, Camden hurry the fuck up. I'm ready for this to end. The seconds felt like hours as I waited on him. It was like everything moved in slow motion and I was on hyper speed. Another minute rolled by and still, nothing. Where the hell was he?

The announcer looked to the judges for a signal, but all they did was shrug their shoulders. They didn't seem to know what was going on either. I grew more impatient with each passing second. "What's the problem?" I asked the announcer.

He shrugged and turned the microphone away. "I don't know yet. We have someone going to check on your brother. If he doesn't show up in five, he forfeits and you win the title."

What? I didn't want to win the title like that.

Danny's eyes went wide and he beckoned me closer. "I don't know what's going on, but I don't like it," he mumbled low. "It's not like your brother to miss a fight. He lives for this shit."

Gabriella got up and rushed over. "Where is he?"

"We don't know," I growled. "If he doesn't show up, I don't know what the fuck I'm going to do. I've been waiting to kick his ass for over a week."

She searched around and held up her finger. "I'll be right back. I'm going to see what I can find out." Ashleigh's eyes went wide when Gabriella went back to her, most likely telling her what was going on. I was going to go in-fucking-sane if Camden didn't show up. I had to have this fight, I *needed* this fight—there was no way around it. I couldn't let go of what he did.

The crowd chanted his name over and over, hoping to get him out there. The minutes ticked by and once the final five were up, it was over. I watched the judges talk it over and call the announcer down to them to discuss the issue. What were they going to decide? My fate was in their hands.

The announcer came back into the ring and brought the microphone to his lips. "Ladies and gentlemen, it appears Camden Jameson has decided to forfeit the fight this evening." The crowd grumbled and some of them booed. They paid for a fight and they weren't getting it. I couldn't blame them. My douchebag brother just fucked everything up . . . again.

"With a unanimous decision, the judges have awarded Ryley Jameson the Middleweight Champion title. I think we can all say he deserves it." He lifted my arm in the air and the crowd went wild, jumping to their feet. I wanted to smile, to run around the ring in celebration, but there wasn't anything to celebrate. There was no victory.

And just like clockwork, Sarah Wilder stormed up into the ring with her camera crew, talking excitedly into the camera. "Good evening, I'm here live with Ryley Jameson, where he was set to fight for the Middleweight title against his own twin brother, Camden Jameson. Under unanimous decision, Ryley was awarded the championship due to an unusual forfeit by his brother." She turned to me. "Ryley, what on earth would possess your brother to give up the title so easily?"

Even though I was raging inside, I knew I couldn't show it. Danny accentuated his smile and mouthed the words 'breathe' when I glanced over at him. "Actually, I have no clue what's going on with my brother right now," I said, looking straight into the camera.

"Do you think he was afraid of fighting you? Afraid he would lose?" Her eyes gleamed with delight. She wanted a story, but I sure as hell wasn't going to give her one.

"As much as I'd like to think that's true, no, I don't think that's it at all. I'm sure he has a reason for not showing up. But I would like to thank the judges for giving me this honor, and more importantly, to thank the fans here tonight. I know they wanted to see a fight. Trust me, I wanted to give 'em one." Nodding to the camera, I smiled quickly and rushed out of the ring.

Ashleigh bolted up to me and put her arm around my waist. Her touch was all that kept me grounded this past week. Without it, I probably would've done something stupid. "Oh my God, this is insane. I told you something was going to happen. I don't like it, Ryley."

"Neither do I," I admitted. "Come on, let's see if we can find out what's going on."

I nodded to Tyler for him and Kacey to follow us to the back. The whole way there everyone congratulated me on the title, patting me on the back, and shouting their delight. If only I could enjoy it. Danny made it to the room first and held it open while we all filed in. Gabriella was already in there, her head down, body stiff.

"Gabby, what are you doing?"

When she turned around, her hand shook as she passed me what she had in her hand. "I saw this when I came in here. As much as I wanted to rip it apart, I think you need to see it. We both know what it means."

Opening the letter, there wasn't much to it . . . but I knew what it meant.

Brother,

This ends tonight. No titles, no rules. Just you and me. Someone will be by to get you.

~C

"Ryley, what does it say?" Ashleigh demanded, coming to my side. I handed her the letter and walked away. She wasn't going to like it.

"What's going on, bro?" Tyler asked.

Tyler knew about the whole underground fighting fiasco because one of his friends from the Labyrinth was a part of it. Now he was rotting in jail. "Do you remember what Wade was involved in last year?"

Tyler tensed. "Please tell me Camden's not involved in that shit? Fighters were murdered, Ryley. What does he want you to do?"

"I'll give you one guess."

Ashleigh

"YOU CAN'T DO this," I blurted out. Everyone turned to me as I stalked up to Ryley and grabbed his arm, turning him to face me. "It's one thing to fight where there are rules and judges, but it's quite another to fight where there's none. You could get seriously hurt . . . or killed."

Tears streamed down my cheeks and I looked down at the letter again. I didn't want everyone to see me break down, but the thought of him leaving to fight in some underground battle where anything goes, was just too damn much to handle.

Ryley glanced over his shoulder at everyone, but they averted their heads, giving us some semblance of privacy. "Angel, I have to go," he murmured regretfully. "Please tell me you understand."

"No, I don't understand. You don't have to go," I begged, holding onto him. It wasn't like I could physically stop him, but I could at least try. "Let your vengeance go and stay here with me. It's not worth it, Ryley. I don't want to give you a guilt trip and tell you stay for the sake of our family, but I'm begging you. Please . . . stay."

He stared down at me, anguish in his clear blue gaze, but I could tell it wasn't going to work. He wasn't going to rest until he made his brother pay. A part of me understood, but I wanted to be selfish and hold onto him.

"Why do you have to go?" Tyler asked. "What do you have to prove?"

Ryley looked at me and brushed his thumb over my cheek and down my lips, keeping his heated stare on mine. "He needs to know that he can't touch what's mine and get away with it. I'm sure you know how that feels."

Over Ryley's shoulder, I peered up at Tyler and he bristled, jaw clenched. He recently went through a whole ordeal with Kacey, where she'd almost been raped. I couldn't imagine how scared she must've been. Luckily, he was there to save her. But who would save Ryley if he needed help? Before another word was spoken, a knock sounded on the door. We all looked at it, but no one moved except Ryley.

I lowered my head in anguish once I saw who was on the other side. It wasn't Camden, but by the look in the dark eyes gleaming at Ryley, I feared it was time. The man was tall and bulky, probably in his early thirties, with jagged scars on both arms—almost like damage from a knife fight. The stench of malevolence poured off of him, and when he noticed me staring, he winked. *Disgusting pig.*

Ryley noticed the exchange and stepped in his line of

sight. "What the fuck do you want?"

"I'm here for you," he barked with a sneer. "Unless you're too much of a pussy."

The tension soared and I half expected Ryley to punch the shit out of him, but instead, he walked over to the table and grabbed his bag. With his back to everyone else, he quickly glanced over at me and mouthed the words 'I love you' before turning around and heading through the door, disappearing down the hall. The guy smirked at us and slammed the door.

"*Ryley*," I shouted, rushing toward the door. Before I could get there and chase after him, Tyler blocked my path and put his arms around me, holding me in place. I pushed against him and fought, punching his chest. I had to get to Ryley.

"Ashleigh, stop," he ordered as I continued to thrash. "You can't go after him. It's too dangerous."

After pummeling him for God knows how long, I got tired and just let him hold me, my tears soaking the front of his shirt. "I don't know what to do," I cried. "I feel so helpless. What if something happens to him?"

Gabriella came up behind me and Tyler let me go so I could hold onto her. "Ryley's strong, Ash. You have to look at this from his point of view. His own brother deceived you. He was going to have the fucking baby results changed for Christ's sake. I hope Ryley beats the shit out of him."

"Wait, what?" Tyler interrupted. "What did Camden do?"

I laid my head on Gabriella's shoulder while she explained what'd happened over the past few weeks.

Kacey gasped and Tyler grunted. "No wonder he

wants to kill his fucking brother."

"If you don't mind me butting in," Kacey began, "I actually know who that guy was."

Lifting my head, I turned around quickly, wiping away my tears. "How?"

She bit her lip and sighed. "As Kyle's sister, I've heard and seen a lot of things. That guy goes by the name of Scar, and he runs an underground fighting ring. I saw my brother and Pax with him a few times. There were nights when Kyle would come back cut up and bruised, but he was always happy, like he enjoyed what he did. I was never allowed to go though. Kyle wouldn't let me."

"Paxton went too?" Gabriella asked incredulously.

Kacey nodded and then her eyes narrowed. "Yeah, but I don't think he was involved with it as much as my brother. If you haven't noticed, Pax is different. He's a good guy."

Gabriella stiffened for a brief moment and then put her arm around my shoulders. "All right, I think I'm going to get Ashleigh back to the hotel. She needs to get some rest."

Tyler moved forward, pursing his lips. "You take her back and stay with her, that's it—no detours. If anyone gives you trouble, I want you to call me, okay?"

"I will. I have experience with kicking ass, so I think we'll be all right. Besides, no one's going to mess with me."

He stood staring at us, like he was trying to figure something out. When all Gabriella did was smile, he rolled his eyes and took Kacey's hand. "Just be careful and go straight back to the hotel. The last thing Ryley needs is for something to happen to you two, not to mention your brother would have all our asses."

"I agree," Danny cut in. "Don't do anything stupid."

Gabriella snorted. "Who, me? Never."

Smirking, Tyler opened the door. "Tell that shit to someone who believes it. Now let's go. I'll walk you guys to the car and make sure you get to the hotel safely."

With her arm around me, she led me out the door and we started on our way to the car. "What are we going to do, Gabby?" I asked quietly. "I don't think I can sit at the hotel, not knowing what's happening to Ryley."

"Just be quiet," she warned. "I have a plan, but I'll tell you in the car. I hope it works."

Ryley

ASHLEIGH'S SCREAMS ECHOED in my head as I walked away. Not once did I look back, I kept on walking, even when Mr. Fuckhead behind me chuckled. "It looks like your bitch is scared for you. Maybe it's because she knows you're going to get your ass handed to you tonight."

Gritting my teeth, I kept my mouth shut. I had to save every ounce of energy and loathing for my brother. The more he taunted, the angrier I got. And the angrier I got, the worse it would be for my brother. When we got outside, I was led to a black SUV with dark tinted windows and black rims.

"Get in," he barked.

"Where are we going?"

The guy laughed and shook his head. “You don’t get to ask questions. By coming with me, you agree to what I say. If not, you’ll pay the consequences. Get in.”

Throwing my bag in the back seat, I huffed and slid in. Once the other guy got in the driver’s seat we were on our way.

“All right, let’s see,” he said, fumbling around for something in the seat. “Oh yeah, here we go.” He threw something over his shoulder and it landed in my lap. “Put that on. Also, you can call me Scar.”

That didn’t surprise me. His whole body was riddled with them. I held up the long scrap of black cloth. “A blindfold?”

Scar glared at me through the rearview mirror. “Yes, jackass. You’re an outsider. We don’t disclose our secrets to those who don’t belong.”

He stopped on the side of the road and waited for me to put it on before he went any further. Once I had it secure, he started back on the way. “Good boy,” he taunted. “Before we get there, I will go over some things with you. Your brother has challenged you to a fight and now that you’ve accepted, there’s no turning back. When we arrive, I’m going to put you in a room, so our bidders can come and take a look at you. You won’t be able to see them, but they’ll be able to see you.”

“They’re gambling on us?” I asked dryly.

“Didn’t I say no questions?” he snapped. “If they bid on the right fighter, they get *rewards*.” The way he said it made it sound like it wasn’t just money these people were gambling with. Unfortunately, I was about to find out.

“After the bidders make their rounds, we tally up the bids and then we bring you out. Both fighters agree to the terms once in the ring. Some make up their own rules and some just go balls out. The bloodier they make it, the more money they make. If you make it good enough, you could go home with half a million dollars tonight."

"I don't want your fucking blood money," I growled. "I'm only going to fight my brother and be done with it, nothing else. After that, I'm getting the fuck out."

Scar chuckled and the car came to a stop. "If you can walk. Sometimes people don't get up. But as far as the money, it's your choice. If you don't want it, it leaves more for me."

He got out of the car and the door to my right opened. "Let's go, Jameson. Everyone's waiting for you."

Grabbing my bag, I jumped out of the car and was led toward the unknown. I didn't know where I was or what was about to happen, but I knew one thing . . . I was ready.

Ashleigh

AS SOON AS we got into the car, Gabriella called Paxton, and to our advantage, he was in Las Vegas. He agreed to see us and it just so happened he was staying at the same hotel. Their conversation was awkward, almost like there was something she wasn't telling me.

"Are you sure this is going to work?" I asked. "The last time you two were together, I sensed some tension. I don't think he'll want to help out after you were such a bitch to him."

Her mouth flew open as she slammed the brakes on the rental car. "I was *not* a bitch," she exclaimed. "Paxton and I just have some disagreements, that's all."

"Yeah, disagreeing over who likes the other one more . . ." I mumbled.

She shot me a death stare.

"Are you sure nothing's going on between you two? I mean, there's like some serious sexual intensity there. If I can feel it, then there's definitely something going on."

Gabriella got out of the car and I followed. Tyler and Kacey stopped behind us and rolled down the window. "You guys okay?" he asked.

Forcing a smile, I nodded while Gabriella waved. "Yeah, we're fine," I shouted. "Thank you for everything."

"No problem. Make sure to call if you need me."

I waved and kept the smile on my face until he and Kacey disappeared out of the parking lot. Gabriella started to walk off, but I caught up to her and grabbed her arm. "Hey, don't walk away from me. What's going on with you and Pax? Best friends tell each other things."

"Oh, really?" she countered with a smug smile. "I seem to remember you flying off to Aspen and keeping *me* in the dark."

Side by side, we walked into the hotel and got into the elevator. "I know and I'm sorry about that. I should have told you, but I thought maybe it wouldn't be real if I didn't believe it." Her face paled as if I struck a chord. "What is it?" I asked.

The elevator doors opened and she pulled me to the side. "Okay, fine. I'll tell you what's going on. I kissed him a couple weeks ago and it was a mistake. That's it."

"Why was it a mistake?"

"Because," she snapped. "It just was. How would it look to be with someone who helped fuck over my brother? I'd be a traitor."

So that was the hold up. "People change, Gabby. He honestly seems like a good person. Maybe a little rough around the edges, but still a good guy."

"It's not going to happen, Ash. I can't allow it. Now, can we go and get this over with? If Kacey says he used to go to these fights, then he has access. He's the only one who can help us at this point."

I waved my hand toward the hall. "Lead the way."

Taking a deep breath, she blew it out and marched down the hall to Paxton's room. My thoughts strayed to Ryley and what he was doing. Was he already there? Was he fighting? Each second I spent away from him made me sicker, but most of all, it made me angry. This was the last time Camden was going to take our happiness away from us. If I knew I was able, I'd volunteer to get up into the ring with him.

Once we stopped at Paxton's door, Gabriella stared at it and froze. I waited for her to knock and when she didn't, I did it myself—pounding on it. She turned to me, snarling.

"What?" I grumbled. "You were taking too long. I don't exactly have all the time in the world."

About ten seconds later, the door opened and Paxton answered, his hair disheveled wearing only a pair of jeans. I snuck a side glance at Gabriella who's eyes went wide, but then turned to stone when he looked at her.

"Did we interrupt something?" Gabriella asked snidely. "I'm sorry if we made your whore leave for the night."

Paxton smirked and opened the door wide. "You're too kind. But, no worries. She'll be back later. By all means, come on in."

She crossed her arms and shoved past him, leaving me uncomfortable, standing by myself at the door. "Hey, Paxton," I greeted warmly. "Thank you for seeing us tonight."

He motioned for me to enter so I walked in and he shut the door behind me. "So what can I do for you ladies?"

"First off," Gabriella advised, "you can call your cum dumpster for the night and tell her you won't be needing her services. You're going to be busy with me."

Oh hell, here we go.

Paxton lounged across his bed and lifted his hands behind his head. "What if I don't want to be *busy* with you tonight? You've already made it perfectly clear that I don't do it for you."

"Guys, stop. This isn't getting us anywhere," I stormed, glaring at them both. When I turned to Paxton his smirk faded and his expression grew serious. "I'm the one who needs help, Paxton. As I'm sure you know, Ryley and Camden didn't exactly get to fight tonight."

"Yeah, I saw that. Never thought Camden would pussy out."

"He didn't," I said, sitting down on the edge of the bed. "In fact, Ryley's gone to fight him now and I don't know where they've gone. I was hoping you could help me."

Paxton sat up. "And how do you expect me to do that?"

Gabriella stepped in this time. "Because Kacey told us that you and Kyle used to be involved with that underground fighting bullshit. She recognized the behemoth who came and took Ryley away. We need your help to find him."

"You can't be serious. I'm not going to take you there, it's too dangerous."

"Please," I begged. "I have to know he's okay. What if something really bad happens to him? Do you think those savages will make sure he gets medical care?"

Frustrated, Paxton jumped to his feet and ran his hands through his black hair. "You don't seem to get it. It's too fucking dangerous, especially for women like you. Do you know what happens if I break the oath?" I shook my head and Gabriella did the same when he peered over at her. "Well, let me tell you. If either one you so much as talks about the Dark Side to the wrong people, you'll find me in an alley with a bullet through my fucking skull. How does that sound? You still want to go?"

My mouth flew open and I shuddered. "Is it really called the Dark Side?"

He nodded and hung his head. "If you saw the place, you'd figure out why pretty quick. It's not for the faint of heart."

I knew I wouldn't tell anyone about it, but it was still a lot to put on Paxton's shoulders. Sighing, Gabriella got to her feet and approached him, her tension ebbing. "Pax . . . I mean Paxton," she murmured. "I know this is a lot to ask, but we wouldn't put you in this position if it wasn't important. I'm sorry for the way I've been toward you, but I'm asking for your help. I think we can both promise we won't say a word about it to anyone. I'll do whatever you want, just please help us."

His stare bore into her, and in that moment nothing else existed. Why did they fight it? For a moment I could see myself and Ryley in them. "Okay, fine," he gave in. "I'll help you, but you have to agree to my terms." And this was where things would either go my way or go to hell.

"Just name them," Gabriella agreed. "I'll do anything."

Paxton bit his lip and tapped her on the nose. "I'll get to that in a minute, sunshine. Right now we have other things to discuss."

Gabriella groaned and came back to sit beside me. "I have a strange feeling I know what his terms are going to be," she whispered. For some reason, deep down I didn't think she'd mind.

Pulling up a chair, Paxton sat down right in front of us. "To get into the Dark Side, you have to be willing to show proof of bids. You can gamble with money, women, cars, et cetera. Our only problem right now is that the banks are closed and I can't pull out the amount I need to get in. The only other option is . . ."

"Us," I whispered as the realization set in. "You would have to gamble with us."

Regretfully, he nodded. "Yes, and whoever the winner is, you would go to them. The deal is that they get a night with you."

"And you were a part of this?" Gabriella asked.

"A long time ago, but not anymore. I would only need one of you to gamble away. The other can stay with me as my guest."

Before I could volunteer, Gabriella beat me to it. "You can gamble me."

Paxton stiffened and clenched his jaw. He didn't like it any more than I did.

"No," I demanded. "I'm the one making us go. He can gamble with me."

Gabriella's eyes went wide and she flung her arms in the air. "Oh, yeah. That's smart. You're a genius! Why don't we let Ryley see you auctioned off in his fight? If he loses and you go to Camden, what do you think that'll do to him? He'll kill his brother for sure."

"He isn't going to lose."

"It doesn't matter, Ash. I can deal with Camden in my own way. You can't. Besides, you have a little bit more to worry about than I do. You're fucking pregnant for crying out loud."

"Oh fuck," Paxton growled. "You are?"

When I nodded, he ran his hands over his face. "Then there's no choice. All I can say is, if Camden wins, he better turn you down. If not, then he's going to deal with me. I'll fight him myself."

"You'd do that?" she asked.

"Let's hope we don't have to find out." Moving his seat back, he got to his feet and opened his bag, pulling out a shirt. "I suggest you run to your rooms and change clothes. You're not going to get in wearing those. Something short, tight, and sexy will do the trick."

"Oh hell," I grumbled. "I didn't bring anything like that."

Gabriella pulled me to my feet and winked. "Don't worry, I did. Now let's go, so we can get out of here. I'm just dying to be auctioned off."

"Maybe you should hear the terms first," I insisted. "It might be something you don't want to do."

She turned to Paxton, who approached her slowly with a devilish smirk on his face.

"That's true, sunshine. It might be something you don't want to do. But then again, maybe you'll like it."

Gabriella rolled her eyes. "It doesn't matter, Paxton. Ryley and Ashleigh are my two closest friends. There's not anything I wouldn't do for them. So, in other words, don't tell me. I'd rather go into this not knowing."

Paxton looked down at me. "All right, you heard her. She doesn't want to know. Just remind her of that when the time comes for her to pay up."

Gabriella turned on her heel and marched to the door, opening it wide.

"I have a feeling she won't forget," I murmured. "We'll see you in just a few."

After we left, Gabriella remained quiet the whole way to our room. It was hard to decipher what was going through her head, but I had a guess. She would figure it all out eventually. All I knew was, I was indebted to her and Paxton.

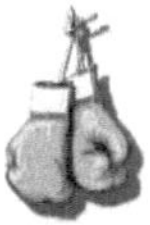

"I can't believe I'm wearing this much makeup," I muttered, looking at my reflection in the mirror.

"Neither can I, but we have to play the part."

Gabriella laid it on thick and put me in one of her dresses; thankfully, it wasn't too tight around the stomach. It was red and strapless, falling mid-thigh. I had to admit, I didn't look like myself. Gabriella didn't either in her midnight blue halter dress.

My stomach was in knots, probably from the pregnancy and being scared shitless. I forced a couple of peanut butter crackers down my throat and guzzled some water, hoping it would help. Nothing was going to help my nerves.

"I don't think I know of any female fighters that look and act like you. It's strange to think that someone so dainty can kick ass."

Gabriella smoothed on her deep red lipstick and pouted her lips. "It's part of my charm, and my cover. Everyone underestimates me. I guess that's why I'm undefeated." She brushed out her hair and turned in front of the mirror. "All right, let's go. We need to hurry. Paxton texted and said to meet him in the lobby."

It didn't take us long to get ready, but we knew we had to look the part. I had to make sure Scar didn't recognize me. "Thank you for doing this, Gabby. Paxton is taking a huge risk taking us."

Grabbing her purse, she opened the door and nodded. "Yes, and I'll keep my promise and not say a word about it to anyone. I trust you to do the same."

Once out the door, it slammed shut and we were on our way. "After tonight, I want to forget any of this ever happened. It'll be like it doesn't exist."

"That's not going to happen, Ash. Sadly, this is a night you'll remember for the rest of your life. I don't know what's going to happen, but you need to keep your feelings in check. If you see Ryley, don't make a scene. He can't fight his brother if he's worried about you."

We got into the elevators and descended the fourteen floors to the bottom. The Bellagio was one of the best hotels in Las Vegas and I loved staying at it. Just a few weeks ago, I'd been here taking a pregnancy test with Gabriella and Ryley by my side. It was strange to think how so many things had changed in a month.

"What if something happens to him?" I asked as the

doors opened. "What if he needs help?"

She stopped in front of me and put her hands on my shoulders. "Then we'll help him. I have no problem getting up there and facing Camden myself."

As soon as she turned around, Paxton was up ahead holding what looked to be scarves in his hand. When his face lifted, he looked at us once and then did a complete double take.

"I guess he didn't recognize us," she murmured. "It *is* kind of hard with an inch of makeup on our faces, dressed like whores."

Paxton approached us, his hesitant smile slowly turning to a frown. "When I said to change, I regret that now," he said, staring at Gabriella. "Unfortunately, we have no choice." He handed us each a black silk scarf.

"What is this for?" I asked, smoothing the silky fabric through my fingers.

"It's part of the rules. They won't let you anywhere near the entrance without it on. Are you ready for this?"

He held out his arms, so I looped mine on his right while he waited on Gabriella to take his left. Sighing, she slowly slid her arm through his and glimpsed up at him.

"I'm ready," she assured him. "Just as long as nobody touches me, I'll be fine. I'd hate to get kicked out because I ripped some guy's balls off."

Paxton pulled his arms in, drawing us closer. "No one is going to touch either one of you."

We started toward the hotel exit, my blood racing in my veins. We were about to cross over to the Dark Side . . . literally.

Ashleigh

THE RIDE WAS silent and judging by the tension in the car, I was afraid Paxton was going to think better of the situation and turn us around. I could see it in his eyes—he regretted agreeing to our demands. He'd put his trust in us, and if we waivered from that trust, he would pay the consequences. Surely, Gabriella could see that he was trying to prove himself to her?

"All right you two, put your blindfolds on. It's almost show time."

I glanced back at Gabby who smiled reassuringly before tying the scarf around her head. I saw enough of our surroundings to know we weren't exactly in the good parts of Vegas. My skin prickled, but I put on my blindfold and sat back in the seat. My world felt like it was quickly spinning out of control.

"I'm warning you," Paxton began, "you're going to hear me say and do things I don't want to do. Just smile and go with it. Ashleigh, you're my guest, which means you'll be glued to my side. For Ryley's sake—stay there. I don't even want to know what happens to women if they venture off into a dark corner.

"Gabriella, as much as I hate you doing this, you'll be taken to sit with the other females who were gambled off. They're going to slap a bracelet on you when we walk in and when the time comes, you'll have to go. As soon as the fight's over, I'll come get you."

"Great," she mumbled sarcastically. "Nothing like being treated like a herd of cattle. I guess I just have to sit pretty until Ryley kicks Camden's ass."

"Let's hope so," Paxton remarked. "If not, then we're going to have some serious problems getting out of there."

The blindfold made me feel vulnerable, weak. I had to protect not just myself, but my babies as well. This was a nightmare. For the rest of the way, I blocked out every sound and movement, and focused on one thing . . . Ryley. He made me stronger, showed me what life was like outside of the box. Colin had always been my safe place, but Ryley was the area outside of that, an adventure. I wanted more adventures with him, and now I was afraid we wouldn't get them because something bad was going to happen.

"We're here," Paxton noted. "Just be quiet while I talk. That especially goes for you, Gabriella."

She snorted. "I know what's at stake, Paxton. I care about what happens to Ryley."

The car slowed and Paxton rolled down his window.

The smell of cigarette smoke wafted into the car and I almost gagged. Smells were a lot stronger now that I was pregnant.

"Show me the mark," the man barked.

I couldn't see what was going on, but Paxton must've done something right because the guy chuckled. "Well, I'll be damned, if it isn't the Reaper. We haven't seen you much around these parts recently."

"Not been in town much, man. I heard there's going to be a killer fight tonight. Thought I'd come check it out."

The man chortled. "Fuck, yeah. We got the Twins of Terror battling it out. And it looks like you came bearing gifts. The one in the back looks mighty tasty. Got a nice set of tits on her."

"You got that right," Paxton agreed. Biting my lip, I waited on Gabriella to start cussing, but she kept her mouth shut.

"You know the rules, Reaper. Surely, I don't need to repeat them, do I?"

"Nah, I'm good. They're not going to use their lips for much of anything, other than sucking my cock."

"I hear ya on that. If you get tired of 'em, let me know." The sound of a rusty gate creaked in the night air and soon we were on our way.

"Good luck with that, cocksucker," Paxton grumbled as he rolled up the window. "Keep your blindfolds on. We're not in the clear yet."

"I can't believe you're a part of this shit," Gabriella snapped. "And you wonder why I don't want to go out with you."

"I *was* a part of it. Let's get that straight right now. And as far as going out with me, you don't have a choice anymore. Shall I discuss the terms with you now?"

She scoffed. "Can we please talk about that later? I don't want to stress Ashleigh out any more than she already is."

"That's fine with me, sunshine. We can discuss it later tonight, alone."

"Joy," she mumbled.

I'd had enough. "You two are driving me *insane*. It's obvious you both want each other, so stop playing the mind games and do what feels right. The more you fight it, the harder it is. Trust me, I should know."

The car filled with an awkward silence, but I didn't care, it just proved I was right. I'd spent a month away from Ryley when all I wanted to do was hop on a plane and beg him to take me back. I wasn't the type of girl to beg, but when you're faced with the fact you could lose someone forever, you'd do just about anything. Gabby kept pushing Paxton away, and if she wasn't careful he'd give up and move on.

"Are we almost there?" Gabriella complained.

Paxton slowed the car until he came to a complete stop. "Now we are. You have to keep your blindfolds on until we get inside. Just sit in the car and I'll help each of you out. There are some expensive wheels on both sides and if I have to pay for damages, you're going to owe me a lot more than what I'm already charging you."

When he got out of the car, I tilted my head toward the stubborn girl in the back. "Stop being a bitch to him," I hissed low.

She sighed. "I can't help it, Ash. He drives me insane. I can't let him wear me down."

"Suit yourself. Be miserable. I can't force you to see

reason."

Paxton opened up my door and took my hand. There were voices all around and then whistles as I stepped out of the car. He put his arm around my shoulders and led me around to the other side to get Gabriella. Once she was out of the car, Paxton walked slowly since he was guiding two blind women into the unknown. The gravel crunched beneath my heels and it was a wonder I didn't trip and break an ankle.

"Once we're through this line you can take the blindfolds off," Paxton murmured. "Gabriella, they're going to put a bracelet on you. Don't fight it when they grab you. You're supposed to be willing."

"I'll be fine," she answered.

"And Ashleigh, do *not* run off from me." Instead of a reply, I nodded my head and kept walking. Judging by the voices up ahead, we were almost at the entrance. "Okay, here we go."

"Well, well, if it isn't the one and only Reaper. Congrats on the title fight. You haven't been here in a while. Wanna challenge someone?" The guy's voice was deep and gruff, and I could just imagine what he looked like, all bulging on steroids with a neck as thick as my thigh.

"Not tonight. I'm here to watch the twins battle it out. Maybe next time though since I have some time on my hands."

"I hear ya. We'd love to see you back in the ring. So what are you offering tonight?"

Paxton's body moved and I knew he was guiding Gabriella forward. "I'm bidding this little kitten," he said. "She may look innocent, but she's a pistol in the bed, if you know what I mean."

I heard a smack sound, like he'd slapped her on the ass. *Here we go.*

"Very nice," the guy added. "It's a shame I'm not fighting tonight."

And just when I thought I had heard it all, Gabriella's voice spoke out and Paxton tensed. "Oh, don't worry, big man. I'm sure I'll be back again sometime."

As soon as I heard him snap the bracelet around her wrist, we were off. Paxton pulled us fast inside the door and let us go. When I lifted my blindfold, I watched him take Gabriella's off, fuming at her. "I swear you're trying to fucking kill me, aren't you? Don't speak to anyone Gabriella. These are not the type of people I want you being around."

Her smile faded and she nodded, especially when she noticed me glaring at her. She had a mouth on her, and luckily, it'd never gotten her in trouble. We weren't exactly in a place where she could joke around.

"Noted. Where do we go from here?"

Paxton looked at us both and sighed. "We're going to go through another set of doors and down a flight of stairs into a basement of sorts. Since it's late, most of the other fights should be about over. There'll be a hallway we walk through that has windows into other rooms. Ryley will be in one and Camden will be in another. This is where you decide on who you want to bid on."

I gasped. "Will he be able to see us?"

We started down the hall and through the other set of doors. It was dark and dank, smelling of mildew. The stairs didn't look too inviting either with only a blinking light illuminating the path.

"No. We can see in, but he can't see out."

Taking the steps one at a time, I half expected a line of people to follow us, but we were the only ones. It was eerie. Eventually, we got to the hallway where it was nothing but separated rooms on each side with a glass panel to look in for each section. There was a man at the end of the hall with a bald head who beckoned us closer with a wave of his hand. He was a fighter as well, judging by the build and stature.

"They must be at the end of the hall," Paxton explained.

Sure enough, when we got there, I looked into the room on my left and saw Camden, lifting a set of weights with his muscles bulging. His body was bigger, more muscular. No doubt the product of steroids. Turning away, I couldn't stomach to look at him anymore. Even Gabriella couldn't stand it any longer. I wanted to say that it wasn't fair, but then again, the Dark Side had no rules.

Next, we ventured over to the other side of the hall and I was afraid of what I would see. Would Ryley be in there looking ravenous like his brother? What I didn't expect was to see him sitting there with his head down and leaning over on his elbows. I could only see his profile, but even then I could feel the rage radiating from him.

With my hand on the glass, a lone tear fell down my cheek and my heart broke. What if he didn't win? Camden obviously wanted to have the advantage in this fight. It made me wonder what else he had up his sleeve.

"So have you decided which one you want to go to?" the bald headed guy asked.

Gabriella jerked in surprise, her gaze torn away from Ryley. "Oh wow, let's see. I think I like that one," she said, pointing at Ryley's room. "He seems mysterious."

"Yeah, we've gotten that from a few of the women."

I bristled at the mention, but Paxton squeezed me around the waist before he spoke.

"Honestly, I think the dude's going to have his ass handed to him. Don't know what drove them to hate each other, but it had to be something drastic."

"Who are most people betting on? If you don't mind my asking," I inquired curiously.

Bald guy looked down at his notebook and pursed his lips. "Most people are rooting for Striker—he's grown to be a legend here."

"Well, ladies, I do believe it's time to go," Pax announced. He nodded toward the bald guy who opened the door behind him and let us pass. It was another dark hallway, but this time the noise was deafening. There were shouts and screams, along with the sound of fighting, like metal clanging against metal. I didn't like the sound of it at all.

Surely enough when we stepped into the doorway of the open room, my whole world came crashing down around me. There were dozens upon dozens of people surrounding the cage in the center of the room. It was a literal cage with barbwire circling around the top. If someone wanted to climb out, they couldn't. My attention was then brought to the fighters in the ring, wielding what looked to be swords. *Holy fuck!* I was speechless, frozen in place.

"Swords, Paxton? What the hell is this shit?" Gabriella protested. "Is Ryley going to have to do this?"

Paxton shrugged. "I don't know. Camden is the one responsible for this fight, so it'll be up to him. There's no telling what he'll come up with."

The guys in the ring were bloody, gashes marring

their skin. The room reeked of blood, making my stomach turn. Slapping my hand to my mouth, I turned away and swallowed over and over, hoping to keep everything down.

"Ashleigh," Gabriella murmured, putting her hands on the side of my face. "Breathe through your nose. You can do this." She watched the fight over my shoulder and we both winced when the guttural scream of one of the fighters echoed through the underground dungeon.

"What happened?" I asked, squeezing my eyes shut. The guy kept screaming until he was taken out of the room, and even then I could still hear his tormented cries.

Gabriella blew out a nervous breath. "The fight's over. Let's just say the guy's arm is hanging by a thread."

Oh, please God, don't let Camden choose swords. "What happens now?" I asked, glancing up at Paxton. Turning my attention to what he was looking at, I saw two men rush into the ring to clean up the puddles of blood. One had a squeegee and was just slushing it off the edges of the cage. It was a scene from a horror movie. Again, I had to turn away for fear of throwing up.

"Right now, we wait until they clean the mat. Then all of the women who were auctioned off have to go sit around the ring. I guess you can say they're the trophies to go along with the money. After that, it'll be time for the fighters."

"What if Ryley sees Gabriella?"

Paxton shook his head, his expression weary. "He's not going to notice, Ashleigh. When you're up in the ring, you can't afford to lose focus. That's when people get seriously hurt."

"Have *you* hurt people?" Gabriella asked, standing

before him.

Clenching his jaw, he looked away, the vein in his forehead bulging. "I have, but a lot of them deserved it. Maybe if you knew why I did what I did you wouldn't think so horrible of me."

Her expression narrowed. "What do you mean?"

I was interested in his answer too. Before Paxton could respond, the bald headed guy from the hallway approached us, heading straight for Gabriella. "All right, sugar tits, it's time. Take your seat with the others."

Huffing, she threw her arms around me. "Stay strong. I'll be fine." Letting me go, she didn't get far before Paxton grabbed her hand and pulled her to him, his lips only a breath away from hers.

"Remember, don't do or say anything when you're up there. As soon as the fight's over I'll come get you."

She nodded and slowly stepped back, her chest rising and falling with her breaths. Turning on her heel, she stalked off toward the ring and looked back once before disappearing into the crowd.

"Can you see her?" I asked.

"Yeah, she found a seat. I think it's best if we stay as far back as we can. We don't want him to see you. It would be disastrous."

Two men strolled by rolling carts toward the ring. I couldn't see what was on them, but judging by the look on Paxton's face, it wasn't good. "What's going on?" I demanded, grabbing his arm. "What's on those carts?"

His face paled and he closed his eyes before turning to me. "I think I know how they're going to fight tonight. It's not good, Ashleigh."

"Tell me."

Chapter 42

Ryley

FOR THE PAST couple of hours, I waited in the tiny cell with my head down. On the other side of the mirror, I knew there were people watching me, deciding on if I was worth bidding on. I didn't give a shit if they did. All I cared about was getting into the ring.

"All right, Jameson, you're up. Ready to go down in history?" Scar chuckled, opening the door wide.

Keeping my stare straight ahead, I stood up and rolled my neck. I had to block everyone and everything out, even if I wanted to bitch slap the smelly bastard in front of me. When I walked out of the room, there was a long hallway that opened up at the end. As soon as I turned the corner, the people exploded into cheers.

There were no announcements or music blaring over

the speakers, only me walking down to the cage with Scar by my side. It was a fenced enclosure with barbwire across the top and spatters of blood across the mat. Judging by the sounds of the fight before mine, I'd say it was pretty bloody.

"Ooh, what do we have here?" Scar pointed out, glancing up to the ring. "It looks like your brother finally figured out what kind of weapon he wanted tonight."

"Weapon? I wasn't aware he was going to be a pussy."

Scar burst out in laughter. "I'll have to tell him you said that. No one's ever been in the ring without one."

"Well, let it go down in history, because I don't need shit," I growled.

"Suit yourself, dumb ass, it's your funeral. The rules are your own."

Up in the ring, there were two gray carts, with two men behind them, dressed in black robes. I couldn't see their faces, nor could I see what was on the carts until I got into the ring. There were three sections with one side being a set of handwraps, the other a platter of what looked to be hot glue, and then the last . . . shards of glass. *You have got to be fucking kidding me.* There was no way in hell I was putting that shit on my gloves.

I was led over to one cart and told to stay put while we waited on my brother to enter. I wasn't a regular, so I didn't get the introduction that Camden did. The people around the ring shouted out his name. Apparently, he went by Striker now.

Eyes wide, I stared at the man who used to be my brother—now my number one enemy. He looked nothing like the man I once knew. Steroids had made him bulkier, but size was never an issue. The real handicap came from Camden and I knowing each other's weaknesses. What he didn't know was, I'd worked on mine until I'd fucking bled.

Climbing into the ring, Camden lifted his hands in the air triumphantly, as if he'd already won. "It's nice to see you again, brother dear," he chided. "Let's get this party started."

"Waiting on you, fuckface."

He wore his usual bright red and black shorts and red robe. When he lifted it off of his body, I couldn't believe the amount of scars on his chest and back. It was a shame I wasn't going to stoop to his level and add more. I wouldn't give him the satisfaction, even though it was tempting.

Camden walked over to his cart and held out his hands, letting the robed guy wrap them. The man behind my cart reached for my hands, but I backed away, snarling my lip. I didn't want anyone touching me. Camden tilted his head back in laughter when the hooded figure looked over at him.

"That's his choice, leave him be," Camden insisted. "It's just a shame I don't feel like playing fair."

"Like you ever did," I snapped, marching to the center of the ring. "You always felt the need to cheat to win against me. What makes this any different?"

Camden's leer faded and he turned away so he could finish getting his fists prepped. He knew I was right. The brother I used to know before my father died would've fought me fairly, but that boy was long gone. In his place was a man full of lies and deceit. How the hell did he get so fucked up?

When all was said and done, Camden dropped his

robe on the mat and one of the black robed men picked it up on their way out of the ring. The glass on his fists reflected the lights around the room, reminding me I was without a weapon. I only had my fists to protect me. In that singular moment, I hated him with every fiber of my being. He'd tried to fuck up my life and then challenged me to this fight. It should've been the other way around.

Scar joined us in the center of the ring, his eyes gleaming in delight. "It looks like this is going to be an interesting fight. Are you sure this is what you want?" he asked me, looking down at my gloved fists.

I wanted Camden to hurt, and feel the pain. *I* wanted to be the one to inflict the damage. "No," I growled. Lifting my hardened gaze to my brother, I undid my gloves and handwraps, letting them fall to the floor. "This is what I want."

Gasps erupted through the crowd as I dared my brother to challenge me fairly. We stared at each other, brother against brother, but the coldness in his demeanor still remained. I was completely unarmed, and he didn't waver . . . he kept his glass fists. *Fucking bastard.*

"This just got interesting," Scar announced. "Do you want timed rounds, or no interruptions?"

Camden and I said it together, "No interruptions." As soon as I started, there was no way I was going to stop.

Scar strolled out of the ring and shut the cage door, locking it with a chain as thick as my wrist. It made me wonder what happened if someone tried to break out before the fight was over. "You know the rules. No one leaves until the other is down."

The energy crackled like fire, but I only had my focus on one thing . . . revenge. I blocked everything out and kept my sights on my brother, ready to strike when we were told to attack. Nothing else existed, except me and him.

"Fight!"

Ashleigh

RYLEY ATTACKED FIRST and pummeled Camden, striking him hard on the side of the face. Camden laughed and spit blood onto the mat. However, Ryley didn't stop there, he kept going. His brother reciprocated by rearing back and kicking Ryley in the shin, before slicing his hand across his back, blood pouring out in rivers and catching at the waistband of Ryley's shorts.

Gasping, I tried to charge forward but Paxton tightened his grip on me and leaned down to growl in my ear. "If you don't stop trying to run away, you're going to have bruises all over your fucking arms."

Fighting against his hold, I gritted my teeth, watching Ryley's blood pour freely. "This has to stop. It's not fair," I shouted. None of my screams could be heard through the deafening noise of the people surrounding me.

"I know it's not fair. None of this is. But he agreed to this, Ashleigh. Now, let him do it."

I didn't want to let him do it. I wanted him safe and away from this place. The world moved in slow motion as I watched Camden and Ryley battle it out, blood blinding my vision. All I could see was red as Camden sliced Ryley's skin over and over with the glass. Ryley never flinched, just kept striking and kicking like nothing was amiss, like he wasn't bleeding out all over the mat.

My breaths were all I could hear. I almost felt as if I was in a different world. Hell would be the best word to describe it. I was in the dungeons of hell, having to spend the rest of eternity watching the only man I loved bleed to death inside a cage. As much as Ryley was ready for the fight, he still needed me. Every fighter needed something to fight for. He always told me he fought better with me by his side. How could he do that if he didn't know I was there?

Lifting up on my tiptoes, I found Gabriella with her hand over her mouth, her stare full of torment. It wasn't until I looked back up into the ring that everything spun out of control. Both guys were on the mat, grappling. My current location hindered a clear view.

"Paxton," I ordered, "let me go. I need to be up there. He needs to see me."

"No. It'll only make him lose focus."

Facing him head on, I stared up into his sea green eyes and nodded toward Gabriella. "Is that how you would feel if it was Gabby who wanted you to see her? What if you were fighting for her? Imagine how alone Ryley must feel being in a place that is clearly not on his side. We make each other stronger, Pax. Neither one of us is good without the other."

Focusing on the ring, he huffed and took my hand. "Fuck, I'm going to regret this. Let's go." He charged toward the ring and pushed us through the crowd. The closer we got, the more scared I became.

Gabriella spotted us and got to her feet, tears streaming down her cheeks and eyes wide. It was then I noticed Ryley on the mat with Camden on top of him . . . a shard of glass at his throat.

Ryley

AFTER THE FIRST slash to my back, I grew immune to the rest of the gashes littering my skin. Everywhere I looked, blood poured down my skin, soaking my shorts and getting into my eyes. I didn't regret fighting defenseless, but I did regret losing my focus. My anger clouded my judgment and I made a wrong turn, over anticipating Camden's next move.

His fist was at my throat, but I could feel the glass jabbing into my skin. I held him at bay, my muscles shaking, and I didn't know how much longer I could hold off. If the glass cut into my neck, I'd bleed out and fucking die. Is that what my brother wanted? To not have to compete with me anymore?

"Why don't you tap out, o' brother mine? And show

these people how much of a pussy you are. Now everyone will know who *I* am. Your time is over. It's a shame Ashleigh isn't here to see you fail."

Grunting, I pushed his fist back, giving me another centimeter of reprieve. "Don't you say her fucking name, asshole. Not after what you did to her . . . to me."

"To you? You should be thanking me. I could've fucked her and she wouldn't have known the difference. She's a goddamn money-grubbing whore who's knocked up with another man's bastard child."

Staring up into Camden's eyes, it was strange to think I was looking at my reflection. Well, my reflection if I was all jealousy and anger. God, I hated him; hated who he'd become. Ashleigh was my family now, not him. I would choose her over him any day, even if that meant putting him out of his jealous misery. I couldn't watch over him anymore, or change him like I thought I could after our father died. He was gone and he wasn't coming back.

"Tap out, brother," Camden grunted. "I'm close to that carotid artery of yours. Only one slip and you're done."

Would he actually go through with it? I didn't know, but I wasn't about to find out. The sound of Ashleigh's voice in my mind brought back my strength, it was almost like she was there, driving me on. If I didn't win this match, my revenge would forever consume me, eating me alive from the inside out. I had no choice but to fight until I had nothing left.

Gritting my teeth, I pushed as hard as I could, Camden's arm giving way inch by inch. His smile disappeared and with one swift move, I jabbed his hand as hard as I could to his cheek, slicing his skin open. Quickly, he jumped off of me and slammed his hand over his face, blood oozing out between his fingers.

Instead of waiting on him to recover, I powerhouse kicked him in the side and watched his legs buckle beneath him. All of the hatred swarmed through my body, giving me the ammunition I needed. As soon as his knees hit the mat, I wrapped my legs around his and my arm around his neck. His blood poured down my arm, but I didn't care. If I had my way, I'd see more of it.

"You're wrong, about everything," I growled low in his ear. "I know what you had planned with Colin." I held him harder, jerking my arm up so that it would choke him. He tried to speak, but he couldn't. "After I had to rush Ashleigh to the hospital, he came clean. I almost lost my fucking kids because of you." His fight started to fade and his skin began to turn blue, but I wasn't done. "We're having twins, you arrogant piece of shit. You were going to rob me of my own fucking family. For that, I want to put you out of your misery. You have no one now. No family . . . nothing. You're dead to me."

"*Ryley.*" Her voice echoed in my head, snapping me back to reality. I heard it again and again until finally her face came into view, almost like an angel, as she stood there staring at me with tears in her eyes.

She was frantic, yelling something I couldn't understand. It wasn't until Camden's body fell limp in my arms that I realized what she had been yelling.

Let him go.

Ashleigh

RYLEY WAS IN another world. Even when he looked at me, he wasn't seeing me. I wasn't going to give up though. He couldn't do this. I stood there screaming, demanding he let his brother go. Paxton even had to punch a man when he tried to put his hands over my mouth and drag me away. They wanted to see death, to see Ryley end his brother. It was chaos and if I didn't stop it, Ryley would regret it for the rest of his life.

As soon as Ryley let his brother go, Camden collapsed onto the mat. Knowing the shit was about to hit the fan, Paxton grabbed my hand and pushed us through the crowd until we got to Gabriella.

"We have to go right now," he commanded. Eyes wide, Gabriella took his other hand and jumped over the seats, but not without the notice of Scar, who was now barreling through the crowd on a directed path. Luckily, we made it to the entrance of the ring where Ryley stood bloody and full of rage. He glared down at us, fuming.

"Paxton!" he thundered. "Me and you are going to have a big, fucking problem when I get out of this godforsaken cage."

Pax glanced over at Scar who was almost there. "I don't think that should be our main worry right now. We have incoming."

Scar grabbed a hold of Gabriella and turned her around. "And where do you think you're going?" he asked. When he got a good look at her and at us, he finally put two and two together and realized who we were. However, he didn't take his hands off of her. Paxton tensed, but I pinched his arm and kept my focus on Gabriella. I was afraid to look at Ryley.

"Ryley won, so we're leaving," she challenged. "I belong to the winner."

When she tried to pull away, Scar held her tighter. "You're not going anywhere, princess. The fight's not over."

"Like hell it's not," Ryley shouted. He beat against the cage, but the door was locked shut. Unless he could break through the chains, he wasn't going anywhere. Behind him, Camden slowly started to get to his feet.

Scar grinned wide and nodded toward Camden. "See for yourself. The fight doesn't end until you both agree, and I was given strict orders that your brother refused to tap, no matter the circumstances. So either you finish him off or look like the coward you are and tap out. It's your choice. However," he taunted, putting his arm around Gabriella. "This sweet ass will belong to your brother. Surely, you wouldn't want that, now would you?"

Behind Ryley, Camden swiped his forearm over his cheek to wipe away the blood, but more flowed down. When he spotted Gabriella, he licked his lips and grabbed his groin. "Tap out, fucker," he sputtered, his voice gravelly. "I'd love to see how much of a fight she gives me."

And right then, everything had changed. Ryley's eyes no longer looked like the crystal blue I loved so much, they were dark and cold. He had hit the breaking point and it terrified me. Snarling, he charged his twin and brought his left arm up as if to strike. It all happened so fast, I didn't know what I was seeing. Camden tried to block on his left, but then Ryley sprung into the air and came down on him with a hard punch to the right. It was something you'd see in a kung fu movie. I had never seen Ryley do that before, and neither had Camden by the surprised look on his face before it struck him. He went down . . . out cold.

Ryley stood over him, his rapid breaths making his chest rise and fall. Camden was done and he wasn't getting up anytime soon. Storming back to the gate, Ryley beat against it and shouted, "It's over. He's done."

"And so it is," Scar remarked dryly, letting Gabriella go. After walking up the steps, he put the key in the lock and opened the door wide.

Ryley thundered out and came straight for me, his dark eyes unreadable. "We're getting out of here," he growled, taking my hand.

Paxton put his arm around Gabriella and before we could start toward the exit, Scar stepped in front of us, blocking our path. Even though Ryley was covered in blood, he put his arm protectively around my waist. Scar noticed the gesture and leered at both Ryley and Paxton. "Remember, stay quiet about all of this and all will be well. I'd hate to see something bad happen to one of your women."

Ryley stepped forward and met Scar head on. "If you so much as breathe on them, I will kill you with *no* hesitation."

"Then keep your mouths shut and there won't be a problem." Scar smirked and moved out of the way. Paxton didn't waste any time getting us out of there as he charged through the crowd.

As soon as we got in the car, I knew all hell would break loose. Gabriella jumped in the front seat, while I sat in the back with Ryley. His body looked horrible, covered in blood and torn open in places. I was afraid to touch him for fear I'd cause him more pain.

"Paxton, we need to go to the hospital. Ryley's going to need stitches," I demanded. There were wounds torn open to the point I could see the muscle underneath.

Ryley scoffed. "I don't need to go to the hospital. Just take me back to the hotel."

"Are you serious right now? Look at yourself!" I shouted. Snapping his attention to me, his nostrils flared and his jaw tightened. "You can be pissed the fuck off if you want, but you're going to the hospital, and that's *final*."

"Do you want to know why I'm pissed?"

I already knew why, but I had to let him get it off his chest. He was going to blow up at some point, it might as well be now.

"I'm pissed because you put not only your life in

harm's way, but our babies' lives as well. How could you be so stupid?"

"Uh-oh," Gabriella mumbled.

"Stupid?" I asked, eyes wide. "If I didn't show up, you probably would've made the biggest mistake of your life. You were two seconds away from snapping your brother's neck. Our children are very important to me, but where would they be without their father, huh? They need you just as much as they need me. You can't be there for them if you're in jail. So right now, you're going to the hospital and then we're going back to the hotel. The next time you think what I did was stupid, I want you to remember that."

Taking a deep breath, I turned away from him to look out the window. The rest of the ride was nothing but silence, even from Gabriella—which was utterly shocking. I'd said what I needed to say and hopefully it got to him. If what I did was stupid, I would do it again in a heartbeat.

CHAPTER 46

Ashleigh

WHILE GABRIELLA AND I waited in the waiting room, Paxton left to run to the hotel to fetch a change of clothes. Ryley didn't have anything on except his fighting shorts, which were drenched in blood. We couldn't have him going into the hotel like that.

"You made a solid point in the car," Gabriella murmured. "I think you got to him when you said it."

"He's still pissed at me though, and I see his point. But I'm still angry at him for leaving. It was reckless and irresponsible."

"We all were irresponsible. The night could've turned out differently, but we're all okay and so is Ryley. All we can do now is be thankful." I was going to be praying and thanking God for the rest of my life. I didn't want to imagine what really could've happened.

About that time, Paxton strolled in with a set of clothes in his arms. "These should work," he said, passing them to me. "Have you heard anything yet?"

I took the clothes and put them in my lap. "No, but I'm pretty sure it's just going to be stitches. Why don't you two go back to the hotel? I can wait here on my own."

"Don't be ridiculous," Gabriella scolded. "I'm not going to leave you here to the wrath of Ryley all by yourself." She sat back in the seat and folded her arms across her chest. *Always the stubborn one.*

"Seriously, guys," I said, glancing at them both. "It might be best if you leave. I can handle Ryley. Besides, don't you two have some terms to discuss?"

They both looked at each other, but Paxton was the one who spoke, "Actually, tonight's not the night for that. We can discuss it later. It's been a long night." Getting to his feet, Gabriella reluctantly followed, but not before checking with me one last time.

"Are you sure this is what you want?"

"Yes, now go. I'll call you in the morning."

Side by side, they walked out of the waiting room and disappeared around the corner. For the first time, I could breathe easily. Ryley won the fight and it was all over. The only thing I had to tackle now, was Ryley himself.

Leaning my head against the wall, I closed my eyes and started drifting off, only to be right back in the Dark Side, staring at blood. Lots and lots of blood. I thought Camden was a nightmare I couldn't escape from, but the Dark Side was much worse. The way it smelled of death and decay would always and forever be ingrained in my mind. It was seriously a place you'd see in scary movies or in your worst nightmares.

Thankfully, I wasn't in the depths of despair long, as a hand caressed my cheek and I was brought back to the present. Jerking awake, I opened my eyes to find Ryley kneeling in front of me, his sunken eyes boring into mine. *He'd lost so much blood.*

"Angel, are you okay?"

"Yes," I answered quickly, handing him the clothes. "It was just a bad dream. Regrettably, I have a feeling there's going to be a bunch of them in my future."

"Where did Gabby and Pax go?" Taking my hand, he helped me to my feet and then slid the T-shirt over his head. His skin was covered in dried up blood and bandages, but at least there weren't exposed wounds anymore. I didn't realize how many cuts he actually had.

"I told them to leave," I said. "I thought it would be best. I should probably call a cab, huh?"

Once the cab was called, we walked outside and waited. We were finally alone. Lowering his bloody shorts to the ground, Ryley quickly put on the pair of khaki shorts Paxton left for him and threw his fighting shorts in the trash.

"Do you want to talk about it?" I asked.

Sighing, he gently took my hand and held it in his lap, clasping his fingers with mine. "Not really. It's over and there's nothing we can do about it now. The only thing that worries me is the way you looked at me when I was in the ring. You were scared of me, weren't you?"

I didn't want to admit it, but I knew I couldn't lie. I'd been terrified. I had never seen him so full of hate and violence. "Yes," I whispered honestly. "It was like you weren't even there."

"I wasn't," he answered sadly. "Deep down, all I could feel was a bottomless pit of anger. I don't want to imagine what I would've done if I didn't stop. If you weren't there . . . things could've ended up differently."

Lifting my other hand, I gently stroked his hair. "It's a good thing we don't have to worry about that. Everything is going to be fine now."

"So we're good? You forgive me?" he asked. The cab finally pulled up and he helped me to my feet.

"Yes, we're fine, I promise. We're going to make mistakes and do stupid shit, but now we have more than just ourselves to think about. Things are about to change and we need to be ready."

Nodding, he put his hand on my stomach and closed his eyes. "You're right. When we get home, a lot is going to change. I just hope you're ready for it."

Lifting up on my tiptoes, I gently kissed his lips. "I'm ready for anything, as long as I have you."

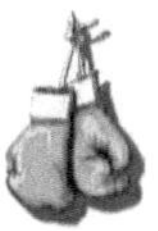

Three Days Later

As soon as we got back home, Ryley couldn't rest until we were out of Los Angeles. I guess there were too many bad memories there. For the past three days, with the help of family and friends, our belongings were packed up and already at our cabin in the Sierra Nevada Mountains.

Today was the last day we would be in the city for a very long time.

Ryley was ready for a new beginning and so was I. His cuts were healing nicely, but every time he would do something strenuous they'd ooze. Needless to say, I was dying to make love to him again, but I wanted him to heal more. Besides, we'd been too busy moving into our new home.

"I can't believe you guys are leaving already," Gabriella cried, flinging her arms around me. "I'm going to miss you."

I held her tight and squeezed my eyes shut. "I'm going to miss you too. But hey, we'll see each other soon. You're coming up for Thanksgiving, right? It's only a couple of months away. Maybe Paxton could come with you?"

She laughed. "Yeah, right. We'd kill each other."

"Have you two talked since this weekend? I'm curious to know what his terms are. You guys were acting kind of strange when you were helping us move our things." Paxton's repentance was basically to help us move. He felt like he owed it to Ryley for breaking the guy code. It basically all boiled down to that it was mine and Gabriella's fault, which it was.

"No, we haven't talked about it yet. He decided to wait until next weekend. He knew I was upset about you leaving." Her phone buzzed with an incoming text so she pulled it out and looked at it, frowning. "Where's Ryley at?" she asked.

"He said he wanted to make his rounds and say goodbye. Why? What's going on?"

Sheepishly, she walked backward to the door, biting

her lip. "Because there's someone who wants to see you before you go. I thought it best he do that with Ryley not around. I think we all need closure in our lives and you need it with him.

"Face it, Ash, you two have history. Yes, he made a mistake, but he loves you, and remember . . . he came clean in the end. He's leaving California and I know after today you guys probably won't ever see each other again. You'll regret not doing this if you don't." By the time she opened the front door, he was walking up the front steps. "I'll just be outside."

Colin joined me at the door, but didn't make a move to come inside until I stepped out of the way. He had his usual green baseball cap hanging low over his eyes, wearing a USC T-shirt and jeans. From the looks of his skin, he had already healed from his fight at the Dark Side.

"I know you probably don't want to talk to me, but I wanted to see you. Gabby told me about Vegas and what went down."

"Yeah."

Taking off his hat, he ran his hands through his blond, spiky hair and looked up at me, his expression full of trepidation. "I heard you're having twins too. Congratulations."

"Do you even mean that?" I asked skeptically.

"A lot's happened in the past week, Ash. I feel horrible for what I did and knowing you'll never forgive me is the worst of all. I'm sorry for everything, and I wanted to make sure you knew that before I left town."

"Where are you going?"

"I'm going to New York to play ball. My flight leaves this afternoon. I just wanted to tell you I was sorry before heading out."

Tears stung the back of my eyes and I looked away, pursing my lips. Colin was one of the loves of my life and his deceit went deep. It hurt more than anything I could've ever imagined. Approaching cautiously, he wrapped his arms around my body. I didn't even move, but let him hold me while the tears fell down my cheeks.

"I love you, Ash. I think I'll always love you. I just want you to be happy," he murmured gently.

Lifting my arms, I circled them around his waist and held him in return. "I *am* happy. One of these days, you will be too. You just have to let it happen naturally. Don't force it."

He pressed his lips to my forehead and smoothed his hand down my back. "I'll try. You're not an easy girl to get over, but I'll keep that in mind. Take care of yourself, Ash. Maybe one of these days I'll be in the World Series." He stepped back and let me go, heading toward the door.

"Take care of yourself too. I have no doubt you'll make it."

"Thanks," he said, placing his hand on the door handle. "Goodbye, Ash." Opening the door, he stepped out and started down the stairs.

"Goodbye, Colin."

I joined Gabriella on the front steps and watched him get in his car and drive away. He looked back once and I waved, my throat closing up the further he drove off. Colin had been a huge part of my college life and now that time was over. It pained me, but I had to move on.

"Now aren't you glad you said goodbye? It's one less regret you'll have."

I nodded and put my arm around her. "You're right,

I'm glad I got to see him one last time. Thank you."

"Do you think Ryley's going to try and find Camden?" she asked.

Clutching my stomach, I took a deep breath and let it out slow. "I don't know, Gabby. As much as I hate the idea of him seeking Camden out, I can't help but wonder if he feels obligated. Ryley had always been the one to look after his brother, almost like he took the place of their father when he died. I just hope he knows what he's doing."

How many regrets would Ryley have if he didn't face his brother again? Would he regret what he did? Or simply just hate Camden forever? I didn't share a sibling bond with anyone, least of all a twin. Whatever Ryley decided to do, I would support him.

Ryley

I HAD SAID my farewells to everyone I knew in California . . . except my brother. There was no telling where he was, or what he was doing. Hell, I didn't even know if he was okay. After I left him knocked out in the ring, I hadn't given much thought to him until now. Even with my body riddled in cuts, I didn't want to give him the satisfaction of ever thinking about him again. What changed my mind was my mother when I went to visit my father at his grave. She had reminded me of something my dad would have said. I needed to face my anger. That I should face my brother and tell him how I felt.

It was a long shot, but I pulled into Camden's driveway in Malibu. His car wasn't there, but it could easily be in the garage. I had a key to get in, but when I got to the door it was already unlocked. A giant cloud engulfed me, bringing with it the stench of alcohol and weed. *What the fuck?*

After shutting the door, I followed the cloud to the living room where Camden sat with his back to me, a fifth of whiskey in his hand. It was halfway gone.

"I thought I was dead to you," he slurred.

When he turned around and I got a good look at his face, I hung my head and sighed. The place on his cheek where I cut him with his own glass fist was jagged and red. It was going to leave a nasty scar.

"I mean, that *is* what you said to me the other night, right? That I'm dead to you." Lifting the bottle of whiskey to his lips, he took a long, hard pull.

"You're right, I did say that. I was angry and I still am. However, you're my brother and I can't let things end this way. So what do you say about a truce?"

Camden bellowed and took another sip. "Are you serious? You almost killed me in the ring, asshole."

"I wonder why," I snapped. "Do you have any idea what you've done to me? And judging by the way you held that shard to my neck, I have no doubt you would've followed through. *I'm* the one who should be pissed at you, not the other way around. I swear, I didn't realize your hatred for me ran so deep."

Camden swayed on his feet and he slammed the bottle of whiskey down hard on the glass table. "It's always because of you, isn't it? So what now, brother? You gonna get married and ride off into the sunset with your girl? Have the white picket fence? Let me tell you, it sounds fucking boring."

In that moment, I actually felt sorry for him. I never

thought I'd settle down with a girl and have a family. My life on the road was what I looked forward to, the chance to see different cities and fuck whoever I wanted. That was the life for me . . . until it just wasn't anymore. If he didn't straighten up, he would never find true happiness. But if I were being honest, at the current moment in time, I didn't give a shit if he found it at all. He was too stupid and fucked up to realize he was pissing his life away on hate and jealousy.

"It may be boring to you, but it's what I want. I'm leaving Los Angeles for good. I came by to tell you that I'm sorry if I've done anything to spur your hatred of me. Believe me, it was unintentional."

Chuckling, he lit up a blunt and sucked in a lung pull, holding it inside until he coughed it out. "So do you want an apology from me? Because you sure as fuck aren't going to get one."

I had a feeling he'd say as much, but I had to try for my family's sake. Backing away, I opened his door wide and let it slam into the wall. "Then I guess you *are* dead to me. I thought you'd come to your senses, but it's obvious you're too goddamned stupid to realize you're fucking up your life."

"Then maybe you should've killed me and put me out of my misery."

"Maybe I should have. That way, I wouldn't have to worry about you fucking up our lives ever again. The only problem is, after all of the shit you've put me through, I still love you." I took a step forward, my voice dripping with venom. "But if you so much as try to fuck with me or Ashleigh again, I will make sure to put you out of your misery. I can promise you that."

With those final words, I stormed back to my car and sped out of his driveway. It was hopeless . . . he was hopeless. He'd fallen so far, I doubted he would ever come back. I know I meant it figuratively, but my brother really was dead. There was no trace of him left in that body of his.

Ashleigh

One Week Later

A WEEK HAD passed and it was pure bliss spending it with Ryley and his family. He hadn't left my side for a moment, yet I knew once his coach moved up here, my time was going to be all over. Training would begin again and my champion would have to make sure he was fit to defend the Middleweight title next season. But for now, he was all mine.

The sun shone down on us as we laid on the blanket in the middle of the meadow by his house. Trees surrounded us with their plush green leaves, and every so often I'd find a twinge of yellow and red amongst them. The smell of autumn lingered on the cool, brisk air and I welcomed it. Fall was my favorite season.

For the past week, I'd let Ryley heal from his fight, not only physically, but emotionally as well. He'd confided in me about visiting his brother before we left Los Angeles, but didn't want to talk about it. His wounds went deeper than just skin, and would take much longer to heal.

Luckily for me, there was no one around for miles, especially since I had plans to seduce him. Hence, the reason I put on a pair of skimpy shorts and a plaid button down, left open with a sports bra underneath. The sports bra wasn't exactly sexy, but it was the only thing helping my sore breasts. Who would've thought pregnancy hormones would make your tits hurt like a bitch?

Running his fingers up and down my bare stomach, Ryley groaned in my ear and bit my lobe. "You look so fucking hot right now. I like the open shirt you got going on." He rested his hand over my belly. "When will I get to feel them move?"

Placing my hand on his, I smiled. "Usually around eighteen weeks. Also around that time, we'll be able to find out what we're having. I say, boys. What do you think?"

A smirk splayed across his face. "I'm going to disagree and say girls. We don't have many in my family. Besides, I don't want them having the rivalry like my brother and I do."

Sliding his hand away, I rolled over and straddled his waist, pinning his hands above his head. His arousal could be felt growing beneath his shorts. I squeezed him with my thighs and he pressed his bulge into my center. It had been too long since we'd made love. His raw gaze bore into mine, untamed. It wasn't just me who had suffered during the week. In a lightning fast move, he escaped from my hold and flipped me over, spreading my legs open wide.

"Is there something you want from me, angel?" he asked, sliding his tongue along my bottom lip.

Lifting his shirt, I pulled it over his head and threw it to the side. "You have no idea how bad I need you right now."

"Well, let's just see if your claim is true," he murmured, unbuttoning my shorts. Once his finger slipped easily inside of me, he groaned and pulled it out, sucking it clean. "I do believe your right. Why don't you take a look at how bad I want you?"

Sitting up on his knees, he lowered his shorts and his cock sprung free. I wrapped my hand around his length and glided up and down, earning a strangled moan from his lips. The tip of his cock glistened with his desire so I did the same thing he did to me and swiped it with my finger and sucked it off. He tasted salty, but I loved it . . . I loved everything about him.

Growling low in his chest, he pulled my shorts all the way off and lifted me up so he could work on the rest of my clothes. It was all so fast, until I winced as he tried to take of my bra. Gingerly, we worked as a team to rid me of the offending garment. He kissed me sweetly on the top of each breast, and spoke to them. "I'm sorry my little fun bags. I will remember to take better care of you."

Once his clothes were off, he covered me with his body and pushed inside, deep. "Fuck, I've missed this. I've missed being inside you, angel."

I moaned and fisted my hands in his hair when he pushed in harder. "I know the feeling."

Taking my hands out of his hair, he held them over my head. My breasts grew heavy and my nipples peaked in anticipation. He licked lightly over one, and I lost it in a matter of seconds.

"I guess I've deprived you," he muttered regretfully.

I moved my hips with his thrusts. "You're here now."

In lieu of playing with my overly sensitive nipples, he licked and sucked his way up my neck. I missed his lips, and would take them anyway I could get them. When he got close to release, his eyes locked on mine, never once wavering. With each push, he grunted with the force, penetrating me not only with his body, but with his mind too. His demeanor held me captive, even my heart fell victim to him.

My climax built with each thrust and eventually I tightened all around his body, screaming my release as he pounded into me, his cock pulsating with his own. I never knew love could be so wild and raw. With Ryley, I never knew what I was going to get. It was always a mystery. I had a strange feeling he liked keeping me in the dark. I think that's what kept the devilish twinkle gleaming in his eye.

Finally, he let my hands go and they almost felt numb with how hard he held onto them. When I brought them down to my stomach, the sun reflected off of something on my hand and time stood still. All I could focus on was the huge smile spreading across Ryley's face and the sparkling diamond ring on my finger. Instead of a clear stone surrounded by twinkling diamonds . . . it was blue. I could barely see it through the tears building.

"Oh my God, how did you –?"

Gently, he pulled out and rested beside me, placing his hand on my belly. "You were a little preoccupied," he teased with a wink.

"So what are you saying? What does this mean?" My heart flip-flopped in my chest and I could barely contain my smile. *Could this really be happening?* Knowing my luck, I was in a dream and I'd wake up any minute.

Brushing the hair away from my face, he pressed his forehead to mine and kissed me. So soft, yet so deep. "I'm saying I want you to be my wife, angel," he murmured against my lips. "I want to spend every day of my life knowing that you're mine. There's nothing else in this world that I want more than to have you with me always."

"Ryley," I breathed, gazing down at the ring. "I don't know what to say. Are you sure this is what you want?" There was no way in hell I was awake. I had to be asleep. Marrying Ryley and starting our family was a dream come true.

"Ashleigh, I've never been so sure of something in my life." He kissed me again and leaned back, searching my expression. "Please tell me it's what you want too."

Closing my eyes, I squeezed them shut and shook my head. "I'm dreaming, aren't I? As soon as I open my eyes you're going to be gone. Pinch me so that I know this is real." When he didn't pinch me, I opened my eyes just a tad and there he was, smirking at me.

"I can promise you, I'm still here and I'm not going anywhere, nor am I going to pinch you. If you want me to prove I'm real, I'd be happy to make love to you again—just give me ten minutes. Okay, fifteen."

I giggled and then I'm pretty sure I squealed like a piglet. I was just so happy.

"But the only way I'm going to do that, is if you give me an answer."

Tugging his arms, he complied willingly and covered

me with his body, settling between my legs. "Then you better get used to this body, Ryley Jameson, because it's the only one you're going to be seeing for the rest of your life, even when I'm old and saggy."

"And when that time comes, you'll still be sexy as hell. Especially when compared to my own hairy, wrinkly body." He playfully nipped my nose. "You still haven't said the one word I want to hear. I need to hear it." Lowering his lips to my neck, he trailed his kisses down my chest and flicked his tongue across my nipple.

Moaning, I held his face in my hands and brought his gorgeous blue eyes up to mine. "Yes, Ryley. My answer is yes. You have my heart and for that, I'm yours . . . always and forever. Now make love to your fiancé."

He smirked down at me. "With pleasure."

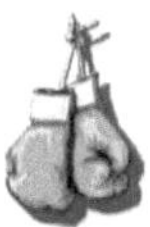

The afternoon had given way to a chilly night, but I was prepared, and snuggled in a blanket on our back deck. I hadn't really noticed the chill in the air when Ryley and I made love under the sun, but then again, I didn't notice much when he occupied my attention. We were actually going to get married. Even looking at the proof on my finger, it was still hard to believe.

"So what did Gabriella say when you told her?" Ryley asked, setting down my hot chocolate.

"Oh, thank you. You totally read my mind."

"I'm learning," he replied, smiling. Sitting down, he

put his arm around me. "Was she excited for us?"

I burst out laughing. "Excited couldn't begin to describe how she reacted." In fact, my ear drum still hurt from her screaming. "She'd already started talking about the baby shower and now the bridal one. She threatened that if she wasn't my maid of honor, she was going to kick my ass. Needless to say, I let her have the title."

I didn't want anyone else taking it anyway. Unfortunately, she still wouldn't tell me what her and Paxton's terms were. Why was she keeping it a secret?

"That's great. I still haven't decided who I want my best man to be. Hell, I never thought I'd get married. And even if I did, it was a given who I'd have. But now . . ."

"I'm sure your grandfather would love to take the role," I offered gently.

Ryley sighed and held me closer. "Yes, he would. Every time I see him, he talks about how pretty you are and how lucky I am."

"He's right, you are lucky," I laughed, elbowing him in the side. "However, Gabby brought up a good point today. We've talked about anything and everything, except the main thing . . . the wedding date."

"I wanted to leave that up to you. I know we haven't been together long and there's still so many things about each other we don't know. If you want to wait another couple of years, that's fine too. We can have a huge wedding or a small one. I'll give you anything you want."

Ever since I was a little girl I knew exactly what I wanted as far as a wedding. It just so happened that I was living in the right place for that dream. "Ryley, have you ever seen the Robin Hood movie? You know, the one with Kevin Costner?"

He glanced down at me, furrowing his brow. "Yeah, a long time ago. I actually have the DVD inside. What does that have to do with our wedding?"

"Well, at the end Robin and Marion get married, right?"

"Yeah?" he said slowly.

"Well, their wedding is how I want mine." I pointed to the meadow, the same place where he proposed and made love to me. "Our meadow is the perfect place. The way the autumn leaves will blow in the air in the fall, blanketing the grass. We wouldn't even need to decorate because the fall colors would make it perfect."

I could see it all play out before me. Me, dressed in a flowing white gown and a vine headdress, just like Marion's. Our families would be surrounding us, smiling as we said our vows. It was perfect.

"So I take it you want to get married soon?" he asked. "It's almost fall, angel."

As much as I wanted to do it now, I knew it wasn't a good idea to jump into it. "I think we should wait until next fall," I answered. "We have so much to learn about each other, and a lot of upcoming responsibilities. I'm afraid of rushing into it. Besides, with these pregnancy hormones, I'd probably be a bridezilla. I don't want to do that to you."

He chuckled. "Me either. If you want it next fall, it's settled. Hopefully, your dad won't hate me when he finds out we're living in sin."

Rolling my eyes, I smacked him in the arm. "Oh, whatever, he's not going to hate you. Speaking of which, I need to call my parents and tell them. I wish I could see their faces when I say that not only am I getting married, but I'm pregnant with twins."

Picking up my phone, I started to dial, but Ryley swiped it out of my hands.

"What are you doing?" I asked incredulously.

Grinning from ear to ear, he stood up and pulled me with him. "I have a better idea. Let's fly out to Aspen and tell them together. It'll be a good time for me to meet them. Plus, you wouldn't have to handle them on your own."

"You would do that? Even if there's the slightest possibility my dad might pull his gun out on you?" He wouldn't do that, but I could see him getting pretty pissed off that his little girl got knocked up and wasn't married.

"I would do anything for you, angel. And facing the wrath of your father is one of them."

Lifting up on my tiptoes, I wrapped my arms around his neck, breathing him in. "I think you're grandfather has it all wrong. I think *I'm* the lucky one."

Ryley bent down and pressed his lips ever so gently to mine. "We're lucky to have each other. I love you, angel."

"And I love you too."

Always.

Ashleigh

Eight Weeks Later

THE VISIT WITH my family went better than expected. Ryley and my father got along great, and my parents were excited about being grandparents. I had to say, things were finally looking up for us. Ryley hadn't spoken to his brother, nor had anyone seen him in a while. Even their mother hadn't heard from him. I guess it was safe to say he was gone indefinitely.

"Miss Warren?" the nurse called.

Her name was Julie and she had seen me the last time I'd been in to hear the babies' heartbeats. She had the most beautiful long, red hair I'd ever seen, with freckles all over her peachy skin. The pink scrubs made her look like a strawberry puff. *Speaking of which, I want some strawber-*

ry puffs.

I smiled up at Ryley and placed my hand over his, as it rested on my belly. Ever since he felt the babies kick for the first time, he'd barely kept his hands off of me. "Are you ready for this?"

The whole time we were in the waiting room, his leg bounced up and down making the chair squeak. Some of the other pregnant ladies in the room thought it was funny. We were both nervous, but I think he was more nervous than me. He nodded and smiled nervously. "I think so. Let's go."

When we approached the nurse, she held the door open and grinned. "I bet you're excited, aren't you?"

I nodded. "More than excited. It's not every day you get to see your children for the first time."

She pointed to the scale and I hopped on, cringing when Ryley stood there looking at it. I don't know if there would ever be a time when I'd feel comfortable with him knowing my weight. There were just some things I wanted to keep secret. I guess it was a girl thing.

After she took my blood pressure and I peed in a cup, we were put in an examination room. While we waited, I peered over at Ryley who sat there texting on his phone. "Who are you talking to?"

With his head down, he smiled at his phone. "Apparently, there's a pool that's up to ten thousand dollars if you guess the sex of our babies right. The tabloids are waiting for the answer. I never thought our twins would become the hot topic of discussion."

"Really? Your people love you, Ryley. This actually doesn't surprise me at all. There are a lot of women out there who want you to be their baby's daddy."

He even got an email from a woman who asked if he would donate sperm to her so she could be artificially inseminated. There were seriously some crazy ass people out there. I didn't realize how much until I started spending every day with him.

As soon as the doctor knocked on the door, Ryley quickly put his phone away and came to my side.

"Good afternoon, you two," she greeted, holding my chart. Her name was Dr. Christine Wyatt, around fifty years old, and a good friend of Ryley's mother. "Is everything going okay? No problems other than morning sickness?"

"No, everything's good. I don't throw up as much anymore, which is even better."

She nodded in Ryley's direction. "So that one's not giving you problems?" she teased.

"Actually, I think it's the other way around. He's the one dealing with my mood swings and late night cravings."

"Well, looking at your weight and blood pressure, everything looks good. You've only gained four pounds, so I'd say you're doing great. Usually with twins, the mother gains a little bit more weight. Don't be surprised if you pack it on towards the end."

"Great," I mumbled sarcastically.

"Don't worry, angel," Ryley whispered in my ear. "If I can't be on top, you're more than welcome to ride me any day."

Rolling my eyes, I pushed him away and laughed. By the blush on Christine's cheeks, I knew she'd heard what he said. Talk about embarrassing.

"All right, I think we're ready for the ultrasound."

Then she looked at Ryley. "If you don't mind, I told your mom that I would do it myself. These kids are basically going to be my own family, so I'd like the honor."

Ryley glanced down at me and I nodded. "Of course, we don't mind at all," he said.

We followed her out and down the hall to the sonogram room. I already knew what to do so I climbed up on the table, lifted my shirt, and lowered my pants a little. Christine typed away on the computer and then squirt a glob of jelly on my stomach. I jumped with the coldness.

"I think we're ready. Let's take a look at your little ones." Once the wand touched my stomach, it was hard to tell what we were looking at, until Christine pointed everything out. "I'm going to give you some pictures to take home." She moved the wand over and captured a picture with both sets of feet. It was amazing. "Now that's priceless. I've never been able to get both sets like that before. But then again, I don't see twin births every day."

Ryley held my hand when I started to tear up and sniffle. When I snuck a peek at him, his eyes were glistening as he regarded his children. Their heartbeats echoed through the room and it was hard to tell which one went to what baby. It was just amazing seeing them in my belly.

"Everything looks good, you two. Now do you want me to see if I can find out what they are?"

"Yes," I blurted out excitedly. "When I talk to them, I want to be able to call out their names. If they're boys I don't want to call them by girl names. I don't think their father would like that."

"Hell no, I wouldn't. My boys need to be manly," Ryley blurted.

Christine shook her head and laughed. "I remember

when you're father was the same way about you and your brother. My, how time flies." She moved the wand around my belly and pressed in a bit to get the twins to move. Then a smile lit up her face. "I think we got one. Say hello to twin boy number one."

"I knew it," I squealed. "I had a feeling it was going to be boys." And there on the screen was the perfect shot of my little boy . . . with everything out. Like father, like son. Ryley smiled at the screen, but deep down I knew he had hoped it would be girls.

"Oh, but wait," Christine remarked happily. "I think I got a good one of twin number two." She slid the wand an inch to the right and giggled. "And here you go. It looks like you get the joy of both worlds. Twin number two is a girl. Ryley, your mother is going to be *ecstatic* when she finds out."

"A girl?" I gasped. I couldn't have heard better news. When Christine nodded and pointed out the little hamburger bun, as she had put it, I openly cried out in joy.

Ryley beamed and took the pictures from Christine, holding onto them like they were the most fragile thing he would ever hold in his hands.

And I just laid there, speechless.

"I'm going to write up my notes and I'll meet you both out front once you catch your breath. I can't begin to tell you how excited I am about this." She hugged Ryley and squeezed my arm before leaving us to ourselves. We both sat staring at the ultrasound pictures in shock.

"I can't believe this," I whispered. "I get my boy."

"And I get my girl," he finished. "Hopefully, she'll look like her mother."

Looking at the picture of our boy, I laughed and held

it over my heart. "Is it bad that I'm scared our boy will look like you? He'll be one good-looking heartbreaker when he gets older. I feel sorry for the girls already. Although, none of them will ever be good enough for my little man."

Ryley put his arm around me and helped me off of the table. "I wouldn't worry too much about him. If he takes after me, it won't be so bad. I mean, I found you, right? That at least counts for something. Our girl, on the other hand, is going to hate me when she starts dating. Maybe I should invest in some rifles?"

"You have a long time before that's necessary," I teased.

"Let's hope so. Now all we need to do is come up with names."

"I want our girl to have Gabriella as a middle name. She's the reason we met and she's my best friend. I think she'll like that. Besides, she'll basically be their aunt anyway."

Ryley nodded, but then his lip turned up in a sad smile. "I don't see a problem with that, just as long as you let our son have my father's name as his middle."

"What is it? I don't think you ever told me." I never wanted to bring up the topic of his father since it was such a sore subject. I couldn't imagine how horrible it would be to have one of your parents die in your arms.

"Alexander," he answered softly.

"Alexander," I repeated. "I like that. Now all we need are first names. I think Ethan would be a great name for a boy. Ethan Alexander Jameson. What do you think about that?"

Ryley pursed his lips, furrowing his brows. "That

sounds good. Just as long as you let me pick our daughter's name."

"Oh, hell. I don't know if I like the sound of that. I'm afraid of what you'll come up with."

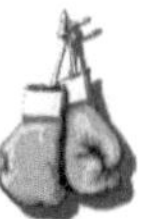

"I think I have it," Ryley murmured. It was late and I could barely keep my eyes open, but I turned in the bed and faced him. His crystal gaze shone bright and full of life as he stared down at me.

"What are you talking about?" I mumbled, snuggling into his chest.

"I figured out our daughter's name. I've been thinking about it all day and it finally clicked into place."

"Oh yeah?" I smiled. "What did you come up with?"

Lowering his hand to my bare stomach, he bent down and kissed the swell of my belly, speaking against my skin. "Emma."

"Emma," I said aloud, trying it out. "It's beautiful. What made you think of it?"

Keeping his hand on my belly, he smiled. "The name Emma means whole. I wouldn't be complete without her, or you, or Ethan. All of us together are what makes me who I am. I would be nothing without you."

Bringing his hand to my face, I held it on my cheek and leaned into it. "I feel the same way. And I know Emma and Ethan feel the same way too. They won't stop kicking me. I guess they're going to take after their daddy."

They were still small, but their little fists and feet were giving my insides a workout. Ryley sat up on his elbow and chuckled each time my stomach would flutter. "They're going to take after us both, angel. I just hope they can handle a father like me."

"They're strong," I said. "I'm pretty sure they can handle anything. They're Jameson's, what do you expect?"

He looked up at me, full of love. "And soon you will be too. I can't wait for the day I can call you my wife."

Me too. *Soon . . .*

The End

READ ON FOR A SNEAK PEEK AT PAXTON'S PROMISE (RELEASING 12-29-14)

PAXTON'S PROMISE

A GLOVES OFF NOVEL

Gabriella

FOR THE PAST week, Paxton had given me time to adjust to my life without Ashleigh by my side. She was gone to her cabin in the mountains, living the dream life. I was happy for her and Ryley, but I sure as hell was going to miss her. I had a feeling I knew what Paxton's terms were going to be anyway. *Maybe he'll forget about me this week.* Fat chance on that.

When the knock sounded on my door, there were two options. It was either going to be Bradley or Paxton. For the past week, I had basically thrown Bradley to the side, and I could feel the hole growing bigger between us. Every time I was busy, I was with my fighters and he didn't like it. We spent more time angry at each other than actually civilized. However, when I opened the door, it wasn't

Bradley. It was a tattooed fighter wearing fuck me jeans and a tight black T-shirt. *Walk away, Gabby.*

"So we meet again," he said simply. For a moment, his sea green eyes flustered me like they did every time I saw him. This time, I couldn't let that happen.

Throwing open the door, I rolled my eyes and ventured back into my living room. He was going to come in anyway, there was no reason to stop him. "It appears so," I grumbled. "You know, I was kind of wishing you'd forget about me. I guess the hundred pennies I threw in that well didn't work."

The door shut and I could hear him chuckle. "Sorry, love. No wish is going to get you out of our agreement. I gave you a week of freedom, but now your time's up. You're not thinking of backing out are you?"

Instead of sitting beside me on the couch, he sat in the chair across from me, his gaze boring straight into mine. "No. I made a promise and I'm going to keep it. I always keep my promises."

"And the same goes for me," he murmured, voice smooth and deep. "Now, how 'bout we get down to business?" My heart sped up at the thought and a small smirk splayed across his lips.

"Fine," I answered, clearing my throat. "I'm sure it's nothing I can't handle."

The deep chuckle in his chest rumbled all the way down to my clit. "Oh, we'll see about that, sunshine. First, I need to know. What's the status with you and the douche bag baseball player?"

I crossed my arms over my chest. "I don't think that's any of your business."

"It is now, considering for the next month you're going to be with me and me only. You're going to have to get rid of him."

My eyes went wide. "Are you serious? What am I supposed to tell him?"

Nonchalantly, he shrugged. "I don't give a shit what you tell him, as long as he knows to stay away from you. If he so much as causes a problem, I'm going to extend the month."

"Don't you think this is a bit extreme? Wouldn't a week suffice?"

His expression grew serious. "You obviously have no idea how far I put my neck on the line for you. I think a month is being very generous."

After experiencing life in the Dark Side, I knew it was a scary place. Those people wouldn't think twice about putting a bullet in my head. In fact, I'd say their humanity was long gone . . . just like Camden's.

"Okay, fine," I gave in. "A month it is. You don't expect me to fuck you do you? That shit's not going to happen."

Paxton tilted his head back and roared in laughter. "Oh, Gabby, as much as I'd love to have you spread out for my delight, I would never ask that of you. But if you wanted it, I'd be happy to oblige."

I scoffed. "Well, that's not going to happen. When does all of this start?"

"Tomorrow," he noted, getting to his feet. "I trust you'll handle everything with your boyfriend today?"

I stared at him in hopes that he'd smile and tell me it was all a joke. Sadly, I didn't get that. "Yes," I sighed. "I'll talk to him."

He strolled to the door and I followed to make sure

the door shut behind him. Paxton opened it wide and stopped. His back was to me, but then he turned around, piercing me with his green eyes. "Good, then we won't have any problems. If he really wants you, he'll wait for you." He stepped closer and circled a strand of my midnight hair through his fingers, his voice dipping lower. "It won't matter though. I know you won't go back to him after I get done with you."

"Sorry to disappoint you, Paxton. That's not going to happen either," I said, glaring at him.

"Oh, it wasn't a wish," he clarified. "It was a promise. And as you know, I never go back on my word." Smirking one last time, he winked and disappeared out the door, his footsteps calm and collected as he descended the stairs.

Growling in frustration, I slammed the door and stormed back over to the couch. *Fuck him with twelve giant cocks.* He didn't know what the hell he was talking about. I was going to make damn sure that promise was a promise he couldn't keep. What an arrogant prick.

Closing my eyes, I leaned my head against the couch and sighed. Only one more day of freedom. How was I going to spend it? The answer came with a text.

Bradley: I need to talk to you. Can I come over?

Here we go. If there was ever a time we should split up, it would be now. There was no way he was going to put up with me being with another man for the next month.

Me: Sure. I have lots to tell you too.

And none of it was good.

OTHER BOOKS BY L.P. DOVER

Forever Fae Series

Second Chances Standalones

Standalone (Romantic Suspense)

ABOUT THE AUTHOR

NEW YORK TIMES and USA Today Bestselling author, L.P. Dover, is a southern belle residing in North Carolina along with her husband and two beautiful girls. Before she even began her literary journey she worked in Periodontics enjoying the wonderment of dental surgeries.

Not only does she love to write, but she loves to play tennis, go on mountain hikes, white water rafting, and you can't forget the passion for singing. Her two number one fans expect a concert each and every night before bedtime and those songs usually consist of Christmas carols.

Aside from being a wife and mother, L.P. Dover has written over nine novels including her Forever Fae series, the Second Chances series, and her standalone novel, Love, Lies, and Deception. Her favorite genre to read is romantic suspense and she also loves writing it. However, if she had to choose a setting to live in it would have to be with her faeries in the Land of the Fae.

L.P. Dover is represented by Marisa Corvisiero of Corvisiero Literary Agency.

ACKNOWLEDGMENTS

THIS IS TO my family, friends, readers, bloggers, and future readers. Without you, I would be nothing . . . because without you, I wouldn't have anyone to share my stories with. Thank you for all of your support and I will always and forever be grateful for you. I hope you enjoy the Gloves Off fighters just as much as I do.

ALSO CHECK OUT THESE
EXTRAORDINARY AUTHORS & BOOKS:

Alivia Anders ~ Illumine
Cambria Hebert ~ Recalled
Angela Orlowski Peart ~ Forged by Greed
Julia Crane ~ Freak of Nature
J.A. Huss ~ Tragic
Cameo Renae ~ Hidden Wings
A.J. Bennett ~ Now or Never
Tabatha Vargo ~ Playing Patience
Beth Balmanno ~ Set in Stone
Ella James ~ Selling Scarlett
Tara West ~ Visions of the Witch
Heidi McLaughlin ~ Forever Your Girl
Melissa Andrea ~ The Edge of Darkness
Komal Kant ~ Falling for Hadie
Melissa Pearl ~ Golden Blood
Alexia Purdy ~ Breathe Me
Sarah M. Ross ~ Inhale, Exhale
Brina Courtney ~ Reveal
Amber Garza ~ Falling to Pieces
Anna Cruise ~ Maverick